Unholy
Ghosts

Unholy Ghosts

Ita Daly

BLOOMSBURY

First published 1996

Copyright © 1996 by Ita Daly

The moral right of the author has been asserted

Bloomsbury Publishing Plc, 2 Soho Square, London W1V 6HB

A CIP catalogue record for this book
is available from the British Library

ISBN 0 7475 2448 3

Typeset by Hewer Text Composition Services, Edinburgh
Printed in Great Britain by Clays Limited, St Ives plc

For Eva Bieler

O the mind, mind has mountains; cliffs of fall
Frightful, sheer, no-man-fathomed.
— 'Carrion Comfort', Gerard Manley Hopkins

'Hands,' Mutti used to say as she slapped globs of Pond's Cold Cream on to the backs of hers, 'hands is where the growing old begins.'

I stand in front of my mirror and see the truth of this. In middle age the signs of ageing are visible all over my body but in the rush towards decay it is my hands that are winning the race.

I raise them towards the light. The backs are traversed by veins which run like swollen blue rivers. Though in flood, these rivers offer no relief to the surrounding skin which appears cracked and parched. They are well-shaped hands, unadorned, unattended even, the nails clipped too short, the fingers ringless.

I have never been married.

The pads of my fingers are worn smooth and shiny. They remind me of the seat of Father Jack's clerical trousers which so repelled me as a child. I used to imagine the bony cheeks of his bottom scraping against the material as he stirred restlessly, flicking his lizard gaze around, seeking out the latest object of his displeasure.

I wonder if my fingertips have been obliterated, rubbed clean through years of work. I would make an anonymous corpse for I have never been to a dentist. My strong teeth and bones are an inheritance from my maternal grandfather, or so I have been told.

'You should get into the habit of wearing gloves, Meyers,' Anto told me when I had been working here for about a year, 'otherwise you'll ruin your hands.'

I never bothered. I tried a pair once but I hated the clamminess against my skin.

He calls me Meyers and I call him Anto. Everybody does. The girls in the kitchen, the porters, the patients. Everybody.

I think it's ludicrous. Even Tony would be a shade matey

but Anto – I ask you. It started with a patient calling him that years ago and he liked it. He would. It's all part and parcel of the man's inordinate vanity, like the fact that he won't wear a tie or a white coat.

Am I beginning to sound bitter?

I asked him once why he never calls me by my first name.

'Because you're Meyers, Meyers.'

'It wouldn't be because you find Belle incongruous, would it now?'

'Such nonsense.'

'Or is it to keep me in my place, keep a distance between us? I mean after all, you are my employer, among other things.'

'Oh go and read a seed catalogue.'

If you were to look at my fingers you'd think I was an ambidextrous, heavy smoker. The truth is I'm a right-handed gardener and the nicotine colour comes from ingrained soil. I've scrubbed and pumiced and soaked in glycerine but I've never been able to outgrain it. This upsets me for I wouldn't like people to get the impression of grubbiness when I am in fact fastidious.

The old blood line. Cleanliness is next to godliness. When we came here first Buba's only reservation about our new home was, 'They are not so clean, I think, these Irish.'

Buba smoked; everybody did when I was a child. Mutti smoked untipped cigarettes made from Virginia tobacco. I can remember the golden threads clinging to the jammy surface of her lipstick and how she removed them delicately with her little finger.

Buba smoked small cigars and Father Jack favoured Sobranies.

Nowadays hardly anyone smokes, even up there. You'd think they'd be puffing their heads off, that they'd be encouraged to, given the circumstances. Only the nurses remain unregenerate.

I keep on remembering, they're there all the time now, Buba and Father Jack and Mutti. I can't get rid of them. When I close my eyes or when I stare into space they pop up and begin to smoke and chat and ask me questions, just like they used to.

It started quite suddenly two days ago. I was taking a bunch of leeks up to the nurses' home and as I passed by a window I caught sight of a young woman standing in the bay, in profile. As I drew abreast she threw back her head and exhaled a thin stream of smoke, blue against the glass and the light outside. Her lips were pushed outwards, bunched into an O. A muscle slid up and down her exposed throat. I put a hand up to my own throat and thought, maybe said, Mutti. Standing at the kitchen window, staring unblinkingly into space, half turned towards the garden and smoking. Always smoking.

I am ten years old. I am filled with rage. Why does she not notice me, why does she not let me in, wherever it is she has gone?

But soon I recover my equilibrium. It is only Mutti, an idle woman, staring out of the kitchen window. Mutti is not important, too idle, too ineffectual, unlike Buba and me, busy little bees.

When she turned towards me I saw that the young woman looked nothing like Mutti. Not as good-looking and without make-up. No scarlet stain at the end of the cigarette then. No residue of Crimson Heart or Raspberry Crush, Mutti's favourites which she kept in a little glass basket on the mantelpiece in the kitchen, handy for renewal throughout the day.

I blamed Anto when I saw him. 'It's all your fault.'

He was innocence personified. 'But, Meyers, that's great, it's great that it's all coming up. You've suppressed all this for years and you didn't want analysis and I agree with you there but now it's come to the surface of its own accord. Nothing wrong with that, it's healthy.'

'I don't want to remember,' I wailed. 'I'm perfectly happy as I am.'

'Then why is this happening?' Anto can seem quite rational at moments like this. I suppose it's a trick he's perfected over the years. 'Nobody has forced you to remember – that's the beauty of it. If I were you do you know what I'd do? I'd write it all down, get it down coherently on paper.'

'I'll tell you why it's happening. Because you've upset everything. You've changed everything, the equilibrium of my life. So all my buried memories have been disturbed and they're on the move now, like a nest of rats.'

I was pretty pleased with that speech but as usual he managed to turn it to his advantage. 'There. You see. You're talking like a writer already. Now, not only would it be helpful to you but it would be entertaining for you and maybe even a valuable record of the times if you turn all these newly surfacing thoughts into an autobiography. How about it?'

One aspect appealed to me. 'I wouldn't mind remembering the early stuff, in Germany I mean.'

'And you will. You were, what, seven when you came to Ireland? Memories should certainly survive from before then.'

'Do you think?' The idea was beginning to appeal to me.

'Absolutely.'

'Well, we'll see.' He could wait. If I did start writing I didn't want him watching over my shoulder, anticipating the first appearance of his name. 'We'll just have to wait.'

HOUSES He was wrong about Germany. No memories leak from across the sea. I begin here in Ireland in a new house in the country. Where two counties meet, Mutti tells me, Wicklow and Kildare. She pronounces the names of the counties carefully, proudly. So are we speaking English? We must be and yet when did I learn?

We are still at the touching and sniffing stage because everything is new to us. Strange and new. Foreign.

Mutti and I stand at the sink doing the washing-up. It is a whitish, stone sink and in front of it there is a window looking out on to a field. There is no garden outside, just this field which rises towards a hedge at the far end.

The house feels raw and damp and as we stand at the sink the grey, cement floor is cold under our feet. Just inside the door there is an imprint of a giant foot, left, Mutti tells me, by a careless builder. I wonder if a giant has built our house as I put my two little feet inside the imprint. Mutti says that this will be covered over, she is glad to say, as soon as the linoleum arrives from Dublin.

We hurry through the washing-up for outside something magical has happened to the dense hedge at the end of the field. Today, overnight it has been transformed, clothed in white. Not snow as I first thought, but blossom. White, lacy blossom.

Mutti swirls the brownish water down the sink. I refuse to bathe in this water but Buba says it is excellent for the skin because coming from the bog it is particularly soft.

'Now,' says Mutti, 'we must pick.' She pulls at the ill-fitting kitchen door and we go out into the field. I trudge behind her through the damp grass, clumsy in my new wellingtons. She begins to hack at the hedge with a kitchen knife. The blossoms release a spicy scent and Mutti tells me to be careful of the thorns.

For a day the house is filled with the spicy scent and blossom-laden jugs crowd surfaces in every room.

Then just as suddenly the jugs are empty, the blossoms thrown out on to the ash heap behind the coalshed.

'Why?' I ask Mutti.

'Because it is unlucky to bring the may into the house. Today in the village I ask what is this blossom and I am told that it is the may and that it must never be brought into the house. It brings the bad luck.'

Mutti is the only one who goes to the village. She has a bicycle. Like the linoleum Buba's car has not yet arrived from Dublin and so we two remain marooned inside our new house.

'Such peasant foolishness,' Buba says. 'Why do you listen to such foolishness, Erika?'

But Mutti was always a one for magic.

Anto rails against the minister who has decreed that the hospital must be emptied by the end of February.

'The man is a fool, won't listen to anyone. I've told him time and time again – '

'You've told him that all large mental hospitals should be closed down. He's only doing what you wanted.'

'Did I suggest the time-scale? Did I suggest throwing sick people out before proper alternative arrangements could be made for them?'

'If you hadn't gone on at him in the first place he wouldn't have got the idea and everything would have been just as it was and I'd still have a job.'

'Meyers. Please.'

'Do you know what I think, Anto? I think that you were fed up with this place, that it was you who wanted out. So you offered him this story and now you're off to rescue Romanian orphans, which is a lot more glamorous than being chief bottle washer in a state mental hospital. That used to be glamorous once upon a time when all your theories about mental health were fashionable. Now that day's gone you want to move on, don't you, Anto, and you don't give a damn about who gets hurt in the process.'

I can't stop myself even though I know it is undignified and unjust. I don't like being dumped, which is what it amounts to, whatever gloss he puts on it. So I say all these stupid things that I regret afterwards.

'Look, we've been through all this before.' His voice has that note of patience that drives me wild. 'The hospital will be sold, eventually, but that doesn't mean that the gardens have to go too. We'll fight to see that they're kept – '

'You won't be here to fight.'

'– and anyway nobody is going to take a battering ram to evict you. The lodge is yours until you find somewhere else to live and if the gardens are saved, which they will be, you won't have to. You can continue to live in this little house.'

The picture that this evokes is so lonely, so startlingly eerie, that I know I will not stay on here, whatever happens.

'Everyone wants the gardens saved, everyone knows what an amenity they are. Now I've got a contact in the Parks Department – '

'Oh God, spare me that. Anything but Dublin Corporation.'

'Turning up your nose as usual. OK. A private patron. We must find you some wealthy person who will save your gardens. Would that suit you?'

'More jokes.'

'I'm not joking but I am starving and I'm going to get us something to eat. Have you got a towel?'

We had been talking in the bathroom while he washed my back and I sat with my head resting modestly on my arm-encircled knees. Now that we are no longer lovers I don't like him to see me without my clothes on but I still cling to the luxury of having my aching back washed. He does it gently and thoroughly and when he rests his hand on my spine I find my spirit ease.

'I'm going to get some rosemary for the chops,' he called from the kitchen. 'Do you want mushrooms or broad beans or both?'

This has been our life for almost thirty years, playing house on stolen afternoons. Separately we have attended night classes in cookery and wine appreciation and have put our expertise to practice in this house, preparing meals, building up my modest cellar. Amateur sybarites, part and parcel I imagine of the adulterous affair.

He gave me two chops, himself three. I sliced the brown bread I had baked earlier and spread it with salty country butter. This butter is made by an ex-patient who brings it up to certain gourmet shops every week from Wicklow and who always has a pound or two for Anto.

People love Anto. I suppose I loved him once myself.

'Have you started the writing yet?'

'No.' I wouldn't give him the satisfaction of admitting to it.

'Try, Meyers.'

'I've decided not to bother.'

'I wish you would. Those memories aren't going to go away, not unless you force them down again and that wouldn't be a good idea. It's healthier to get it all down, trust me, and we can deal with whatever comes up together. I don't want to leave you with unfinished business.'

'Some might say I am unfinished business.'

'Oh, Meyers.'

The may is withered when we get the word that we are to move again.

Mutti and I are sitting outside in the sunshine. She has spread a rug on the kitchen step and I think how pretty she looks in her short-sleeved fluffy jumper. She wears her blonde hair rolled at the neck, a glossy, sausage-like roll which I have tried to copy, but my hair is kinky and stubborn, and besides, it is the wrong colour. Black.

Buba comes out waving a letter. Her pink cheeks are pinker than usual and her little black eyes are sparkling.

'It has come, he has written to us,' she says. 'Father Jack has summoned us. By the end of the month we go to Dublin and our lives will begin again.'

I don't ask how our lives have stopped. Buba and Mutti often use phrases which make no sense to me and I am used to them. Perhaps it is because English is not their native tongue.

I am called indoors to have my face scrubbed and my nails checked in preparation for Father Jack's arrival.

'But who is he?' I ask, irritated at being dragged in from the sunshine. 'Is he a relation? Is he from Germany?'

Buba smiles, looping a blue ribbon behind my ears and tying it in a bow on top of my head. 'He is most Irish but he is also an old friend. And he is our benefactor, Liebchen, remember that always. Father Jack is our benefactor.'

When I meet him I decide that I do not like benefactors.

He is sitting motionless in the front room. It is this reptilian stillness that comes to characterize him for me and which will continue to chill me over the years when I will come upon him in our house in Dublin, sitting somewhere in the shadows.

'Pleased to meet you, Belle,' he says and I watch, fascinated, as the moist, pink lips break open and outwards into a smile. They seem incongruous in the midst of all that dried-up, yellow skin, like some luscious fruit lying rotting in the desert.

His suit is black and shiny and the material rasps when he moves. His eyes are hooded, slits of blue.

'I'm sure you are looking forward to your move to the

city,' he says, dipping a biscuit in his coffee and sucking it in between his teeth.

'No,' I reply truthfully.

'Then you should be,' he says coldly, dismissing me and turning to address Buba.

I wait for her reprimand. I am the centre of this house and cannot be dismissed so easily. But she smiles at me vaguely and says to Mutti, 'Take her for a walk, Erika. Father Jack and I have much to discuss.'

He is standing on the steps of our new house when we drive up in Buba's black Wolseley, also new.

The journey has been fun, especially when we went slithering around corners as Buba spun the wheel. I haven't been able to see out because of all the piled-up luggage.

'Welcome,' says Father Jack, jangling keys.

I gasp in wonder at the steps, embedded with fragments of stars. I kneel and begin to scrape at the fragments with my fingernails.

'Come in, child,' says Father Jack. 'Come in and see your new home.'

The hall is full of tea chests and dusty sunbeams. More dust rises from the bare boards as we step on to them.

Buba puts an arm around me and another around Mutti. 'This is our new beginning.' Her black eyes glint with unshed tears. She looks towards Father Jack. 'Here our new life begins and it is all thanks to dear Father Jack.'

He smiles. 'You must get a brass plate for the door. Dr Meyers, MD. Now that we've got your papers in order you must set about establishing your practice.'

There are panels of red glass in the hall door and inside the light is wine red. Then Mutti opens one of the panels and sunshine pours in, changing the red to gold.

When someone knocks on the door I won't open it. I'll open one of the panels and answer mysteriously through the wrought-iron grille.

'There's a door at garden-level as well,' says Father Jack. 'That could be handy for the surgery.'

Buba takes his hand in both of hers. 'Father Jack, the worker of miracles. First you bring us to Ireland, then you find us a home and now you make it so that I can work here.'

He withdraws his hand and slides it behind his back to join its mate. 'Ireland's gain, dear lady. We cannot have your talents lying hidden.'

I leave them to go and explore. I walk to the top of the house and then down again, three flights of stairs to the semi-sunk garden-level. Even here light floods into empty rooms. Soon this will change when Mutti gets busy hanging the heavy, velvet curtains that we have brought with us. Dark-green velvet will occlude the light and change the character of the house so that it becomes inward-looking.

In a scullery or back kitchen a tap drips. There is a sweetish smell which I trace to a door beside the window. I open it to discover a floor-to-ceiling cupboard with shelving made of wooden laths. On the bottom shelf half a dozen wrinkled apples lie and it is their scent that still lingers in the air.

The others have followed me down. Buba claps her hands.

'So nice,' she says. 'So nice, so cosy. Better, I prefer to upstairs.'

She walks along the corridor, peering into each room.

'We live down here, I think. A sitting room and a big kitchen where we can eat. Then upstairs the surgery and room for the people to wait. What do you think, Erika? A good plan?'

Father Jack tuts his admiration at the back of his throat. 'Isn't that so like you, dear lady. No swank or nonsense where you're concerned.'

Mutti begins to unpack things from a tea chest. I am sent to fill a kettle from the dripping tap in the scullery. Mutti makes tea and we drink it standing up from cups without saucers.

'Thank you for the milk,' Mutti says to Father Jack.

He slurps a mouthful of tea. 'Something I always remember from the old days. The Meyers put milk in their tea and that used to make me feel so at home.'

I am remembering something too. A milk bottle. I am standing with it in my hand and I let it fall. It breaks on to red tiles. Such a mess. Buba will be cross.

There is someone with me. 'Don't worry,' she says and begins to push the broken glass and spilt milk into a corner under a sink. She is using a long broom, much taller than herself.

Suddenly Buba appears, grabs the broom. 'Deceitful little girl,' she says, 'showing bad example to Belle. Such a religious family, won't even eat here because of your kosher rules and still you are not taught to tell the truth, to own up when you do something wrong.'

Who is this little girl of my own age? Did she exist or have I invented her?

Father Jack nudges me. 'Off in a daydream, Belle, lost in a wonderland. Well, your grandmother has brought you to a veritable wonderland. It'll take you weeks to explore all the nooks and crannies.'

That night we three sleep together in Buba's big bed. The rest of the furniture will arrive tomorrow. It is too hot under the eiderdown between the two of them but I don't mind.

Buba puts an arm round me and says, 'You like that we bring your little bed in here so that you sleep beside your Buba? It is the biggest room, we can share and Mutti next door, all cosy together. I think you like that, *Liebchen*.'

*   *   *

When Mutti got upset she used to make strudel dough.

At the kitchen table she rolled sheets of cream-coloured pastry, thin as tissue paper, with blue, bruisy bits where the light shone through.

I, her robust daughter, heave manure on to my gardens when anything is bothering me.

I can become quite excited about manure, especially the wonderful stuff I get, which is the texture and colour of a rich chocolate cake. A man who takes tourists round the city in a horse-drawn cab keeps it for me. He lives down the road in Chapelizod but he wasn't aware of the treasure that lay at his feet and used to cart it off to a municipal dump miles away. Now he delivers it up here and he tells me he is grateful to me for taking it off his hands.

I started muck-spreading this morning before it was bright. I should have started a month ago to give it as long an exposure as possible to the winter frosts. The worms do the rest.

For an hour I worked without raising my eyes any higher than the tines of my fork. My back began to ache, I skinned my knuckles on the wheelbarrow but I could hear the whirring in my head begin to slow down.

I prefer the gardens at this time of year. I love the bare branches of winter trees and the stems and seed pods in the herbaceous border. I am not a cutter-back and tidier in the autumn. Like William Robinson I consider neatness an overrated virtue in the garden.

And look how many things have been burgeoning while I sulked indoors. Hellebores and virburnum and mahonias are in flower, yellow and red dogwoods have been painted afresh. I sniffed up the scents and admired my gardens lit now by that strange winter sun.

People who do not work out of doors are often unaware of how much sunshine there can be in an Irish winter, more than in an Irish summer when the monsoon sets in. Winter sun does not hang from the heavens but seems to be caught on a cusp of the earth so that its rays slant low and angled and strong. I have stood under a black sky in winter even while the earth around me shimmered in the sunlight. It is a strange feeling to be out in such a landscape.

I had taken the netting off the pond – for the leaves are long since down – and I was eating a picnic lunch under the alders when Anto came bounding down from the hospital. Unlike my drying carcass his body still seems well-oiled. I found myself admiring him, his grace, his pewter curls. Not for the first time it occurred to me that I might have done better for myself if I hadn't been so susceptible to male beauty.

'The gardens are saved, Meyers,' he said, grabbing one of my sandwiches.

'What are you talking about?'

'It's true, I've been out to RTE and I met a young guy, a producer in Current Affairs who's keen on gardening. I think we could persuade him to make a film about the fate of these gardens once the hospital goes.'

I felt like demanding my sandwich back I was so annoyed. Because of the love affair between him and the media he thinks that exposure on telly is the answer to all problems.

'Did you bring any beer?' he asked, beginning to root in my knapsack. 'Have you nothing to say about my good news?'

'Leave that bag alone.'

'Co-operate with me on this one, Meyers. Meet the guy and talk to him at least. You'll see how enthusiastic he is.'

I distrust enthusiasms, Anto embraces them, other people's as well as his own. Of course he has two mammies to run home to, two homes to choose from when hope becomes forlorn.

I stood up and shook out crumbs for the birds. 'I'm off. Some of us have work to go to.'

'And the writing, Meyers,' he called after me. 'What about the writing? I hope you're getting down to it, making room for it every day.'

To be fair, Anto has been more of a father to me than I've ever been a mammy to him. In *loco parentis* he saw himself in those early days after he had rescued me and found me a home and a job. Now in my new life I had acquired my own benefactor.

In his office, where I had been summoned, he took my face in his hand and turned it towards the light. He was frowning over me, wondering what to do with me.

'I cannot go back to my grandmother's,' I said. 'Even if it means spending the rest of my life in a mental hospital I cannot go back there.'

The hug he gave me was distinctly fatherly but I was aware of a hard, male body, familiar yet unknown. 'No need to worry about that. I've had a word with your mother and she's agreed that it is best if you stay here but in a different capacity. I'm going to offer you a job.'

'But my grandmother – '

'It's your mother I've been dealing with – she seems to be making the decisions. Now, about the job. It's an apprenticeship really and there's a house going with it. All I've got to do is swing it with old Jimmy, if you're interested.'

Old Jimmy had been head gardener and then sole gardener in the mental, as he called it, for over thirty years. He had been a bedding-plant man in his glory days, with several under-gardeners and several greenhouses on the go. When I came on the scene he was clapped out, cantankerous and arthritic, taking me on because I was better than nothing.

That winter I worked as I've never worked before or since. Taking advantage of my young back old Jimmy had me spreading manure, clearing out sheds, moving plants, tidying up forgotten and neglected corners.

But I learned from him and when he was leaving at the end of the following summer he presented me with his coverless copy of William Robinson's *The English Flower Garden*. He shook my hand and advised me not to stay in the lodge any longer than I had to.

'They offered it to me thirty year ago,' he said, 'but I wouldn't have rested easy in my bed knowing that one of that lot up there could break out and come down and murder me in my sleep. That Anto should have more sense than to let a bit of a girl like you sleep there on your own.'

I had come to love my little house, snug inside the high granite wall, screened from the hospital by an overgrown shrubbery which had turned into a wood. It was a secretive house that suited my secretive life. If Father Jack and Buba came searching for me, they would never find me there.

Every fortnight Anto came and gave me my wages, refusing the seat I offered him, flicking the money down on the table with a twist of his slim, elegant wrist. He was tall and spare and elegant. I used to speculate on whether he would look older or younger with his clothes off, acknowledging his ancientness, knowing that the love of my life had come and gone and yet wanting this man, this good, kind benefactor.

It took me almost two years to seduce him, full as he was of notions of honour and responsibility. I was only interested in survival, knowing that I had to have him or I would wither more serely than any of the plants in my herbaceous border.

Could you call what we had a love affair?

Winter afternoons, summer mornings as the light changed inside my bedroom and I grew familiar with a body which seemed just as vigorous if not as perfect as that other one. Laughter over spilt sauces, arguments over bottles of wine, jokes told, endearments exchanged, both of us aware that we must keep things light, maintain a brightness of mood, never descend to the serious where we might find ourselves discussing his marital status or my past. In so far as any two people can, we lived in the present, spending our money on expensive food, silk-covered cushions, scented bath oils and bottles of wine from Tuscany and the Rhone valley, places we would never travel to together, any more than we would go to a restaurant or a cinema in town.

'Don't go home.'

'I must.'

'You don't love me.'

'You know I do.'

'Then stay.'

'I can't. Oh God, can I – '

'Go. I love you too.'

I'd say you could describe it as a love affair.

FRIENDS   Did I have any friends? Not in the early days.

Did I mind? Not in the early days.

In the early days, despite Father Jack who hovered over our lives like a malign black crow, I had no needs that weren't met by my grandmother and my mother. I was loved extravagantly, the centre of those women's lives, although Mutti's attention could stray into absent-mindedness from time to time as she took up her position at the kitchen window, pulling on a cigarette, staring into space.

When Father Jack wasn't around I got all Buba's attention. Every night she brushed my hair and rubbed my back, telling me as she eased the stiffness of scholarship that she believed the school day was far too long. I was her *Liebchen* and she petted me and fed me squares of rich, dark chocolate which arrived every month through the post, neatly packed in brown paper and sent by a cousin in Switzerland, our only living relative as far as I knew.

Buba was the dominant figure in our world so that I now remember Mutti as a sort of unreliable older sister, someone whom Buba and I would shake our heads over because of her flightiness.

I remember her nervousness and Buba describing her as 'highly-strung'. She jumped at noises and was forever reapplying the thick, jammy lipstick she wore or playing with an unrolled strand of her hair.

Yet this is not the whole picture.

Mutti ran our household with ease and efficiency. Along our road with its large, ugly, solid houses, ours was the only one without a maid. Ours was the cleanest too, I've no doubt, where carpets were taken out each morning and beaten, where brasses were polished and terrazzo floors scrubbed. Mutti cooked soups and stews and potato dumplings and loaves of puffy white bread and apple strudel and steamed chocolate puddings.

My little mother, running upstairs in her high-heeled shoes to admit Buba's patients, then back to the kitchen to take something out of the temperamental oven of the Raeburn, nails newly varnished, lipstick newly applied. And yet I see her as limp and ineffectual, idle, yearning, to be pitied somehow and not to be taken seriously. Buba's assessment obviously and I willing, indeed eager, to concur.

We loved our ugly new house built with unimaginative sturdiness at the turn of the century. We never hankered after anything more graceful and turned our backs indifferently on the lovely eighteenth-century squares and roads all around, retreating gratefully behind the rawness of the red-brick façade.

We hid ourselves away, drawing the heavy green curtains throughout the house. In winter some of them remained closed day and night. Winter was their season and became mine. Evenings began soon after lunch when fires were lit and lamps switched on. After tea I did my homework seated between the two women while they chatted and smoked and listened to Schubert songs on the wind-up gramophone.

I had a special reading lamp which threw a pearly circle on my school books spread out on a low table. They had no need of strong lights for they seldom read. They didn't have a wireless and never bought newspapers. They had no interest in the outside world nor need of it.

And yet again this is not the whole picture. I was encouraged to go out, to mix, to bring back news from the outside world.

'Gut little Irish girl,' Buba would say proudly. 'Soon that is what you will be, the good little Irish girl and nobody can tell the difference.'

And she would question me about my day at school and about my friends.

But in school I wasn't fooling anybody. I was seen as foreign and my foreignness evoked hostility. They laughed at the way I spoke and at my ignorance, especially my ignorance of someone called InfantJesusMeekandMild.

I don't remember any of this making me unhappy; I don't think I cared. I had Mutti and Buba, especially Buba.

When I finished my homework I would rest my head on her knee and listen to the Schubert while I looked into the fire and she smoothed my hair. Did I understand the words? I'm sure I did although this is contradicted by the fact that I never understood the conversations between Buba and Mutti when they spoke German. Perhaps I continued to remember the meaning of the lyrics after I had forgotten the language. Or perhaps the cadences of the music, its rise and fall within our silent room, conveyed to me all of Gretchen's longings, for example, making Goethe's words redundant.

When I started to yawn and rub my eyes Buba would say, 'Time for the good night's sleep to begin,' and Mutti and I would go to the kitchen where she would break squares of the Swiss chocolate into three china mugs, boil some milk to frothing point and then pour this on to the chocolate.

By the time I had changed into my night clothes and reappeared with my face and hands washed, the drink had reached the tepidness I liked.

Buba and I would go upstairs together while Mutti doused the fire and tidied up. Buba supervised my teeth-brushing and then in our nighties at the foot of Buba's large, mahogany bed we did our physical jerks. We would stretch our arms up to the ceiling, swing them round in circles and touch our toes, each twenty times. Buba was very keen on physical jerks and better at them than I was.

'Look at me,' she would say. 'Do you see an old woman with the aches and pains? No, you do not. And why? Because of the physical jerks.'

She had other aids to health: a heavily carnivorous diet, a spoonful of cod-liver oil every morning, sleeping without pillows and an avoidance of draughts.

She feared draughts particularly and excluded fresh air from the house except for ten minutes every morning when all windows were flung open to allow for what she called 'the displacement of airs'.

When we were both safely in bed and she had extinguished the overhead light by pulling a cord that hung over her headboard, she encouraged me to talk. She liked to listen to my accent which she said was becoming more Irish every day.

She wasn't a great talker herself and any time I asked her a question about our old life in Germany she deflected me. 'No, tell me more about that girl who never has a book. What did you say was her excuse?'

I was easy enough to deflect.

*   *   *

Though we didn't have any friends we did have our benefactor and Buba never allowed us to forget it.

He arrived every Sunday in the early evening and immediately Buba would begin to fuss, placing his chair, issuing orders to Mutti and me to go and get some coffee ready. He didn't even pretend to an interest in me, something that Buba would not have tolerated in anybody else. He seemed afraid of Mutti, never meeting her eye, only looking at her when she was turned away from him. Then he would flick up his eyelids and dart covert glances along her legs and up her body.

I was fascinated and repelled by the way he ate. He liked Mutti's cherry cake and would pick out the cherries and leave them till last, piling them on the side of his plate, something I knew I would have been reprimanded for.

He'd accept a second slice and a third, eyes darting towards the cake stand to check on how much was left. His horrid fleshy lips would part and his red tongue flick out to receive the cherry. Munch munch munch. Swallow.

Those lips had a life of their own. Busily and sensuously they moved, smacked, widened and pouted and were kept permanently damp by a flicking, snake-like tongue.

I couldn't understand why Buba liked him, why she seemed to enjoy talking to him. I felt a crawling sensation at my scalp as I watched the long yellow fingers carry cake crumbs and cherries to his mouth and the red fleshy lips part moistly to receive the offering.

'You don't like him, do you, Mutti?' I whispered in the scullery as we prepared his snack. I knew she didn't.

All she would say was, 'We owe him much.'

'What – what do we owe him?'

'I've told you. We are refugees, we are not in this country except for Father Jack.'

'How come?'

'Before the war. He knew us then.'

I was used to that phrase – before the war. There was our life in Ireland and there was before the war. I learned early not to ask questions about the war itself. I learned from Mutti's nervous white hands straying around the corners of her mouth and from Buba's beseeching eyes. I learned not to probe, sensing that some things could not be talked about because of pain or fear.

I grew up with secrecy, accepting the resulting ignorance not only of my own early life but of world history as perfectly normal. It was years before I began to ask questions about it.

Anto is learning Romanian. Breda Shields told me. Shields is a senior nurse up at the hospital and she loves Anto. She thinks he's a saint.

'What good will it do?' I asked her.

'Do you imagine everyone in Romania speaks English? Cop yourself on.'

'I mean what good will he do going over there? Psychiatrists are a bit of a luxury anywhere but the idea of someone like Anto trotting out all that nonsense to those poor people – that is sick.'

'Don't be such a bitch, of course he can help. Have you seen the photographs coming out of some of them hospitals?'

'That's what I mean. They've enough simpletons of their own without importing the likes of Anto.'

Over the years I've learned to talk like this about him, to deflect attention from our relationship. Even when I trembled with love for him I would force myself to say harsh things about him. Nowadays I don't have to force myself. Every time I think of his crazy decision to run off to Romania they come trippingly off the tongue.

He's leaving me high and dry and going off to offer his

services where they are not needed. What can he do for the twisted limbs and vacant eyes, the nodding heads and lolling tongues that we see nightly on our television screens? I don't know what Romanian orphans need but it sure as hell isn't Anto.

'He's not being paid,' Shields offered as justification for his craziness.

'I should bloody well hope not.'

'The Red Cross offered him a job. I suppose you know better than the Red Cross.'

'I know Anto better than the Red Cross does.'

'Ah shut up, Belle.'

Not a great one for sustaining an argument, nevertheless I enjoy sparring with Shields. She's the nearest thing I have to a friend and she's been good to me over the years. She's insensitive, casually brutal on occasion, but never malicious.

When she gets drunk, which is about once a week, she tells me of her hopeless love for Anto.

I offer her sympathy, protest that nobody would ever notice her slight moustache and that she isn't putting on weight. But I've never told her about Anto and me and now there's nothing to tell.

'Is it true they're going to make a film about the hospital?' she asked, licking beer froth from her moustache.

'So Anto seems to think.'

'Jesus. We might be discovered at long last. I want a starring role in it. I've no intention of allowing myself to be played by some actress who couldn't even stick a needle in someone's bum. That sort of thing gives nursing a bad name, particularly mental nursing.'

She and Charlie Lennon are the only ones who have been in this hospital longer than I. They were both trainee nurses when I was committed. Then Anto arrived about nine months later.

Shields has no family; I don't know about Charlie. This

hospital has offered a sort of home to all of us, a home for the bewildered, as Charlie says.

'I used to want to be a film star when I was young,' Shields said. 'I had an aunt in Boston and I used to think that if she'd only take me out I'd make my own way to Hollywood and once I got there I'd be discovered right away. Do you remember the lovely films they had in those days?'

We went to the cinema every week. Buba said it was good for our English but we really went because we loved it.

The early show on Sunday afternoons was the one Buba chose. The queues were shorter and we got out on time for Father Jack's visit. We liked musicals and romances. I fell in love with Betty Grable. I wished I could look like her, as Mutti did with her blonde hair and long, long legs. But I had black hair and short legs, like Buba.

We speculated about the celluloid lives, more real to us than our own. To Mutti in particular who would sigh and look out the window and say, 'It must be wonderful in America. It must be such a wonderful place to live.'

When summer came we stopped going.

'Why?' I asked Buba.

'Because the cinema is for the winter. In summer the germs increase inside the cinema and it is not a healthy place to be.'

I knew this to be an excuse. Now I believe that my grandmother didn't want to risk daylight sorties with the chance of sunshine and skies so distantly blue that they offered no cover at all. Buba could have been a close relation of Count Dracula so strongly did she fear bright days. As the summer progressed Mutti stopped lighting a fire in the sitting room but Buba continued to sit resolutely with her back to the window looking towards an empty grate.

And I am not enjoying this summer either, our second in

our Dublin house. Last year I was happy to follow Mutti around, shadowing her with my own little dustpan and brush, my own wisp of duster. Now this all seems childish and I long for distraction.

Then, by magic, my first friend appears in our garden one day. I am not all that surprised for I have always known that the garden where I play is an enchanted place. Buba and Mutti, brought up in city apartments, never venture out here and it becomes my domain. The high walls, like the front steps, are made of granite. The lawn has reverted to meadow, a pond has turned into a swamp, evil-smelling and mysterious; beside the clothesline a rosemary bush grows lank but fragrant and by a far wall white roses dazzle.

I am making rose-petal perfume when a voice calls, 'Would you give us some of that?'

The head seems not to belong to a body as it bobs on top of the wall. 'I bet it smells great. I'm real fond of perfume.'

She grasps the top of the wall, swings herself upwards and over and lands in a heap at my feet.

She smiles up at me. 'Isn't it just as well I'm not too skinny. Here, give us a hand.'

When she stands up she is not much taller than I but quite grown-up with lipstick and a perm and bosoms that point more extravagantly than Mutti's do.

'I know who you are. I bet you don't know who I am.'

I shake my head. I have never seen her before.

She laughs. 'I knew it. Nobody knows I live in that kip. I could die there and nobody would be any the wiser. And I've been there for years and years. I even remember the day ye moved in. I'll probably die soon because they don't give me enough to eat and I'm killed working.'

She doesn't seem unduly depressed by any of this. 'Do you live in there?' I nod towards the next-door garden.

'I'm the maid, the skivvy is more like. I know all about ye. The old lady, the lady doctor, I'd say she must be your granny?'

'Yes.'

'And the blonde?'

'My mother.'

She sighs. 'God, she has lovely clothes. You know that coat she wears, the one with the astrakhan collar, I'd give anything for one like that.'

'Where do you come from?' I ask, for she speaks with an unfamiliar accent.

'Oh miles away, down the country – but I'm no daw. And I can dance real well. I'll teach you if you like, only we'd need a bit of music.'

She begins to twirl around on the rough grass, humming to herself. Then she comes back to me and puts an arm round my shoulder. 'You and me are going to get on,' she says. 'We'll be real great, I know we will. I'll come and see you every day.'

As she starts to climb back over the wall I hold up a milk bottle to her. 'Here, you've forgotten your perfume.'

She smiles again. 'Keep it, I'll put some on tomorrow and we can have a dance. I always wear swanky perfume when I go to a dance.'

I forsook Buba for my new friend. Eileen Joyce must have been six years older than I at least but from the first we met as friends and equals. Every afternoon she escaped from her employers and waited for me to come out after my dinner. Although she would have eaten too she was always hungry, and I brought her Mutti's cakes and home-made lemonade, which she said was nearly as good as the real stuff in bottles.

I became her confidante and she told me all her problems: how she hated Mrs Mooney who didn't give her enough to eat, how her boyfriend was stuck in the army and couldn't get out, how she couldn't stop biting her nails. (She had admired Mutti's hands as they stood together in the butcher's waiting for meat.)

She shared trade secrets with me, offering me tips on make-up and on developing my bust. She thought my name was lovely. 'I never knew anyone called Belle before. Is it foreign?'

I wasn't too sure but I said it was.

She considered this, then asked, 'Does that mean you're foreign?'

'I suppose so.' By this time I felt quite Irish but Buba and Mutti were definitely foreign.

'Where do ye come from?'

'Germany.'

'Germany.' She savoured the word. 'Are ye Catholics then or does that mean ye're Protestants?'

This was a query I was familiar with from the school playground, followed by the taunt, 'You don't even know your prayers – you must be a Prod. A Prod, a Prod.'

Indifferent to the good opinion of my classmates I hadn't minded then but I did now. I wanted to secure Eileen as a friend and I was determined that nothing would jeopardize our friendship.

I took a deep breath. 'I'm certainly not a Protestant.'

She beamed. 'Catholic then.'

But I lost my nerve. 'No. Not that either. Something different entirely.'

And I ran into the house to have it out with Buba and Mutti.

I confronted them that evening before Mutti had a chance to wind up the gramophone. 'What are we?' I asked. 'I mean, we're not Catholic so does that mean we're Protestant?'

It seemed a straightforward enough question and I was

surprised by their reaction to it. Instead of answering me they began an agitated conversation in German.

'What? What are you saying? Tell me.'

They glanced at me, glanced away, signalled with their eyes to one another over my head.

'Please.'

Buba patted her untidy bun, cleared her throat, looked around as if she were seeking a means of escape. 'We – Why do you want to know?'

'I just do.'

Buba smiled but I knew she was just pretending, moving her mouth in the same way as Father Jack did when he greeted me. 'It's not for little girls to – Erika – '

I had never heard her appeal like that to Mutti before.

Mutti said something in German, then she turned to me. 'Sometimes your Buba finds things painful to say. It is simple enough. We are not Catholic and not Protestant because we are Jews.'

That was fine by me. All I wanted was an answer for Eileen. Jew, Catholic, Protestant, I had heard of them all from the back of the religion class, half listening when I grew bored with the sums or spelling I was supposed to be learning.

'That's all right then,' I said and watched as Buba closed her eyes, then opened them again and smiled at me, a proper Buba smile this time.

'Just so long as we're something.'

Eileen Joyce was not so easily satisfied.

In the middle of teaching me to foxtrot, having drowned herself in my strongest bottle of rose-petal perfume, she backed me up against the garage wall and fixed me with a glittering, bluish eye. 'You're only codding me, aren't you?'

'About what?'

'About being a Jew?'

'No, I'm not.' I was indignant. 'I told you, I even asked Buba. We're Jews.'

She considered this for a moment, then shook her head. 'Ye can't be.'

I was getting annoyed now. 'I've told you. You needn't believe me if you don't want to.'

'But, Belle — there's no Jews in Ireland.'

I didn't even bother to answer this. 'Come on, Eileen, let's do the dance.'

She left it then but came back to it. As she was leaving, sitting astride the wall, she looked down at me and said, as if she had been considering it all afternoon, 'Where do you go to Mass then?'

'What are you talking about now?'

'If you're a Jew you must have a church that you go to on Sunday. Where is it? Where do you go to Mass?'

I went to Mutti this time. 'Where is our church?'

'Us? Our church? We don't have a church.' She seemed amused. 'We are not the people of the grand house with our own church — what are you thinking of, Belle?'

'Not that,' I said impatiently. 'The Jews' church. Where do Jews have their church?'

She shrugged. 'I don't know, I've never thought about it.'

As if Eileen would accept an answer like that. 'Think now, Mutti. If we are Jews you should know where our church is. And why don't we ever go?'

'But we are not religious. Why should we go?' And she widened her blue eyes at me as if it were the most obvious truth she spoke.

I went to Buba. She patted the sofa beside her chair and took my hand.

'Before the war — ' We were off again.

'Before the war, you have to understand, *Liebchen*, we were not the religious people. Not at all. In 1922 your grandfather and I made the *Frei Religiös* declaration to say that we were not religious Jews. Then you do not have to pay the religious taxes. Many, many people did this thing in Germany, Jews and Christians. It is hard to understand here in Ireland where everyone is the Catholic. *Gut* people like Father Jack. In Germany, not so. People are born into a religion but they have not that religion. It is most common.'

When I told this to Eileen she hooted with derision. 'Sure I knew it. I knew all along you were a pagan – a pure pagan.'

She reached over for another slice of cake and smiled at me. 'But sure don't worry, I couldn't care less. As long as you're not a Protestant like them Mooneys. Protestants are very mean, I've always known that.'

Although I wasn't a pagan then I am one today, or a pantheist at any rate.

I've had no truck with conventional religion since I was let down by the Holy Ghost. I prayed to him for years but when my prayers weren't answered I decided that I was wasting my time.

It was a snowdrop that turned me into a pagan. A common snowdrop, *Galanthus nivalis*.

It had rained all summer. In autumn the wind had torn leaves from the trees before they could cheer the sodden world. December was dark and cold, January colder.

Or so it seemed to me, locked up in the madhouse, looking out at a dead world through dirty glass.

Although I was in the madhouse I was sick, not mad. Sick from fear and sorrow and disappointment and loss. But I knew that I would soon be mad if they kept me much longer locked up in this place.

It was a truly dreadful place, a hell established inside the shell of a large Georgian house. Lost souls wandered its corridors, some silent, others sobbing or shouting. The linoleum that covered the floors was dark brown and sweating; the walls were painted brown and splashed with gobbets of food.

Far above our heads the original ceilings remained incongruously intact with rococo cherubs leering down at our suffering.

Windows were never cleaned, paintwork was scuffed. Nobody seemed to think that the mad needed, indeed had a right to, clean, pleasant surroundings. Living amidst squalor and ugliness was the price they paid for being a damn nuisance to society.

At mealtimes we dribbled and moaned. I say 'we' for by this time I too had begun to vocalize my pain. Every day I felt sanity slip away as my pain mingled with the general and all erupted in a collective howl for help which was either unheard or ignored.

I managed to escape by going to sit on my bed while the others were at occupational therapy. I'd pretend I was going to the lavatory and then slip upstairs to sit in a freezing room and stare out at the world. I was docile, a threat to neither myself nor anybody else, so nobody minded. As long as I sat quietly and came down for meals I was left alone.

Then one day I saw it, staring in at me from the window box outside; shaking its ridiculous white head at me, rising out of the compacted black earth, the only sign of life there was.

It was pretty, it was frivolous, words which had become redundant since I had come in here. It reminded me that there was a different life to be had outside and I became determined to hold on to my sanity until I could get out into the world again and take up that life.

So I went to the medical director and asked him if I could

grow things. As I was a 'good' patient I was given this privilege. I started with a window box. Mutti brought me a packet of nasturtium seeds. They germinated and flowered and I became a gardener.

Today I am grateful to nature. As Anto is grateful to God, so I am grateful to nature. The parallel stops there for Anto believes God to be merciful whereas I know that nature is totally indifferent. I can worship, I can offer it sacrifice of blood, bone and fish meal, and still I know that if it suits its purpose it will strike down my clematis with wilt, my tulips with *Botrylis tulipae* and my roses with a plague of aphids.

Anto says, 'God is good,' unfazed by famine, earthquake and the bestial nature of man. Well, good luck to him. He's going to need that thick-skinned certainty where he's going.

A lesser man would despair, Shields says. She's right of course. Anto will soldier on, cleaning the bottoms of incontinent teenagers, cradling the giant heads of deformed babies, smiling at the *Gauleiters* who oversee the orphanages and murmuring, 'God is good.'

A saint. Let's see if he can save my gardens.

RELIGION   I've been trying to remember what Eileen Joyce looked like and I can't call up her face. I have a general impression of fuzzy hair and a lot of make-up. I think the hair was permed. I loved her but I didn't think she was beautiful, not like Mutti. Did she wear glasses?

Those bluish eyes that glittered, especially when she was in zealous mood.

'Ye'll turn, I'd say.'

She had bought me an ice-cream cone and we were sitting on the rotting garden bench, licking contentedly. It was hot, too hot for dancing.

'Turn what, Eileen?'

'Change your religion, gom. Convert to the Catholic Church.'

I thought about this as I licked. 'But why should we?'

'Mostly they do, when somebody's praying for them. I'm praying for ye.'

My ice-cream was melting. I licked sticky white rivulets from my hand.

Eileen poked me in the side. 'You could say thanks. I'd love it if somebody was praying for me.'

'Thanks.'

'And ye'll have nothing but luck from the day ye turn. Like that girl at home.'

'What girl?'

'A Protestant girl. She wanted to marry Junior Lynch and when she turned her family created blue murder.'

'But why did she turn?'

'Because Junior was a Catholic. How could she marry him if she didn't turn? Honestly, Belle, you know nothing.'

'I do so – '

'Well anyway. When her family heard what she'd done they threw her out on the street. They just packed a suitcase with her belongings and left it at the gate and told her never to darken their door again. I never heard of anything so cruel.'

'But how did she have the luck?'

'Will you wait. They got married in spite of everything and Junior started to mint money. Soon he could buy his own shop and it's the biggest butcher's in the county today. Even all the Protestants buy their meat there. What do you think of that?'

I was impressed and not averse to turning. 'I'll turn,' I said.

Eileen's eyes glittered brighter than the sun. 'Have you ever been baptized?'

'What's baptized?'

'I knew it.' She jumped up and began to examine my doll's

tea-set lying on the grass. 'I'd better do it quick, in case you die and go to hell.'

'What's hell?'

'Oh my God but you know nothing. Here.' She pushed me down on the grass. 'Kneel. Join your hands and look holy. Now.' She raised the teapot over my head and began to pour. I squirmed as a smell of ancient stagnation accompanied the stream of water which just missed my head.

She yanked me back. 'Stay still. I baptize thee in the name of the Father and of the Son – ' At this stage the water ran out. She patted the upturned teapot on to my hair and I felt something slimy land on my scalp. I wriggled but her grip was firm.

'– and of the Holy Ghost. Amen.'

I got up.

'Don't rub it off or I'll have to do it again.'

I felt cold and wet but otherwise no different. 'Am I a Catholic now?'

'Of course.'

'Will I say the prayers before class so?'

'Do you not even pray?'

'I don't know how and the teacher said I was excused.'

'Don't you worry, I'll teach you.'

Eileen took her job as a catechist seriously but I soon grew bored.

'I don't want to pray to Infant Jesus,' I told her.

'Maybe the Blessed Virgin would be better.'

'Could I not pray to the Holy Ghost?'

She seemed uncertain. 'I never heard tell of it.'

'Well that's who I'm going to pray to.'

He was the only one of the lot of them that appealed to me. I liked the idea of a ghostly bird. I imagined him fluttering around my bedroom at night, then settling on a perch on top of my wardrobe. He would protect Buba and me as we slept, better than an old man with a beard or a small baby. And I didn't want another woman around, another mother.

'Can I tell Buba that I'm a Catholic now?'

'Don't be a daw. It has to be a secret. But you can pray for her so's she'll turn quick. I still pray for her and for your mother, every night.'

It was a summer of secrets. I remember looks exchanged between Buba and Mutti, silences, German conversations after I had gone to bed. I don't know if they always spoke German when I wasn't around but I remember these going on late at night, these guttural, argumentative conversations.

Buba was full of some fat secret which was putting a smile on her face. Father Jack was in on it, constantly hovering now and being whisked away to Buba's surgery for secret conferences.

'He's coming to lunch tomorrow,' Mutti told me.

'But he never eats with us. Does that mean we'll miss the pictures?'

'I'm afraid so. Father Jack will provide the entertainment tomorrow.'

Buba came bustling into the scullery. 'Horse radish for the beef — have you got, Erika?'

'I've got, I've got.' Mutti sounded sulky.

'Tomorrow is a special day after all.'

'Why is it special?' I asked.

'Patience. Tomorrow you will see.'

Mutti brought the roast in and placed it on a mat on the table. She began to carve but Father Jack, smiling at her efforts, stood up and reached over for the carving knife. 'Shall I do that, Erika?'

Complacently he hacked his way through the beef, piling

ragged slices on to plates. 'Lovely meat, Erika. Perfectly cooked.'

He sat down, looking pleased with himself. Buba glanced towards him expectantly, taking up her knife and fork but not beginning to eat yet.

Father Jack stabbed with his fork, loaded cabbage, beef, half a potato on to the prongs. He raised the load, began to chew, his jaws creaking, his horrid pink lips more repulsive than ever under a shiny coating of fat.

'So.' He swallowed, looked across at Buba, then down at me. 'The time has come to tell this child the good news, what, Dr Meyers?'

Buba nodded.

'This is a great moment in the life of any priest, Belle, a moment I have been waiting and praying for. Now my prayers have been answered and your dear, good grandmother has asked me to start preparations to receive you three – my dearest friends – into the Catholic Church.'

I wasn't really surprised because Eileen had assured me that this would happen but I wanted to tell him that it had nothing to do with him and his prayers. Eileen had got there first, I was sure of that. It was her prayers that had been answered and which were responsible for Buba deciding to turn.

Buba took up her napkin and waved it at me playfully. 'Such a long face. Soon with the instruction from Father Jack you become a perfect little Irish girl. Soon no one can tell the difference at all.'

My long face denoted disappointment. Some secret. After all the build-up, I had been expecting something a bit more exciting. This was hardly worth missing the pictures for – I was a Catholic already.

Father Jack flicked up his eyelids and gave me a disapproving look. 'Aren't you pleased, child? Don't you realize that your grandmother is thinking of you and of your welfare?'

'I'm a Catholic already,' I said and began to eat my sweet.

'Now, Belle,' Buba began but was cut across by the sound of Father Jack clapping his yellow hands together. 'Well, thanks be to God. Did you hear that, Dr Meyers? The beautiful simplicity of it – "I am a Catholic already." Out of the mouths of babes indeed.'

So Buba smiled at me and offered me another slice of Mutti's linzertorte.

Only Mutti remained unmoved, turning her head towards the window as she struck a match and lit a cigarette.

I remember that Sunday as the day that broke the summer in two. Before there was sunshine, heavy golden afternoons spent in the garden playing with Eileen; afterwards grey skies, boredom and a feeling of generalized unease.

I suppose the weather did break for I don't think that it is my own internal weather I am projecting on to events.

Eileen disappeared. One day she just didn't come over the wall. I waited for her the next day, standing on the bench, calling her name, but she didn't appear.

On many an afternoon I stood there in the rain calling her name until Mutti said, 'I'm locking that back door, Belle. You are forever coming in wet, you have no sense now, less than when you were little.'

I don't think Mutti liked being a Catholic. It was making her bad-tempered and she quarrelled with Buba, especially over Sunday Mass which we had started to attend and for which she was always late. I didn't blame her. I found it long and the seats uncomfortable and the church chilly. I warned Buba about germs but she just smiled.

Worse than Mass were my visits to Father Jack to receive

instruction. The others didn't go, saying that it was different for adults, as it invariably was when it was a question of getting out of something.

Father Jack lived in a house with other priests, a house of long, dim corridors where I was occasionally and unpleasantly brushed by the skirts of a soutane as a black shadow swished up and past, and disappeared into one of the many narrow doors on either side.

The sweating walls of these corridors were hung with religious prints of unbelievable horror and goriness: bodies being consumed by fire or livid with wounds from arrows still stuck in the bleeding flesh. Pictures of Jesus and his mother, their chests torn open to reveal their bloody hearts, pictures of Jesus on the cross, nails in his feet, thorns sticking out of his head. Blood, blood, agony and blood. I longed for the tranquillity of the Holy Ghost. I looked in vain for his feathery presence.

Father Jack smiled at my white face and issued me into a room which he called the library. We sat at a circular table of blood-red wood with a dead pheasant under a glass dome in the middle and little piles of religious periodicals at intervals around the edge. Father Jack kept the circumference of the table between us and threw religious truths at me with an uncompromising air.

'I'm not interested in God the Father and God the Son,' I told him, 'only the Holy Ghost. And I'll only pray to him. You can't make me pray to the other two.'

'As we sow, we reap,' he replied. 'I knew you were getting far too much leeway, I could see it clearly. Oh you are a true daughter of Eve.'

'And I don't want this tea.' It was grey and tepid and had that nothing taste which I so hated about tea.

'Spoilt and selfish. Children are starving in Africa and you are turning up your nose at good tea. I'll have to have a word with Dr Meyers. A young Catholic girl must behave in a certain fashion. I'll see to it that she hears all about this behaviour here today.'

I feared his influence over Buba so I closed my eyes, swallowed the tea and prayed to the Holy Ghost to strike him dead.

Father Jack and I were rivals, rivals for Buba's affections. From this rivalry grew dislike, which blazed periodically over the years but was kept doused down most of the time, by me more than by him. I was afraid of him, of his malice towards me, which I had recognized almost from the first time we had met. Perhaps he really did pray for me as he continually told me he did, but I always felt that looking at me he was reminded of something that he would prefer to forget; something distasteful, something that smacked of the sins of the flesh against which he waged unceasing war.

As I remember him now I am filled again with that childish rage as I stand impotently in front of him and watch as Buba smiles on him, blind to the malice with which he smiles on me.

'He hates me, Buba,' I would periodically complain.

She would shake her head and say, 'Silly Liebchen. He is stern, a man, but he loves you just the same.'

Stupid Buba. My anger is turned upon her.

I appeal to Anto. 'All this emotion the past is bringing up. It's too much, I can't handle it. I don't care what you say, Anto, this can't be good for me.'

'Trust me,' says Anto. 'Just let it all come to the surface, let it all come out. It's been dammed up for years; I never realized that, Belle, until now. This is very healthy, believe me.'

I had another problem. 'How do I know what's true and what I'm inventing? The emotions are so strong I don't know if I remember people as they were or I've just screwed them around for my own purposes.'

He put on his intellectual pus at that. 'Your truth will come out, Belle, your imagined truth. The way you felt then, the way you feel now. There's nothing particularly sacred or even superior about facts. Fact and truth are not synonymous. Just let it come out.'

I don't trust that sort of talk.

'We never know with memory,' he said. 'Ask two people who have shared a common event in the past to recall it for you and you will often, more often than not, get wildly different stories. People remember differently because events, facts – there's a sort of plastic dimension there. Do you know what I mean?'

'No.'

'The essence is what survives over the years. Events filtered through an individual sensibility. True for you if not in absolute terms – '

'OK. OK.' When Anto starts talking about absolutes I know it's time to make a quick exit.

I went out into the gardens. As I walked down the avenue and noticed the signs of early growth I could sense myself swing into a different rhythm. I breathed in the smell of damp earth and something sharper, a suggestion of tartness, a hint of spring. Soon the regular labour of seasonal tasks will have begun. The snowdrops will need dividing and then be replanted green. Slugs and snails are out, lured by the uncertain mildness. Already they've made inroads in the buds of the bergenia and I picked them off, stamping on them with extra venom. I'll soon have to start my twilight mollusc patrols. I seek them out with my torch and drop them into a bucket of heavily salted water. Stamping is not an efficient method of destruction for the slug can elude one's boot and sink deeper into the ground, to re-emerge when he's recovered his wind, determined to wreak even worse havoc. A slug has no sense of fair play.

Of course I didn't have to indulge in this manual slaughter when I had a hedgehog, but he was run over by Shields when she was coming home drunk one night. He was on the front avenue where he shouldn't have been and wouldn't have been except that he was disorientated coming out of hibernation. She had no excuse for driving far too fast. She couldn't understand my grief or the burial I gave him. She wanted to know why I didn't go the whole hog and give him a wake. She thought this was hilarious and fell around laughing.

As I said, crude but, I still maintain, not unkind. She offered to buy me another hedgehog and was quite upset when I explained to her that they didn't sell them in pet shops.

The details of her redundancy package have come through. It will be a shame if she gets out of nursing for good; her sort of stolid literal-mindedness is what the profession needs. I know that it was her gruffness that helped me through the worst years up there. She didn't have the imagination to pity us and anyway she was too busy pitying herself. Life's a bugger was what she seemed to be saying as she doled out the pills or yanked us out of bed. Life's a bugger so you'd better get on with it.

Remembering this I cut her armfuls of quince, long curving branches with their bracelets of pink flowers. I've kept one of the quinces in bush form so that I can have it for cutting. The other two are trained against a wall and their blossoms now are brazen and beautiful against the grey. They remind me of those factory girls who used to brighten the grey world of the fifties when they came home on holidays from English Midland towns, determined to cut a dash among the drab natives.

I've decided I'm going to join Anto in the fight to save the gardens. Up till now I've been sulking, punishing him for deserting me. But I'm really punishing the gardens which is silly, for my affair with them still continues.

I've agreed to see this producer who's such a keen gardener. It can't do any harm to have a preliminary chat. I hope he won't be too disappointed when he sees my monochrome borders. The daffodils are past their best, the pulmonaria is late, the lovely, billowing sheets of purple-and-white crocus have disappeared, disintegrated into the brown earth for another year. Easy to see where the idea of resurrection came from, standing in a garden.

It has been a strange season, mild spells followed by nights of severe frost followed by more mild weather. The result is nature all in a dither of confusion, precocity in some corners, premature death in others. Like a boxer a gardener has to learn to roll with the punches. I fear my ceanothus dead. Frost? Disease? Sheer bloody-mindedness?

I loved it especially because of the depth of that blue. Intense, fathomless, you could drown in it. Not any more. Dead, without so much as a by-your-leave. I shall be more circumspect with my affections when its successor arrives. If it arrives, if I am still here, if the gardens survive.

BETRAYAL I loved Buba and I had complete belief in her: in her calm good sense, in her fairness, in her generosity. I knew that I could depend on her and that she would never let me down. I had more trust in her than I had even in the Holy Ghost who never manifested himself to me although I occasionally heard the beat of his wings if I listened carefully at night.

'Go and bring your toys in from the garden,' Mutti said. 'It is almost winter. No more playing out there now.'

The garden already had a winter smell, a breathing out of

musk and decay which had formed into a compound that was suspended in the cold, still air.

I hadn't been out for over a month and I found it a depressing sight with everything battered and defeated by the incessant rain.

I walked along the path slimy with fallen leaves and I almost didn't see her, my eyes searching the ground for discarded toys.

'Eileen. You've come back.' I flung myself at her. 'Where have you been? Where did you go to, Eileen? And you won't believe what's happened; wait till I tell you.'

She stiffened her body against my embrace, then pushed me away. 'I only came to say goodbye.'

For the first time I looked at her. Her face was blotchy with pink patches around her eyes and nose. 'You've been crying.'

She gulped in air and began again, howling up at the sky.

'Oh Eileen, what is it? Tell me what's wrong.'

Her words came in shuddering gusts between sobs. 'What'll I do? What'll I do at all? I'll be killed if I go home but I've nowhere else to go. What am I going to do?'

I put my arms round her, holding on to her this time and beginning to rock her, the way Buba rocked me when I was upset.

'They wouldn't even let me explain, they wouldn't listen to a word I said. They said I was a pure disgrace and that no decent family would have me in their house.'

'But what did you do?'

She looked at me and I could see that even her hair had gone limp with only a few straggly curls left at the ends.

'I'm up the spout. I'm going to have a baby.'

'Is that all?' I hugged her closer, wondering momentarily as I felt the bony outline where a baby could be lurking. 'I thought it was something awful. A baby's good news. And now you and Jimmie can get married and you can leave the awful Mooneys for ever.'

When Buba had been telling me about babies she had mentioned that they sometimes arrived before the wedding but that this was not a good idea.

Eileen wiped her nose on the sleeve of her cardigan. She had a little round mouth with a soft uncertain underlip which she now pulled inwards so that her face suddenly appeared harder and older. It was difficult to read any expression in her eyes for they seemed to have retreated into their sockets.

'He's skedaddled.'

This was difficult to understand. 'But — how? I mean, the army and all.'

She pulled back from me. 'I don't want to talk about it, I can't, can't.' Then she began to cry again.

I took her hand and led her over to the wet bench. We sat down together with Goldie, my eyeless blonde doll, between us.

After some seconds I tried again. 'Could you not go home then? I mean to your own family down the country where Junior Lynch has his shop.'

She made a dismal attempt at a smile. 'You're a funny kid.'

'But couldn't you?'

'If my father was dead, God forgive me. But if I was to go home now I'd be the one who ended up dead.'

As we sat in silence the rain began to fall. I heard Mutti call me from the house. I couldn't leave her like this, alone in the rain in the gathering dark.

'Come in, Eileen, and Mutti will give you — '

I stopped suddenly. I had found the solution. 'Eileen, listen. You can come and live with us.'

She shook her head.

'But you can, I'm sure you can. Buba loves babies. People

bring sick ones to her from all over Dublin and she cures them. And we've two spare rooms.'

She shook her head again but I could see her looking at me from the corner of her eye.

'Really, Eileen. And you could even help Mutti, not as much as you do in the Mooneys' but just help. Buba is the kindest person you've ever met, I know she'd take you in.'

Her arm crept round my shoulder. 'It would only be for a while. When the baby was born, I could maybe go over to England – there's great jobs in the factories over there.'

'Will I go and ask and I can tell you tomorrow?'

'I get sort of nervous even thinking. I wouldn't eat very much.'

'Except for Mutti's cakes.'

We both laughed at this.

'Now you see how much better it is already. I'll come tomorrow before school. I'll be down here at half-eight and I'll tell you then.'

I waited until after tea when we were settled around the first fire of the season. Mutti had closed the curtains tight although there was still light in the sky. Buba had lit a cigar and Mutti was searching for her cigarettes. Soon she would wind up the gramophone and they would sit back while I did my Irish spelling at their feet.

I was lucky, I was loved. I thought of poor Eileen in her cold bedroom next door.

'Buba,' I said, nestling against her knee.

She exhaled, directing the smoke upwards, away from me. '*Liebchen?*'

'Buba, could Eileen come and live with us?'

'Eileen – who is this Eileen?' Her voice was dreamy, her attention wandering.

Mutti seemed more interested. 'The maid from next door,' she said, staring at me.

Buba stroked my hair, then gave me a playful push. 'But why on earth should the maid from next door come here to live?'

'She's up the spout.'

'Up the spout?'

'She's going to have a baby.'

Buba shook her head. 'What a strange expression — up the spout. Never have I heard that expression before.'

'Buba, please. Will you listen. Can she come and live here, the Mooneys are throwing her out.'

She looked at me, laughing. 'And what a strange little granddaughter. She cannot come and live here. How could a next-door maid come and live here?'

I tried to explain. I explained that she was my friend, not just the maid next door, how she had prayed that they would turn, how her father would kill her, how she had nowhere to go.

Then Buba explained to me. I didn't understand, she told me, I was too young. We were guests in this country and we couldn't offend against its mores. We couldn't offend the Mooneys and we couldn't offend Father Jack.

What I didn't understand was Buba's change of character.

Mutti said something in German and Buba gave her an angry reply. Mutti laughed without amusement.

'What are you saying?' I asked. 'What are you talking about?'

'Nothing,' Buba replied, 'nothing that concerns you.'

Mutti laughed again.

'Buba,' I pleaded, 'can't you think of poor Eileen? She really has nowhere to go. What will happen to herself and her little baby? We have to take her in.'

Buba stroked my hair. 'Such a tender heart but you mustn't worry. People of that sort survive. Even in Ireland I am sure illegitimacy is not so condemned by the working class.'

I turned to Mutti for support but Mutti was looking into the fire. She had absented herself as she so often did, standing at the kitchen window, but now her expression was sad rather than wistful.

'And you must try for other friends, Liebchen, nice little girls from school. That is what I wish for you, friends of the proper sort.'

I wanted Eileen to console me when I met her in the garden next morning. I wanted to explain to her, in so far as I understood it myself, that my Buba had disappeared. There was someone who looked like her there now but she was not my Buba. She was an impostor, a cold-hearted impostor, and when I looked at her I could only grieve the loss of my real Buba.

Eileen didn't even seem surprised, as if she had known all along that I could not help her. She wasn't angry and she didn't cry. She was just very quiet.

She began to fumble with the catch on the chain round her neck. When she had undone it she placed the chain with its medallion in my hand. 'You like that, don't you? Well, I'm giving it to you for keeps. Here, put it on.'

I looked down at the medallion. A silver oval with the Holy Ghost embossed in pearly relief.

Her only piece of jewellery, given to her by her godmother when she had been confirmed.

'I want you to pray for me when you look at it. Pray to him. Will you do that, Belle? I think I might need a few prayers and I haven't that many to pray for me.'

Then I felt shame as I thought about her predicament for the first time. And of her generosity and of how much she had given me in fun and love since we had met.

She closed my hand over the medallion and gave me a hug.

'I won't forget you, Belle. Hey, give us a smile.'

But I couldn't look up. I felt the shame pouring over me, a scalding liquid fire.

'I will pray to him,' I called after her.

There was only silence from the other side of the wall.

She looked so like Buba, sitting waiting for me in the kitchen with a loving expression on her face.

'Your breakfast, you must eat or you cannot go to school,' she said in Buba's voice.

'I'm not hungry.'

'You must not sulk, Liebchen, you must not spoil the pretty mouth by pouting.'

I shut my fingers more tightly round the medallion and prayed to the Holy Ghost to kill this impostor and send back my Buba.

When did they begin to merge, Buba and the impostor?

A month after Eileen's departure the process was already under way.

I tried to keep my loyalty intact through the rainy autumn days but each day it became more difficult. By the beginning of December I was like a cat allowing itself to be rubbed as I sat at night at my grandmother's knee. By Christmas the amalgamation was complete and Buba and the impostor had become one.

This was our first Christmas as Christians and it was impossible not to be sucked into the excitement generated by my family as it flung itself, with indecent haste I thought fleetingly, into the new dispensation. I noted too how familiar both women were with the new ritual.

Mutti had put a fir tree in a bucket in the window of our

sitting room and decorated it with apples and oranges and angels made of golden bread dough.

'A German tradition, the Christmas tree,' she told me as I helped hang the angels on the prickly green spurs.

German but not Jewish, surely?

Buba said, 'I think you chose goose, Erika, and with apple sauce, perfect. So delicious, goose, and to remind us of the old days.'

On Christmas morning Buba presented me with my present. 'From both of us,' she said, kissing me.

I looked at it lying on its bed of ruched, purple satin. Beyond anything this is what I had desired. Mutti said I mightn't have it until I was twelve – that was the age when a girl got her first wristlet watch. Now I lifted it from its bed and held it by its black suede strap. The golden face was the size of a teardrop with strokes instead of figures and two tiny hands. Never before or since have I desired an object with such passion. I held it out to Buba with my wrist.

'You like?' she asked.

'It is perfect, Buba.'

'Then give your old Buba a kiss.'

I gave it without reservation and clung to the familiar round little body with grateful recognition.

'Thank you. A million times thank you.'

That night I could not sleep. The day had been too full of incident, too full of emotions which I was still sorting out. I put the watch to my ear and listened to its tick.

I loved Buba but I was no longer part of her. I was separate, on my own now. That seemed very lonesome, and as if to emphasize my mood a dog started to bark. I listened above the ticking of the watch. The sound moved as sounds do at night, now coming from a great distance and now close at hand. Next door perhaps in the Mooneys' back garden which lay in prim hibernation behind the granite wall. Eileen wouldn't be there to feed the dog for Eileen had been thrown out.

I buried one ear in the pillow and placed my palm over the other one with the little watch in between.

In school I would shoot out my wrist to tell somebody the time. Nobody had a watch in my class except the teacher and that was a cheap, tinny thing.

Eileen would be fine. Of course her family would take her in. Or maybe she would get married. Maybe at this very moment she was lying in bed somewhere raising her hand above her face, moving it back and forth so as to make the diamonds in her engagement ring sparkle.

I pushed her out of my mind. I closed my eyes tight. When a glittering blue eye somehow inserted itself into my line of vision I pushed that away too and replaced it with a picture of my new watch.

I was a big girl when I came down to breakfast on St Stephen's Day. I had undergone my first rite of passage into the adult world.

Gardening has taught me a certain ruthlessness. I've tried to pass this lesson on to Anto but to no avail. He is a sentimental man, a marker of birthdays and other anniversaries, a hoarder of faded postcards, old hotel bills, holiday snapshots best thrown out.

I have learned to throw things out, to recognize mistakes, cut my losses and start again. I used to keep plants that had sickened, stricken with guilt as I watched them begin to show signs of disease: choice hybrid alstroemerias grown from stolen cuttings, meconopsis that I had raised from seed and tended over the difficult, unpredictable months of spring. Now it is off with their heads and out with their entrails. I pull them from the soil and fling them on the compost heap if they do not repay my love.

'I still love you, Belle,' Anto says to me. 'I always will. But I can't take you with me, I can't have two wives and she needs me more. You know I won't say anything else, it wouldn't be honourable.'

Should I view this as saintly behaviour, I wonder, outside of human understanding?

Shields said to me, 'You think he's doing it for himself but that's where you're wrong. Sure look at the fortune he could make on the telly if he stayed here.'

'Doing what?'

'Solving people's sex problems like that woman with the foreign accent. Telly is dead keen on psychiatrists.'

'He can't solve his own.'

The remark was indiscreet but Shields was too outraged to pick up on its implications. 'You're a right bitch,' was all she said.

'Or perhaps saints don't have sex problems.'

She considered this for some time then nodded her head sagely. 'You know I think you're right, Belle. They wouldn't, would they?'

I took a walk down the front avenue today. When I started work here the west side of this avenue was bordered by a stand of mournful conifers. I couldn't bear the wretched things, ranked in dull and gloomy uniformity, crowding out the light. Sad visitors were made sadder by their passage under the doleful shade as they made their way up to visit their mad friends and relations. I wanted to cut the trees down but I wasn't allowed to. As a compromise I grew things up through them, clematis and Virginia creeper. I got the idea from the equine Vita Sackville-West, not a particularly appealing human being but a gardener of genius. Not as great in my book though as William Robinson who brought something of Irish anarchy into the heart of English gardening.

I've learned more from Robinson than from anyone. I've modelled my bog garden on his and my fernery.

I am passionate about my fernery. All that arching green engenders such peace.

A green thought in a green shade.

Some gardeners are afraid of green because they think it boring and commonplace and it is if we are talking about the unyielding green of conifers. That is a green that depresses as it hurts the eye. It is like the gloss paint on the corridors of Father Jack's house, without gradation of shading, uniform and dull. But the green of grass and moss and fern, the new, tender green of deciduous trees in spring, that is a colour that refreshes and gives hope.

Books often say that ferns demand shade but I've not found this. Some of the American maidenhairs will grow in the open in an Irish garden. Ferns like lots of leaf mould and I think a mixture of ferns, Japanese, native and American, makes a very pretty garden. Pride of my collection is *Lastrea fragrans*, a lovely evergreen that smells of violets. The uninitiated get a whiff, shove their noses in and come up looking puzzled but delighted.

My fernery is approached by the lavender walk. I chose a site on the cool side of a high granite wall where *Cystopteris alpina* was already naturalized. There's still some planting to be done because I only work in it at mealtimes or when the patients are locked up for the night. They favour this over any of my other gardens. Shy, woodland creatures so many of them, I watch them flitting about, touching fronds, hiding behind the giant *Dropteris goldiana*.

It's their garden, not mine; Anto and I have always been agreed on that. Before he came here patients were not allowed into the grounds. He shot back bolts, opened doors and encouraged me to create an oasis of beauty where sore and damaged spirits could rest and breathe.

And another thing in his favour, he never talks about his wife. This infuriates me but wins him my grudging admiration. She's been at a few functions up in the hospital but I've always chickened out at the last minute and stayed away. Shields says she's good-looking but hoity-toity. She says that women like that, the big-bosomed sort, are often frigid.

Anto caught me today, idling up the front avenue.

'Any progress?' He was wearing a track suit. His body looks best in those sort of loose clothes because he is so loose in himself, so relaxed and graceful.

'Do you know what I fancy, Anto, at this minute?'

'What?'

'A good shag.' I was deliberately crude but I meant what I said.

He looked stricken. I could see the pain in his face and I wanted to hit him. 'Don't be angry with me, Meyers.'

'I'm not. I'm just angry with hypocrisy. And I'm angry with myself for not having seen through you years ago.'

I did hit him then, thumped him on the chest before running off to hide in my lair and drink enough wine to dull the fear.

I am terrified: of losing my house and my job, of loneliness, isolation, madness. Of having to live for God knows how long.

I retreat to the past because it is the only place left to me. Clever Anto. He must have known that this would happen.

But I'm glad I never loved him, I'm glad it was only sex. I loved another once and the sex was different then. That's how I know about love.

I craved him, I couldn't be without him. My body became deliquescent with longing for him. I lay beside him and could not distinguish our separate heartbeats. I touched my finger-tips to his and willed the flesh to become one so that we need never be apart. I ran my hands over his lovely opaline skin and wanted him, wanted him even as I was having him.

And his name wasn't Anto.

FATHERS 'Who is my father?'

I am in secondary school now, self-conscious, worried about an absent father that nobody ever mentions.

Mutti supplies the answer. From a writing case which she always keeps locked, wearing the gilt key as a charm on her charm bracelet, she produces a photograph.

I stare blankly at the face: an arrangement of features under a uniform cap. They tell me nothing.

'He died on the Russian front in '44.'

'He doesn't have any eyelashes.'

'They were very fair. Blond. He was a blond from birth, not like me, from the bottle.'

I am momentarily distracted by this display of hidden vanity. All these years and I've never guessed that she is a bottle blonde.

'The photograph does not do him justice,' she says. 'He was more handsome still.'

'Was he Jewish?'

'No.'

'Not Jewish,' Buba echoes.

I stare again, willing the photograph to give up some hint, some flavour of the dead man.

'I think you look like him,' Buba says.

'I'm not blonde.'

'Not the colouring, more the shape of the face. Look.'

We all look together.

'What was his name?' As I ask the question it occurs to me that his name should surely be mine.

'Wolfgang Elsner. His family was from Austria. They were Catholic, like you now.' Buba smiles at me, nodding reassuringly.

The more I stare at the photograph, the more the man in it recedes from me. I will never know him now.

Mutti replaces it in its yellowing envelope and returns it to the writing case. Delicately turning the tiny key she smiles beyond my head, a smug smile, excluding me. Is she glad that she does not have to share her lover, her soldier boy, with me?

'You shouldn't dye your hair,' I say to her in sudden spite. 'It's no good pretending to be what you're not.'

But it's not just the hair dye. We three live in a cocoon of deceit. The air is thick with evasiveness and unanswered questions. A remark of mine will provoke blushes, frowns, pursed lips. A question will be met with embarrassed silence. I know from his manner that Father Jack is in on it, whatever it is. In the thick of it. As I grow older I have begun to notice all of this; as I grow older they become wary of me. What are they afraid to tell me?

'Tell me about my father,' I demand.

Buba examines the tip of her cigar and when she looks up again her eyes are veiled, not through deceit this time but because she is gone somewhere else, retreated to a world where I know I cannot follow. But I'll try.

'They were in love, your Mutti and Papi. Such lovers as those two were. Your Mutti would stand waiting for him to come, looking down on the street from the big windows of our salon. We lived on a corner where two streets met and he could have been coming to us from either street.'

'Was that before the war?'

'Before the war. But your Papi was already in the army. That is how they met, when he came to Magdeburg. Erika was beginning to train as the infant-school teacher. And they met and fell in love . . .'

Buba's voice trickles into silence and she turns to look at her daughter. Mutti, her face averted, is pushing back the cuticles of her red-painted nails so that the half-moons show up. She paints them every evening, which is why, despite all the housework she does, I have never seen them chipped. It is the fashion to leave the half-moons unpainted.

'We lived on the first floor,' Buba continues. 'As soon as Erika saw him coming she would cry to me, "Here he is, Mutti. Where is my handbag? Are my seams straight?" Then when they went off I would stand at the window and watch the two of them walking along arm-in-arm. To keep in step your Mutti would have to take a little skip now and so often. He had such long legs.'

The room is choking with memories. I can feel them rise from the complex scent of the room, made up of cigar smoke, the dusty fibres of the Turkey carpet and Mutti's heavy perfume. They rise too from the dim flush of light thrown by the opaque glass of the lampshades and from the absence of the two women, for they have left, gone somewhere else.

I think that I can understand the deceit of their lives. I decide that they have to build, to fabricate a new existence for all three of us or they will die of sadness mourning the old.

'Did Mutti not have any brothers or sisters?'

Immediately I see that this is one of those wrong questions that cause embarrassment. Immediately I ask another. 'Did you not used to dye your hair in those days, Mutti?'

She picks up a strand from her shoulder and examines it critically. 'That is why it is so bad today, so like straw. In the war there was no dye so I used all sorts of things. Every girl who wanted to be a blonde had a special tip for lightening her hair. Pee-pee even, if you can believe. That is why it is so bad.'

Buba claps her hands together and smiles at the two of us. I can see that she is trying to shake off the past. Her voice when she speaks is jolly. 'What do I keep telling you, Erika? What do I say? No good to put things on the hair. If you take a tablespoon of cod-liver oil every day, by next summer your hair will be shining, shining. Like your daughter's, and she takes her cod-liver oil for her old Buba every morning.'

We are united. I am included in the woman's world of decision making and beauty tips. I am no longer a child.

A photograph I found last night confirms this. I didn't think any photographs from the old days had survived; I thought I had got rid of them all. This one fell from the pages of a book. *Justine* by Lawrence Durrell.

My books have been divided into two lots – those I'm keeping and those I'm dumping. I'll keep *The Alexandria Quartet*.

I remember a summer when everyone was reading those four books, when everyone wanted to go and live in Egypt. The photograph is not from that summer but predates it. On the back is written in Mutti's hand: July 1952.

The summer of my fourteenth year. A hot summer, as all summers were in those days. I look hot, even in the black-and-white photograph as I lie on the crushed grass.

The background is fuzzy, a suggestion of leaves. In the foreground the figure is in focus, caught with surprising sharpness by the box camera.

I lie with my head turned from the camera, my hair, which I have at last succeeded in growing, pouring over my face. My neck is exposed, vulnerable. My body, though still lanky, is just beginning to take on the contours of womanhood – the swell of a breast just visible, the rounding of a hip.

My legs are lovely, long and shapely, my feet incongruous in T-strap Clark sandals.

I am swamped suddenly by the sensuality that the snap is

57

giving off. What is it? I run my finger across the shiny surface, sniff, gaze. A memory begins to surface. A man who visits our house. He only comes once and I cannot recall his name or if I ever knew it.

Buba and Mutti are in the kitchen quarrelling more vehemently than usual.

'I didn't want him to come,' Mutti is saying.

'He is Father Jack's friend, he is our guest – '

'Not mine. I won't be here.'

'Such bad manners, Erika, so unnecessary.'

'Then stop in my life. If I want a husband I find him and not through oh-so-busy Father Jack.'

Buba sighs. 'I do not know why you dislike that good man.'

The other man arrives for tea and is seated opposite Mutti who has not fulfilled her threat. Father Jack is there too, smiling, nodding, opening and closing his moist pink lips as he pushes food into his mouth.

The man is of no interest to me. He is old. I escape outside as soon as I can.

Later I am called from the garden to say goodbye. Maybe my hair is tousled, maybe I am flushed from the heat which is still heavy in the garden, trapped inside the high walls.

I take his hand, noting its dry texture.

'Good-night,' I say and look up politely.

He doesn't reply and I get a shock as our eyes meet and I cannot look away. It is the shock of sudden sexual desire, coming at me, elemental and unmistakable. I recognize it, understand it, without being able yet to give it a name. For seconds I am encompassed by its energy. We both know what has passed between us. I withdraw my hand and step back.

Father Jack clears his throat, raspingly. 'Well, child, surely it must be your bedtime. Run along. You're still only a child, whatever you might think, and you need your sleep.'

He draws in his plump lips in disapproval.

That night in bed I wriggle around like a puppy. It is too hot for more than a sheet and already I have taken off my nightie. I do not share a bedroom with Buba any more. I am too big for that.

I get out of bed and go to stand by the window. Everything droops in the blue evening light. I press my body against the glass. The cold is delicious.

I am happy and not for any particular reason that I can fathom. I am just so beautifully relaxed, so easy within my skin. And I have this sense of empowerment that I've never had before. At this moment I know that I can achieve anything.

Anto met his wife at university when they were both medical students. She was two years behind him but she never finished because they got married the year Anto was doing his finals. One of the male nurses told me this. He's only been here a year so he hasn't developed this code of loyalty yet which means that he hasn't been infected with that extreme discretion that the others suffer from. At least where Anto is concerned.

He told me also that they're very well off because she inherited money from her parents.

I was right so to think of her as spoiled and pampered, a little rich girl who's never had to earn her living like the rest of us. I've spent a lot of time imagining what she looks like and how she lives. I bet they have a big, ugly modern house with a garden full of bedding plants and a fountain. I can see her with a year-round tan, gold bracelets on her arms, dressed in one of those power jackets in some strident colour. Odd to think that we could have been mates if I had gone to college as Buba wanted me to. She had always hoped that I would be a doctor.

Today the worm turned. Anto attacked me back when I started blaming him for what was happening up at the hospital. The only way I can get through his visits now is to start haranguing him. As each day passes I become more shrill. I am alarmed by the venom that I spit. Where does it come from? It gave me some relief when he cracked today.

He shouted at me, told me to shut my mouth for Jesus' sake.

'Stop trying to make me feel guilty, Meyers, because it won't work. What did you expect me to do anyway? I know it is right to try and get these places closed. Bins, Jesus, you should be thanking me.'

He rubs his eyebrows when he gets excited. I tried to break him of the habit years ago, telling him that his eyebrows are his best feature, which they are, arched and black, giving his face an aristocratic air.

'What did you feel like up there, think about that. Can you just remember what it was like being banged up with poor drooling idiots and the senile and the violent? All in that huge barracks of a place. It used to be that the biggest building on the approach to any Irish town, standing there grey and stark and ugly, was the mental hospital. Thank God that day is gone or going fast.'

'I'm not talking about that.'

'Yes, you are. You go on and on and on. And if anyone should be glad, you should. Nothing can change those places, nothing. No matter what frilly curtains you put up or what colour you paint the walls. The joists, the bricks, are saturated with the pain of generations. If I had the dynamite I'd blow them up myself.'

You have to harden your heart against him when he starts that sort of talk, so I changed tack quickly.

'I've decided I'm not going to see that producer,' I said.

The eyebrow-rubbing became more furious. He stood up, rearing over me like an angry dragon. 'You are infantile, you are totally irresponsible. You tell me you'll meet him, that you'll co-operate because you think, you agree, that it's important to get the public on our side if there's going to be a battle with the Eastern Health Board. I set up a meeting and now, out of the blue, you change your mind. Well, it won't do, Meyers, you're not a child, so you can change it back again.'

'But is there going to be a battle, with the Eastern Health Board, I mean?'

He stopped breathing fire at that. He had been striding back and forth in my small sitting room; now he sat down, collapsed on to a chair opposite me. 'What do you mean?'

'Well, think about it. The EHB are closing down the hospital, we know that, but nobody said they were going to sell it, did they? It's just as likely that they keep it for some other use – a geriatric hospital, maybe. Don't you think they'd keep the grounds then? What would be the point of selling?'

I was as startled by this new perspective as he. So hysterical had I been about losing my house and my job and the possible destruction of my life's work that I had treated my fears as if they were reality and had convinced Anto along the way.

'One thing is sure,' I continued quickly before he could recover from the shock and start apportioning blame. 'One thing is sure, if that film is made blaming the baddies in the EHB and accusing them of environmental vandalism, every square-inch of this land will be sold before the hospital is even closed.'

I felt sorry for him then. I think he's been working hard getting this film project off the ground. And he was doing it for me. That made me into a bit of a bitch. I relished the novelty of the role. It made me quite generous and I invited Anto to stay and have tea with me.

I'm not very good at fancy food. I was whisked away from my mother's knee before I had learned to make anything except apple strudel. Afterwards it never seemed worth the bother, poking around on my own except for Anto's irregular visits and he cooks like a chef in a restaurant.

I made us bacon and sausage and black pudding, cut slabs of fresh bread and wet a pot of strong tea. I actually love this sort of food, especially if my nerves are a bit jingly. All that ballast has a wonderfully settling effect.

Afterwards, when I was checking around the grounds for wind damage, it seemed to me that I can survive here quite happily when Anto is gone. He's been gone anyway for years. He has been no more than a shadow in my life since those early days when I did think that he was going to leave his wife and we were going to live together.

The wind had been howling for days. William Robinson says that the two greatest enemies in the garden are wind and the jobbing gardener. I'd been ignoring that howling wind and now I saw to what cost. A young daphne was beyond repair and I just pulled it out. My walnut tree which has been in for five years needed staking, as did several rose bushes. Many shrubs looked blasted, foliage torn, limbs broken.

I worked until the light went and then returned to my little house which smelled of turf smoke. A deep bath, a warm bed and a glass of whiskey. I can live like this. And I can never be as lonely as I was in my twenties on those Bank Holiday Mondays when all the world was at play and Anto had gone to the seaside with his wife. As long as the EHB allows me to, I can live like this.

HORRORS We are going backwards now. I am eight, maybe nine, too short to see into the downstairs windows of our house.

I am curious about what goes on in Buba's surgery.

She has become quite famous – the lady doctor. Women come to her from all over Dublin and children too. She has no male patients, not from choice but because, she tells me, no Irish man would ever trust his body to a woman doctor.

Mutti answers the door to a constant stream of patients: untidy women trailing children, smart women wearing fox furs and worried expressions. Mutti's fox fur has a pointed snout and merry glass eyes. He seems quite happy to hang around Mutti's neck. I think Father Jack would be happy there too although he pretends otherwise.

Mutti calls me from the kitchen but I ignore her and continue on round the side of the house. The surgery windows are closed so I don't think that Buba will hear the scraping of my shoes on the wall as I try to get a foothold.

I grasp the window-ledge and heave myself up. The stone is rough but I am wearing gloves. I peer inside. At first I can see nothing but as my eyes grow accustomed to the weaker light I can make out Buba, her back turned to me, wearing her white coat. She always wears this white coat in the surgery. She has five and Mutti hangs them out on the line with the sheets and pillow cases when she does a white wash. Like the sheets they smell of rosemary from the overgrown bush beside the clothesline.

There is a movement in the shadows at the far end of the room. A woman emerges, stumbles towards Buba. She heaves herself on to the couch, stretches out, pulling down her skirt.

Buba comes and pulls up the skirt, impatiently it seems to me. The woman is not wearing stockings, her legs are white with knotted blue veins.

Buba grabs her heels which are pink, not white like the rest of her, and begins to push them into the stirrups.

I know that those iron cups that swing apart are called

stirrups because Buba has told me so, though she has never told me what they are for.

The woman's heels are wedged into them now and Buba begins to pull them apart.

I look at the woman's face and see her expression of agony. How can Buba do this? Why is she doing it?

The woman is going to split in half if she continues. I can hear the flesh tearing. Buba – Don't –

I jump down, unable to take any more horror, careless now of any noise I may make. I run away and hide at the bottom of the neglected garden, tearing through sodden winter vegetation.

At dinnertime Buba eats a hearty meal and asks for a second helping of potato dumpling. She smiles down at me and I begin to think that I have imagined it all.

The stirrups again. This time it is a young girl who is on the couch. She smiles at Buba deprecatingly but Buba's movements are rough, even angry, as she forces the heels into the stirrups. I imagine them cold, freezing.

The girl seems to be putting up a fight, refusing to co-operate. I can tell that she is frightened. I can smell her terror, seeping out through the cracks in the putty.

Then Buba speaks. A bit late for modesty now, she says, but we'll see what can be done.

Buba's hands are not gentle, she has some sort of shining implement in them. She yanks the girl's legs apart so that the implement can be got inside. The girl begins to sob.

Am I saying that my grandmother was a back-street abortionist? This is fiction. This memory has been invented by me because there is some other cruelty about Buba that I cannot face. Or not yet.

I've warned Anto about the unreliability of memory.

Now perhaps he will believe me when I bring him this example.

Every year at this time I say that I'll get ahead of myself. I never do. Last year my back packed in; this year it is fear and sadness that have paralysed me.

I forced myself to sow seeds yesterday. The back room upstairs is full of seed trays now and in six weeks they will be going into the cold greenhouse. Now I think that the EHB will sell. All this land is just too valuable.

We've had frost for the last two nights but only today could I force myself to cover the wall-growing peaches and nectarines and the camellias. My camellias bloom late and are therefore susceptible to that lethal combination of frost followed by early morning sun. They have already suffered damage and I found several swollen buds lying on the ground.

I haven't got the heart for this so I'll just do it. That's what Mutti used to say about unpleasant tasks. I think she was confusing her heart with her stomach. In my case it really is the heart that quakes.

The grass is growing. If I feed it early it will encourage the finer grasses and give them a sporting chance against the coarser strains. There's going to be a real problem with moss this year because of the wet winter.

I invited the television producer round for Friday afternoon. I've changed my mind about the programme because, as I said, I'm sure the EHB will sell the land. A couple of JCBs could turn my work of art into a site worth millions in about half an hour. So I may need the media after all.

When I told Shields the news it turned her into a red-head overnight, with purple highlights. She says that this is the era of the older woman and if she doesn't succeed in launching herself into television she may land a toy boy.

'What about Anto?' I asked. 'Out of sight, out of mind?'

'You're a right bitch when you want to be.'

She told me that there are only twenty patients left up there now. Ten of those are going to be transferred to some kind of small unit and the other ten are going home or into sheltered accommodation.

'Anto fought for every single one of them. We've had nothing but bloody meetings – I'm whacked. It just goes to show, though, doesn't it – they're all people to him.'

She started to caress her moustache, her eyes dreamy. 'He is amazing, you have to admit that. Every single family, he knows them all. And he loves all his patients, Belle, really loves them.'

'I suppose that's why he's leaving them.'

'Why do you twist everything – you know it's not like that. It'd suit you better if you did a bit of praying for him. I've started a novena for his safe return.'

I began to laugh. I'm going to miss Shields more than Anto.

'You're better than the telly, Shields. A novena. I haven't heard that word in years.'

She pouted at me, sticking out her lips so that I could see the cracks in her baby-pink lipstick. 'You're so sharp you'll cut yourself one of these days.'

I am preparing for these changes. Really. Today I went out and got my hair cut short. It's a symbolic gesture, a severing of my ties with the past. I want to let Anto go freely. Cleanly. Then I can begin my new life.

When Mona McCarthy got hers cut she did so because she had seen how Audrey Hepburn had been transformed in *Roman Holiday*.

HEROINES Because I have become such a grouch they leave me alone at school, ignoring me. So I am the last one to find out that Sister Frances has broken her hip and won't be returning for the rest of the term. I am surprised when a new teacher walks on to the rostrum. She is small and slight and she moves silently, quick as a cat. She has cat's eyes too, large and green and unblinking. Her black hair is cut in a fringe and she is about twenty years younger than any of our other teachers.

'Right,' she says, looking slowly along each row. 'Stop glowering at me. I haven't done anything to you. Yet.'

This gets a grudging laugh.

She hooks a foot under the chair on the rostrum, pulls it back, slides her bottom on to it, one leg folded under her. She is tiny, like one of the first-years, except for her face where faint, feathery wrinkles have begun to settle here and there.

She seems in no hurry to teach us.

In the silence someone giggles nervously.

Miss McCarthy appraises us. 'I know school is bloody awful,' she tells us. 'I remember what it was like. Anyway, it's not much better from this side of the desk.'

She smiles and we smile back, enslaved now. *Bloody.*

As she has replaced Sister Frances she must be going to teach us history, but for the first day she shows no signs of this although she does mention de Valera several times.

She talks about herself and us. Tells us that we look revolting in our brown gymslips. She doesn't wear an academic gown, unlike the other lay teachers, and she hasn't begun the class with the statutory Hail Mary.

She says that we might as well know that she's not too pushed about exams but she will try to develop our minds.

'And I don't want yes-women,' she says. 'You won't please me by agreeing with everything I say although much of it will be worth listening to. But I like a challenge. I like people who at least try to think for themselves.'

Used as I am to dozing through the school day I am surprised to find myself awake and listening. She is cutting through the fog of boredom and inertia which have engulfed this building for me since I stopped being an eager new girl.

By the time her forty minutes is up we know that she lives with her mother, that she has a dog called Henry and a brother called Cathal, that she is trying to give up cigarettes because of her terrible cough and that Eamon de Valera has both betrayed his country and disgraced it before the eyes of the world.

History is going to be my favourite subject from now on.

I fight with Buba all the time now. Buba is patient with me, smiles when I try to provoke her, saying it is my age and natural. I slam out of the room but at night I am filled with remorse. I worry that she will die for she is not getting any younger.

In class Miss McCarthy stops when she comes to my name. 'Belle. I like that. It suggests optimism, confidence.' She smiles at me, a smile that seems too big for such a small face. 'And justified.' She looks down her list. 'Meyers. Is that German?'

Have I noticed a changing inflection which suggests disapproval? Whatever the reason I answer, 'German-Jewish,' although I have stopped thinking of myself as Jewish since we turned.

At the end of class she calls out, 'Hang on for a sec, Belle.'

I wait as the others file out, indifferent to their jealous sniggers. I am enchanted, under a spell. I have studied every detail of my new heroine, noting the cameo on her little finger, her distinctive scent made up of chalk and coffee and cigarettes.

She smiles at me sleepily. 'Most of my Jewish friends are

from a Russian background; I don't think I know any German Jews. Has your family been here long?'

I am suddenly embarrassed by our *arriviste* status. And she seems embarrassed by my embarrassment, looking at me with alarm.

'My God, I'm sorry. It never occurred to me that you were there during – that you didn't leave till after – '

Now she will think me a complete fool when she discovers that I don't even know about the war.

'We don't talk about it at home.'

She reaches across and touches my hand. 'Belle, forgive me. I'm such an oaf, about as sensitive as a steamroller.'

She stands up and begins to bundle our copy books into a basket on her desk. There is already an apple in the basket, a hairbrush and three Penguin paperbacks with orange covers.

'And I've used up all your breaktime. Here, have this.'

She puts the apple into my hand and closes my hand over it. 'Sorry. Really. Next time just tell me to mind my own business.'

On the way home I puzzle over why I have no memories from Germany. I was there, after all. Why does nothing come through? When I try to remember, all that comes up is a picture of Mutti skipping along on the arm of a tall young soldier. But that is Buba's memory, passed on to me.

Perhaps early memories don't survive and what we think we remember is simply what others tell us. Buba and Mutti tell me nothing, they have erected a blank, white screen in front of the past and I cannot see through. I am not sure whether I will try to hide this from Miss McCarthy or explain it to her. I wonder about her Russian-Jewish friends.

She tries to teach us history. Conscientiously she opens a textbook, clears her throat and begins. Occasionally she succeeds and we listen and learn. About Juana La Loca, for example, who refused to bury her dead husband's body and travelled all over Europe with his coffin beside her.

Mostly, though, the far-off battles are as meaningless to her as they are to us and she talks to us about Life, warning us against the dangers of complacency and mediocrity.

'And timidity,' she adds. 'Look at me. "Those who can, do, those who can't, teach." Get out there and do, girls. Let me be a dreadful example to you all, my life blood turning to chalkdust as my youth fades away. Out you go. Do. Do.'

She likes to talk about the villains of history, plucking them from the centuries, finding a parallel between each one and the biggest villain of them all, Eamon de Valera.

Sometimes she hurls the history book on to a shelf behind her and opens *The Collected Poems* of W.B. Yeats. She tells us that he was a genius, even if he was a bloody fascist, and that we should listen to what he has to say about love and ignore his politics. She informs us that human beings are inconsistent. 'Look at me, driving a Volkswagen.' She pronounces it 'volksvagen' like Buba, acknowledging me with a smile.

We all adore her, with one dissenting voice. Olive Tierney thinks she's cracked. Olive Tierney is solemn and takes education seriously. She has loaf-coloured skin and fuzzy hair. She pursues me, much to my embarrassment, favouring me with her attention because, she says, girls with a medical background should stick together.

She wants to be a doctor.

I don't care how I'll earn my living. I'll even settle for teaching if there is a chance that it will make me one tenth as fascinating a person as Miss McCarthy.

When I close my eyes today I can see Mona McCarthy but I cannot hear her speak. Her voice has disappeared down a shaft of memory. Was it low? High? Did she have an accent?

She must have talked to me a great deal, for so many of my ideas, the ones I have lived with over the years, have come from her.

I can see her but I can't hear her. I can smell her and this smell evokes a sort of excited longing in me as I almost catch that amalgam of sensations that I used to feel then whenever she was around. She gave off an energy which swept us all into its field.

I imagine her sharp little body, the dryness of her papery skin. It was skin that would not have aged well, unlike her eyes which I cannot picture as extinguished, ever.

Why did I say 'Would not have aged'? What do I know?

I open my eyes in a panic and instead of Mona see Anto sitting opposite me, watching me with the sort of attention he always pays to his loonies.

'Good, Meyers. You can't imagine how good this is for you. It will heal you and release you. Help you to move on.'

I grab his hand. 'There's something bad there, something about Mona. I keep on seeing bodies suddenly. They're tumbling round like clothes in a washing machine.'

'Write it down. Write it all down.'

When Mona McCarthy used to talk to us about Juana La Loca, I came to know her well. I used to imagine her long Spanish face, yellow under its black mantilla. I used to picture one of her hands, steadying the coffin as it was jolted over the rough roads of Europe. The knuckles on her hand were large, the skin roughened through age and neglect.

When I saw those knuckles I began to understand why she kept her husband's dead body beside her.

It is through our bodies that we get to know one another: we look, we sniff, we touch. You can know someone without ever talking to them. You could know Mona if I could make you feel the texture of her hair. If I could make you see how her eyelashes grew, bunched at the outer rim of her eyes. If I could make you see how she bit her nails and how it sounded, how laughter caught in her throat and came out sometimes in a bubble of saliva, how she picked at a mole on the back of her hand so that it bled sometimes and how the blood when the air hit it turned a rusty brown, if I could make you sniff up the salty, not unpleasant tang of her sweat, if I could make you do all this, then Mona McCarthy would live again, reincarnated.

I'll remember Anto's body when he's gone to Romania. I'll remember how his back arched up into my hand as I slid it downwards; I'll remember the swell of his buttocks; I'll remember his wonderful springy hair, more wonderful recently since it has turned such a colour. I'll remember his smell and the tender roughness of his eyelids, fluttering like moths under my kisses.

And is this all love is?

Not that I ever loved him.

Sometimes he says things that cut me open and leave me bleeding.

'I want us to have a last meal together. I want to cook it and remember you in your Hansel and Gretel house in the woods. That's how I'll think of you. And you must think of me. All our times.'

The first meal he ever cooked for me was a curry. I was surprised that he wanted to cook for us. Mutti cooked because she had to, Buba had other skills. And now here was the head of the hospital offering to cook supper for his lover because he liked to cook.

In those days there was only one shop in the whole of Dublin where you could buy Oriental spices. We went there together, holding hands. The spices were arrayed in glass jars like the old-fashioned sweet jars. They formed a twinkling backdrop for the brown man standing behind the counter who smiled up at Anto. They had been students together at the College of Surgeons on Stephen's Green and it was he who first introduced Anto to Indian cooking.

I was shy, out of the madhouse no more than two years, but he was shy too. Anto was the only one at his ease. Expansive. He pointed at jars, demanding that some be brought down so that he could sniff at the contents or press the spices between finger and thumb. He asked his friend's advice and then discarded it. Showing off his friend to his mistress, his mistress to his friend. Showing off. Isn't he doing the same thing today, rushing off to rescue Romanian babies?

The shop man smoothed a sheet of white paper on the counter and began to pour on to it little pyramids of various spices: brown coriander seeds, green cardamom pods, lacy curls of cinnamon, tiny chilli peppers, red and wrinkled like new-born babies.

'She will make you a very good curry,' he said to Anto and it was minutes before I realized he was referring to the spices and not to me.

For days the exotic oriental smells clung to my little house, filling me with desire every time I caught them, not for curry but for Anto.

'Make a curry,' I said now. 'Make a curry for our farewell meal.'

'A curry? You know, I haven't made a curry in years.'

He went over to where my books were packed and began rooting around. Eventually he came back with *Spices, Salt and Aromatics in the English Kitchen*. He began to turn the leaves, then flipped to the index. 'This is the only decent book Elizabeth David ever wrote,' he said.

'You gave it to me.'

He laughed. 'Did I?'

'Yes, years ago.'

'I had a friend once who kept a spice shop,' he said, his eyes on the book.

'Really.'

'Before your day. He was from Goa. A nice chap but a terrible businessman. He used to give credit to all the Indian students in Dublin and apart from me they were his only customers.' He paused, resting a finger where he had been reading. 'Then there was some sort of scandal – I can't remember – but he left and the shop changed hands. Sells lampshades now or something.'

'An Indian student murdered a Dublin girl. The story went round Dublin that he was using her body in curries in an Indian restaurant where he used to work. All the spices came from your friend's shop. There was no truth in the rumours but the shop and the restaurant both had to close down.'

Anto stared at me, then slammed his hand down on the open book. 'By God, you're right. I'd forgotten all of that completely.'

'You haven't got a very good memory, Anto, but then being a psychiatrist you wouldn't have to, would you? It's only the loonies that have to remember, isn't it?'

He put his hands on my shoulders, looked into my eyes.

'I admire you more than you'll ever know,' he said. 'You've come through more than most people and you've made a successful life for yourself. But the past has come back and you must deal with that. Then you can move on, like I said.'

I wanted him to go on holding my shoulders. His hands felt solid, dependable, impersonal. His great, square body was releasing energy which was warming every bit of me, turning my blue toes pink. Plumping up my muscles, pouring iron into my backbone. Leaving my heart untouched, though. Honestly.

THE PAST Miss McCarthy couldn't leave the past alone. She wanted to know about Germany, although I suppose you could say that it was I who started her off again.

'Hop in,' she said, pulling up alongside me as I turned out of the school drive on to the road. She leaned over and pushed open the passenger door.

The car was smaller than Buba's and very untidy. There were empty cigarette packets on the floor and screwed-up balls of paper. The back seat was piled high with books and copy books.

'We're not Jews,' I said, wanting to get things straight before they became intractably muddled.

She took her hand off the gear shift and turned to me. 'I thought you said – '

'We used to be but we turned because Buba – my grandmother – said we would fit in better as Catholics over here.'

She considered this as she ground out a cigarette, then snapped the ashtray shut. She turned the ignition key.

'I'm not all that surprised, I can understand. This is Ireland after all.' She had begun to drive fast, heading along the main road away from my home. 'Irish people,' she said, 'xenophobic, monocultural, bloody Catholic bigots. They'd wonder why you hadn't got over the gas ovens considering how well they've recovered from the Famine. And Jews after all – well, they're not Catholics. I'm sure your poor grandmother was thinking about all of that when she decided to convert. And who can blame her.'

She leant forward, groping in the glove compartment and bringing out a packet of cigarettes and a lighter. She told me to light a cigarette for her.

I did it as neatly as I could, making sure not to get the end of the cigarette wet. I had watched Mutti doing it for years.

She inhaled deeply, narrowing her eyes against the smoke.

'Look, if you want me to mind my own business, say so. But this isn't just idle curiosity, Belle, my brother nearly died fighting the fascists. He was wounded at Jarama.'

She must have read my blank expression for she added, 'Spain. The Spanish Civil War. Then Dev thought that he mightn't have suffered enough so he slung him into the Curragh for a while. Poor old Cathal.'

The car slewed to the right as she turned the wheel suddenly. 'I forgot where I was going for a minute.'

At this stage I was wondering too but I didn't want to say anything in case she took her eyes off the road completely or her hands off the wheel. She was a very different driver to Buba.

'Belle, if you don't mind my asking. Did you all get out?'

Get out? 'Do you mean from Germany?'

'Yes.'

I thought. 'My father and my grandfather aren't here.'

She took her hand off the wheel and touched my arm. 'You poor thing. You poor, poor thing.'

We drove along in silence but I could feel her tenderness towards me, her special concern. I had never thought of myself as an orphan before, someone to be treated with extra kindness and sensitivity.

Miss McCarthy crashed down through the gears as we began to slow down. 'Now do you see where you are? Not as dozy as I look, am I? What number?'

However she had done it we were back in my road.

'Thanks for the lift.'

'You're welcome. Here.' She leant over and gave me a hug. The gear shift stuck into my hip but it was a small price to pay.

'You're a great kid.'

As I walked up the path and saw the light go out in Buba's surgery as she shut up shop for the day I knew that from now on I was different. A girl with an interesting, even heroic past. All I had to do was find out more about it.

I had a crick in my neck from poring over an Irish essay. I stood up, stretched and looked around me with a sense of dissatisfaction. Buba was sitting back with her eyes closed, listening to a Schubert song. Mutti was examining her nails, a cigarette smoking in the ashtray beside her.

They would let me go on like this for ever, night after night, denying me knowledge about the past. My past.

'What were the gas ovens?'

The song had finished and the question was dropped into the tiny pool of silence which always separated Schubert from Buba's sighs of pleasure and Mutti's renewed rustlings.

Mutti's red mouth split apart as Buba opened her eyes. They stared at me, struck dumb.

'You know, in Germany. Tell me about the gas ovens.'

I could feel the confusion pouring off them, the embarrassment boiling over.

Mutti said something in German but Buba flapped a hand at her, signalling silence. 'You do not ask such questions,' she said to me, her voice high with annoyance.

'I jolly well do, I've a right to know too. I felt such a fool today in front of Miss McCarthy. Why shouldn't I know? It's my past too.'

They stared at me, their faces rigid except for their flickering eyes.

'I mean I do know bits about it. In general like. But I want to know about us, what about us.'

This brought on more excitation. Mutti pressed her fingers to her mouth as if to stop herself from talking; Buba stood up and began to back away from me, putting the sofa between us and groping for the door handle behind her. Escaping is what she was doing.

As she found the handle she pulled the door inwards and, one foot already in the hall, said, 'I cannot answer. Father Jack, go to him. He will tell you what you want to know.'

I turned to Mutti.

She nodded. 'It is better, Father Jack. He is calm, it will be easier with him.'

Father Jack had stared down at his hands folded in front of him while he offered me an explanation. Now he looked at me, a quick darting look before the eyelids descended again.

'So you see it is not surprising that your grandmother did not want to talk about it.'

'But what actually happened? I can't really understand what you are saying.' I guessed that I had been offered a highly censored version of events. Things stated, then contradicted, other things hinted at but a larger horror hanging unacknowledged over the whole account. 'The gas ovens. I mean – it's just too hard to grasp.'

He raised a grey eyebrow. 'At school? What did you learn?'

'That place. Nobody ever mentioned anything until Miss McCarthy. And history stops as far as they're concerned with the coming of Saint Patrick.'

'That young woman.' He drew his plump lips inwards in disapproval. 'And of course Irish people are sensitive. If it wasn't for her busying herself this might never have come up.'

I forced myself to be polite. 'Father Jack, I need to know. Were there gas ovens where people were murdered? Jews? My family?'

He shook his head, exasperated. 'Look, Belle, it's all very

78

complex. Truth is difficult. The older you get, the more you'll realize how complicated truth always is.'

'Yes, but – '

'Just accept what I've told you. When you're older. And your poor grandmother has had enough suffering in her life.' He drummed his yellow fingers on the blood-red wood of the table. 'And it wasn't just Jews, to put the record straight. Catholics too, many Catholic priests.'

He raised his head to look out over my shoulder through the library window where a spidery fire escape crawled upwards along a grey, pebbledash wall.

His voice as he continued sounded almost dreamy. 'And perverts. I'll say that for Hitler – he made short work of the perverts.'

'Perverts?'

'Nothing for you to worry about. Now, enough is enough, like a good girl. My advice to you is to leave well enough alone. Forget the past. Get on with the present – and the future. University in a year or two, Belle. Then you can think about the debt you owe to your dear grandmother. And to this country, come to that.'

I had no intention of leaving it there.

Buba was busy and elusive but I caught her the next night as she was getting ready to do her physical jerks. Her hair was in its two wispy plaits and her long, cotton nightdress fell in stiff folds from her tiny body. She looked pathetic and old and I felt a stab of regret that I had abandoned this nightly ritual which she still remained faithful to.

I heaved myself on to her high, mahogany bed. 'You're still very good at them,' I said.

She paused, smiled. 'I try.'

I watched her for some seconds, then said, 'Were we, our family, were we ever in a camp?'

She didn't pause this time. 'Rescued, by good Father Jack.' She bent and touched her toes. I couldn't tell if her knees were straight inside the nightdress.

'But you know, what happened to other people, the gas ovens.' I was afraid of upsetting her but I had to know.

'Was grandfather – did he –' I couldn't finish and I waited till she turned towards me and I could see her face.

She was laughing!

She came over and I helped her up on to the bed. '*Liebchen*,' she pinched my cheek gently. 'What awful things go on inside that head. Your grandfather, he died of the natural causes. He was a very old man and he had already done his duty for his country in 1914.'

'And nobody – '

'Nobody. Nobody.'

But I didn't believe her. I knew by the way that she said it, by the manner in which she avoided meeting my eye, that she was hiding something from me. Shielding me, I thought with sudden guilt. Protecting me from something painful.

'Now, no more talk about the past. It is over. We have made a new life here for ourselves and you are the little Irish granddaughter.'

'Yes, Buba.'

'*Gut.*'

'But why do you two talk German then?' I couldn't let that pass. 'I'd have thought you'd hate the very sound.'

She sighed and reached up to stroke my hair. Her little Irish granddaughter was now towering over her. 'Still our language, *Liebchen*, that doesn't change. And just because some things happen doesn't mean that everything about Germany is bad. Remember Beethoven. And all the others. Now. No more

80

talk. I'm tired. Leave the past, listen to your old Buba. Leave the past.'

Mona McCarthy didn't see things like that. She said that you couldn't forget about the past because if you forgot about things like fascism and the Nazis then it would happen all over again.

'Of course there's nothing to forget here in Ireland,' she said, 'because nothing was acknowledged in the first place.'

We were sitting outside my house in the Beetle, screened from Buba's surgery by the chestnut tree that hung over the garden wall. 'We didn't have a war here, we had an emergency.' She laughed and rolled down the window to flick a cigarette butt on to the pavement. She often gave me a lift home but I kept her from Buba's eyes, protecting her from possible criticism. Buba, I felt, might have been influenced by Father Jack who had dismissed her as 'that young woman'.

'I'd have said myself that an emergency is when you run out of drink on Christmas Day. Or when you've a burst mains and you can't find a plumber. Somehow when six million people are being slaughtered you'd think that there would be a more appropriate word for it than the Emergency.'

I was an eager disciple, desperate to match her passion but aware of my inadequacies, the tepidness of my responses, particularly where Dev was concerned.

'This country would put years on you. Look at this.'

She was leaning back, reaching into her basket on the back seat. 'Where is it? I know it's here somewhere.' Copy books went flying upwards. 'Here we are.'

She handed me a crumpled copy of the Irish Press. 'Look at that. That about sums up this country.'

It was a photograph of de Valera kneeling to kiss a bishop's ring. The bishop looked splendid and lordly with his wonderful ribboned mitre.

'The great revolutionary. Huh.'

'Who's the bishop?'

'For goodness sake, Belle – what does that matter? I wish you'd get your priorities right. Look at that expression. Pious. He wouldn't bend the knee to the King of England but he'd be down flat on his face before the Bishop of Rome.'

'Did Ireland – '

She interrupted me. 'Jesus, what am I saying? He *did* bend the knee. I was forgetting altogether about the oath which he accepted when it suited him.'

'Miss McCarthy, I thought Ireland fought during the war?'

'Your ignorance would be astounding if you hadn't been subjected to the Irish system of education. We were neutral. Held on to our ports to spite Churchill. A gallant stand. Then just to prove how neutral we were, this fool,' she stabbed her finger into Dev's face in the photograph, 'this fool went and offered his condolences at the German Embassy on the death of the Führer. Fine gesture that was. Really made them sit up in world capitals. Protocol, you see. All revolutionaries have a great respect for protocol.'

She threw her arms into the air. 'I weep, Belle, I weep when I think of this poor benighted country.'

She gave me a little push towards the door. 'Off you go, your granny will be wondering what kept you.'

As I turned at the gate to wave goodbye she summoned me back. 'We won't give up the fight, though. One of these days I'm going to introduce you to some of my friends and then you can really get involved. Fascism must never rear its ugly head again.'

*   *   *

Olive Tierney cornered me in the toilets at break. 'Why is she always giving you lifts?'

'She isn't.'

'Yes, she is. Every time I see you you're sitting in the front of that Volkswagen of hers. She's a Red, you know.'

'She's a what?'

'A Red. A commie.'

'Who told you that?'

'Everybody knows. Her brother fought in Spain for the commies.'

Was that all? I laughed with relief. 'I know he fought in Spain. He fought for the Republic.'

'And what do you think they were? A load of commies.'

'They were not.' I hoped I sounded sufficiently scornful.

'My uncle should know. He went out to fight for the Catholic Church – '

'What has the Catholic Church got to do with it?'

'Are you stupid or what? The Reds were butchering priests and raping nuns. My uncle told me. And Miss McCarthy's brother was there right in the middle of them.'

I was shaken by her conviction but I rallied. 'I don't believe a word of it.'

'And she wouldn't have got a job here except for Mother de Lourdes. De Lourdes' brother and her brother were interned together in the Curragh. Sure she was kicked out of her last school because of her commie ideas. And my uncle said she'd better watch her step here. I'm to tell him if she starts anything here.'

I stared at her in the mirror as she struggled to tame her fuzzy hair in a French pleat. Was Miss McCarthy a commie?

'And another thing – isn't it about time she started teaching us some history? I've had about as much of the Life and Times of Mona McCarthy as I can stomach.'

*　　*　　*

The next time Miss McCarthy gave me a lift home she said, 'I'm thinking of starting a debating team, with you fifth-years. What do you think, Belle? You've plenty of time this year and I could start working on you, knocking you into shape.'

'Try Olive Tierney.'

'Olive Tierney?' She shook her head. 'I don't really think – '

'She'd be good, honestly.'

'But she seems so lifeless. No spark. I always think of her as docile but uninteresting.'

'That's just the side you see because she's shy. But she's very interesting, she's always going on about the political situation in Ireland and how awful it is. She can't stand de Valera.'

'Well, now.' Miss McCarthy narrowed her eyes in concentration. 'Who'd have thought? Never judge a book by its cover, to coin a phrase. I'll have to watch out for her hidden talents, if that's what you're telling me.'

Miss McCarthy was clever but she needed to be protected from herself and her generous heart. I had listened to what Olive Tierney had said and although I was too ignorant to be able to evaluate it, I recognized the malice behind the telling. Olive Tierney was out for blood.

When she asked me home for tea I didn't dare refuse in case she took it out on Miss McCarthy.

She lived in a house with a name instead of a number. *Sans Souci* was written over the door and on the gate in case you missed the door. Typical, I said to myself, so suburban. I viewed its red-tiled roof and Virgin Mary blue-painted doors and windows with distaste. Since coming under Miss McCarthy's influence I aspired to an attic, a country cottage or a flat in the heart of a city. Suburbia was death, inhabited only by the bourgeoisie. Although we lived in the suburbs I had discovered that we could not be called suburban because, despite Buba's efforts, we did not fit in.

Buba anyway was ambivalent. She had made us turn, she was forever going on at me about being a little Irish granddaughter but she herself was careful to keep the world at bay. Her manner towards the neighbours was cold. Nobody was ever asked in for a cup of tea and our one invitation from the Mooneys was turned down by her on the grounds that we could not go to a sherry party where we would know nobody.

I think she must have been a very good doctor and I know that her many patients held her in awe. Other doctors referred people to her and she worked long hours in her surgery, so long that perhaps she had no time or energy left for making friends.

Mutti on the other hand was lonely. She would have made friends in the neighbourhood but her beauty decreed that she would remain an outsider for ever. Like a bloom from some distant and sophisticated botanical garden she dominated the dull little wild flowers all around her. Younger than the other mothers in the neighbourhood, better groomed, more beautiful, she evoked nothing but envy and fear. And perhaps a touch of moral superiority on their part as they caught the flash of her scarlet-painted nails.

I was grateful for all of this, doubly grateful now as I greeted Olive Tierney's mother who had not quite made the transition from farmer's daughter to successful doctor's wife.

She was red-faced and stout; not fat which can include the voluptuous, but stout with its implications of control, of flesh restrained inside rigid corsets. Nowadays that word has almost become redundant but it suited Mrs Tierney perfectly.

She smiled at me, took my hand in both of hers and squeezed it painfully. 'You're the lady doctor's granddaughter, aren't you? I'm delighted now that Olive brought you home. Her daddy and I are always encouraging her to bring home nice friends.'

Mother and daughter beamed at me in approval.

'Now let you go on up there to the drawing room and I'll get Mary to bring you up a little snack. Then you can get on with your homework and nobody'll disturb you.'

The maid brought us a plate of ham sandwiches and two glasses of very weak orange squash. The drawing room was cold with that fusty air of unused rooms. I sat back in a huge, ugly chair, part of a suite, and looked at the improbable navy-blue roses blooming under my feet in the acres of carpet.

This epitomizes the bourgeoisie, I gleefully told myself, opulence without taste.

The ham in the sandwiches was pale pink and slimy under my tongue. The bread was stale. I thought of Mutti's pastrami, of her liverwurst served with pickled cucumber.

'She's starting a debating team,' Olive Tierney said. 'Has she asked you to be on it yet?'

'No.'

She gave me a look of sly triumph. 'I'm sure she will.'

I stuck my tongue firmly in my cheek. 'She obviously approached the best debaters first.'

Olive nodded complacently. 'Probably. But I'm sure there'll be room for you.'

She stood up to pass me the plate of sandwiches, throwing herself an admiring glance in the mirror over the mantelpiece.

'She said she was looking for people with political awareness – I suppose that's why she chose me.'

'I'm sure that's it.'

The things I did for Mona McCarthy.

*　　*　　*

We had a row today because Anto refuses to vote. The elections are next week and I said he must, particularly as he'll be out of Ireland for God knows how many years.

'Why should I?'

'Because, well, you're part of society, aren't you? You're not a hermit or something.'

'I don't trust society – how can I when I'm surrounded by society's rejects.'

He has a point. People who froth at the mouth, the self-mutilators, people who set fire to their homes or starve themselves to the point of death, what have political parties and systems to offer them? Whatever government has been in office Anto's had the same difficulty wresting money from them.

He spends the money on drugs and alternative therapies but that's not what helps his patients and cures many of them. It is Anto's love which does that, the strength of that love focused on each one individually.

Yet he's so bloody naive.

'If you won't vote,' I said to him, 'at least go and talk to the minister.'

He looked at me, puzzled, crinkling up his forehead, widening his eyes. 'Why would I talk to the minister?'

'For God's sake, Anto. Nobble him. Go and tell him what a great job he's doing and if he could only give you a guarantee that the gardens will remain as gardens whatever happens to the hospital. Get it in writing and the Eastern Health Board won't be able to do a thing.'

When he began to rub his eyebrows I knew that I was in trouble. 'Oh I couldn't do that.'

'And why not?'

'I've built up a relationship of trust with those people. They've always treated me decently. I'm not going to try and exert political influence on them at this stage.'

I didn't bother to argue. The righteous are always immovable.

I'll obviously have to save the gardens myself, which is why I welcomed the two John-the-Baptists who arrived on my doorstep this afternoon. Researchers, they called themselves, precursors of the director who will phone me next week.

I could see the disappointment on their faces when I was showing them around. They found nothing appealing in the skeletal loveliness and were unimpressed by the viburnum, shining and glossy and smelling of nectar. I hope the director has more imagination.

Shields said I blew it by offering them wine. 'Only middle-aged housewives drink wine nowadays,' she told me. 'All the trendies drink Mexican beer by the neck.'

'You should keep your mind on what you're doing and leave that oul' writing alone,' she said, looking with disapproval at the mounting pile of school copy books on the table. 'What are you writing anyway?'

'A novel,' I told her.

She thought about this then asked, 'Am I in it?'

'Of course, need you ask?'

Her chest expanded with pride and she threw back her purple head. 'I'll let you get on with it so.'

And it is coming to seem more like a novel to me. I'm coming more and more to see memory as an amalgam, a mille-feuille of fact, interpretation, desire, invention.

When I think and think and think about the past I believe that I only ever approach near to truth through sensations.

Thinking about Mona McCarthy I feel myself shaking with terror; then this sensation is replaced with a sweet pleasure that floods through me. It is a sensation which the body recognizes before the mind gets at it and begins to re-interpret.

If I am to arrive at any sort of truth it will be through the senses.

SONS AND DAUGHTERS My eyes smart from the cigarette smoke and it is hard enough to see anyway in this dim light.

'Sit down, girls,' says Mona McCarthy, 'and call me Mona, for God's sake.'

She has taken us to the Coffee Inn to celebrate our victory.

We've won the Cup. We've gone through the opposition like butter and finally we've come up against the Jesuit spawn and dealt with that too. In two months Miss McCarthy has fashioned us into the best debating team in Dublin. We've come through five rounds and now we sit with our individual miniature replicas of the Hibernian Cup. Tomorrow our photograph will be in the papers. As we wait for our coffee we recount our moments of glory: how we undermined them by not taking them seriously, how we wounded their male egos by laughing at their pomposity. How right Miss McCarthy had been in forecasting their complacency.

'As far as they're concerned you'll be only girls. When they start to patronize you they'll be expecting confusion, maidenly blushes, anything but a proper fight. Your great advantage will be surprise. Just look them in the eye when you demolish their arguments, no hint of female diffidence. They won't know what hit them.'

The coffee comes in glass cups with froth on the top. Some of mine slops on to the saucer as the girl hands it to me. 'Sorry, man,' she says.

You couldn't call her a waitress with her pale lipstick and her languid manner. A student. All the waitresses are students, wearing black polo necks and pale lipstick.

Miss McCarthy is having wine. 'I think I'll have something to eat – what about you lot? Spaghetti bolognese, I think.'

Olive Tierney whispers in my ear that we shouldn't chance it, it's bound to be far too spicy.

I don't care about the spice but I know that I'd never manage to get the spaghetti to stay twirled round my fork.

The third member of the team says she'll have a doughnut. I cannot remember her name now although I can see what she looks like: lank blonde hair and freckles. She is good at thinking on her feet, surprising us with her witty retorts to the hecklers who had been planted in the audience.

Olive Tierney drags me to the Ladies. It is a difficult journey squeezing past chairs and avoiding outstretched feet, hard to discern in the semi-dark.

'Tell her we want to go home now,' Olive Tierney says.

'Why should I? She's ordered more coffee for us.'

'Have you not noticed the amount of wine she's drinking? She'll be in no fit state to drive us home.'

'Don't be so bourgeois,' I reply, drunk myself on glamour and excitement.

'Anyway, I don't like this place, it's full of beatniks and you know what they go in for.'

'What?'

'Free love.' Although I know that she means to sound disapproving what comes out in her voice is hot, breathy excitement.

When we get back I move my chair as far as I can from Olive's and stretch out my legs. At the next table a girl is sitting by herself. She doesn't look as if she is waiting for anybody, she is just alone. I watch her, admiring, envious. Her hair is cut in a fringe, dead straight. When she flicks a lighter I see the title of the book lying in front of her. *Cry the Beloved Country*.

I take a swig of coffee, then refuse to cough as it goes down the wrong way. The effort makes my eyes water.

Miss McCarthy finishes her spaghetti, lights a cigarette and looks around her. 'I haven't been here for years. God, I feel so old.'

I realize that she is indeed much older than anyone else here and I move the candle on the table further from her face, to protect her from Olive Tierney's heartless, probing eyes.

It must be spring or early summer for it is still bright outside. Light seeps in through the door which is ajar. As I look it is pushed inwards. A beautiful young man appears in an aureole of light. He is like the risen Christ in the calendar in Mother de Lourdes' office. I think I am having a caffeine mirage for nobody else has reacted to this apparition.

But now he is moving towards our table. He stops. 'Mona.'

'God, Max. You shouldn't creep up like that.'

He sits but on the very edge of the chair. His mouth is wide and sulky, his eyes seem very dark in the dark light. His hair is thick, blunt-cut. There is something caged about the way he positions his body, as if he is ready to spring, to escape.

As they talk his hand plays with Mona's cigarette case. He looks towards us and then away, dismissing us. Perhaps she has introduced us, I hope not. To be introduced like that, in a bunch with the other two. And in school uniform. And long-haired beauties at every table reading Cry the Beloved Country.

I could cry myself.

'No, I won't stay. I just looked in . . .'

His voice trails away. This is a characteristic that I will learn about him – the trailing voice and the eyes that suddenly glaze over.

'I'll see you on Thursday then.' He says goodbye to us and is devoured before my eyes by the thick fumy air.

Miss McCarthy lights a cigarette. 'He's so restless, that boy. I thought he might have sat down and had a coffee with us but he's always on the move.'

Three pairs of eyes stare at her, willing her to say more.

She laughs. 'Good-looking, isn't he?'

'Is he your brother?' Blondie asks.

'Don't be daft, he's far too young.' I don't think Olive Tierney means to be insulting, she just never thinks about the way other people might feel.

Miss McCarthy doesn't heed her although she has become sombre, staring at her glass which she is turning round and round on the table. 'Poor old Cathal,' she says. 'No golden boy he.'

The fizz has gone out of the evening, we have nothing left to say to one another. Miss McCarthy grinds out the cigarette which she has just lit and empties her glass. 'Come on, I'd better get you lot home.'

When she has left the other two off I hop into the front beside her. She turns the car round and turns back the way we have come. We both live in the same direction, nearer the city.

The streets are empty but Miss McCarthy drives slowly through the blue evening light. She is humming a few notes of some tune, then breaking off, then repeating them. The tune sounds melancholy, high and plaintive.

'The funny thing is,' she says suddenly, 'Max often reminds me of Cathal, the Cathal I remember, I mean, when I was about the age you are now.'

She begins to hum again; it is getting on my nerves.

I want to ask her about Max. 'Is that fellow, Max, is he – '

'Max is Max. Like Cathal, a young god.'

We both use the same word, see the same image.

She gestures towards her handbag and I take out her cigarettes and light one for her. She inhales as if she hasn't had a smoke all day and begins to tell me a story. 'Your life can fall apart overnight, you know. Mine did. Other people do it to you so that you have no say in it.' Her voice wobbles a bit as she says this, I stare straight ahead of me where it is safe to look.

'He ran away, the bastard, and I can never forgive him for that. Then I look at him today and sometimes I feel the anger inside me will tear me apart, destroy me just as he's been destroyed.'

Her brother Cathal left university to go to Spain. Ran away to fight fascism when she was fourteen and he was her god. Their father was dead, he was the man of the house and he left them with a quick embrace and a cheery goodbye at Westland Row Station.

Mona and her mother returned home determined to be brave and get on with their lives, praying to God to keep Cathal safe. The following Sunday they found that they had become outcasts when the priest read Cathal's name from the altar, together with the names of ten other young men who had gone to do the devil's work in Spain. The mother was not angered by this, she was mortified. She agreed with what the priest had said but she loved her son.

The Beetle slouches to a stop opposite our front gate and Miss McCarthy lights another cigarette, still talking.

'I remember being sick with anger. Angry with my mother because she hadn't got up and walked out of the church, angry with the priest for his attack and angry with Cathal for causing all the trouble in the first place.'

She exhales, throws back her head. 'He was so wonderful. His voice, his eyes − so alive. And sure of himself, arrogant even. Immortal. I never worried about him coming home alive although Ma was sure he'd end up with a bullet in his back.

'Then there was a headline in the *Independent* about nuns being raped by Republican soldiers in a convent near Madrid and a brick was thrown through our front-room window. People wouldn't serve us in shops. It was after that I started reading his books to try and find out why we were suffering, if it was worth it.'

She laughs suddenly, turning towards me. 'And you know something, Belle – I'm still not too sure.'

'But what about your brother?'

'What about him? What happens to old revolutionaries, the ones who botch it up and don't get killed? He lives in a caravan in Rush. Can't be near people. I have to go out and collect him every Sunday so's he can come in and eat Ma's Sunday joint. He's still the apple of her eye.'

She doesn't say this with any pleasure, there is a sour note in her voice. Outside it is growing darker. In our garden the uncertain topiary of some jobbing gardener who has conned Mutti into giving him some work is filling dark corners with crouching men touting guns. Does Cathal sleep with a gun under his pillow, lying in his caravan in Rush with the Irish Sea outside noisily chomping at the rocks?

'What is it with mothers and sons anyway, answer me that. Christ and Cathal both telling their mothers where to get off and both getting away with it while I'm older than either of them and I'm still expected to go to Mass every Sunday like a good little girl.'

A light goes on in Buba's bedroom, throwing a bright oblong on to the scrubby front grass.

'I must go,' I say.

'Indeed you must. And I must shut up and sober up. Too much wine, Belle, that's what brought all this on.'

As I stand on the doorstep waiting for Mutti to answer my knock I find the little cup in my pocket. I take it out to present to Mutti, to explain why I am out so late. The strange thing is, I've forgotten all about the debate. It seems to have taken place a long time ago and in a much simpler world.

I'm beginning to use the past to justify the present or at least to explain the shabby state of affairs between Anto and me. It's adultery, isn't it? Ugly word, ugly deed.

What's his excuse?

Maybe saints don't need excuses. It seems to me they're a rum lot most of them with little or no consideration for their family and friends. None of them could resist a desert or a hermitage, a tyrant, a murderer, a rapist, any old excuse to get them out of the washing-up or driving the kids to swimming on a Saturday morning. I suppose, give or take the intermittent adultery, you could say that I'm a stylite myself, but then I have no family obligations whatsoever, I can afford to indulge my whims.

I saw him today, my saint, when I was hacking away at a neglected *Buddleia davidii*. He was sitting on a bench in the sunshine with a young man. They faced one another and Anto had his hand on the young man's shoulder. I couldn't see either face but it was easy enough to recognize the boy's pain, the foetal curling of the spine, the head twisted aside, doing violence to a slender, tender neck.

The mad are not touched. Even those who love them do not touch them. Mothers don't touch children, husbands don't touch wives.

But Anto touches them all. He holds their hands, puts his arms around them, reaches out to squeeze a shoulder, to run a finger down the length of an unlovely cheek. He touches them all, the smelly and the ugly, even those outcasts among outcasts, the smelly, the ugly and the old.

You see crazy faces smile when Anto passes by; eyes, blind as those on antique statues, look at him with sudden recognition; people open up like flowers as he walks past.

And all this despite the fact that he's none too bright, at least I don't believe he is. Who could believe in his intelligence in the face of his gullibility?

He practises every unorthodox theory; he has brought charlatans from all over the world to the madhouse. They have come from California and India and Tibet – shamans and monks and gurus and healers, the seventh sons of seventh sons and pubescent girls who claim to have had visions of the Virgin Mary.

When I question him about all this he taps my nose and says, 'More things in heaven and earth, Horatio. Keep an open mind.'

He hasn't a very open mind where drugs are concerned. He is highly suspicious of what he calls chemical control and resorts to its use with great reluctance. I tell him that electric shock therapy helped me but he says that he cured me, rescuing me just in time before serious damage was inflicted on me.

I had been doing so well. In the old, disused porch of the hospital rows of empty margarine tubs were filled with clay and turf mould and sprouting tiny green shoots. They were pleased with me, the powers that be, and as a reward they brought Buba and Father Jack in to see me.

I attacked him, naturally. I hit him with a gardening fork, just missing his eye.

So they yanked me off, strapped me to a table and ran electric currents through me. Some people, knowing all the facts and looking objectively at the situation, might say that their behaviour was a lot madder than mine.

When Anto arrived to clear out the ancien régime, I was swimming up through space, trying to free myself, body and mind, from the cotton wool that surrounded me.

He held my hand. I could feel the pressure of his fingers, the first thing I felt.

'You're not mad,' he said. 'You've been wounded and I am here to heal you.'

I found his eyes and locked mine on to them. They were fathomless but I knew that I wouldn't drown while I held his gaze.

'I am here to heal you and soon you will be better.'

'Don't send me home.'

'It's too early to think – '

'Don't send me home, you must promise me. Never, never. Not home.'

So he moved me here to this little house and gave me a job.

Perhaps I've lingered too long. Perhaps he thinks that his diagnosis may have been wrong all those years ago. By staying put for thirty years haven't I proved that I'm insane?

It wasn't like that, it never is. I slid into the crevice that he showed me and stayed there, one day at a time. I didn't plan on a thirty years' tenancy, for God's sake. It just happened. Life just happens. Like the seedlings that have drifted into the crevices in my little terrace and have been living there quite happily ever since. When terror fills the space inside my head, causing my ears to buzz and my eyes to bulge, I try to emulate those seedlings. As my uprooting seems inevitable I must just be. I will make no decisions, I will just be.

POLITICS AND THE HEART As I let myself in by the side gate I saw Mutti standing at the kitchen window. She was looking up at the moon which was looking down at her. I stopped to stare at both of them. They had a lot in common, the moon and Mutti: a luminous beauty, secrecy, mystery, isolation. It was the first time I realized how isolated my mother was.

She called to me, 'Belle, you are so late. We worry.'

'Is Buba gone to bed?'

'Yes.'

'I'll go up and say good-night to her then.'

I kissed Mutti who smiled and returned to her former pose, head raised looking up at the distant moon.

Buba was still asleep. Her face was paler than her daytime face but still rosy. Her hair released from its bun was formed into two wispy plaits. She slept on her side, one hand under her head. I pulled the string at her headboard and withdrew, leaving the door ajar. Buba never liked to sleep in complete darkness. Since I had moved into my own room she always slept with her door open.

Night silence is denser. I could feel it part as I moved through it, then gather again behind me. Round the two women it was so thick as to be impenetrable. As one watched and the other slept the silence expanded, then enfolded all.

In my room I stretched out on my bed and took out the book that Mona had given to me. Its blue-and-white cover was stained, its edges curling. I had noticed the distressed condition of Mona's books, as if she didn't merely read them but fought with them, forcing them perhaps to give up their meaning.

'Read that,' Mona had said to me earlier, scraping the book off the floor of the car as we sped along parallel to the grey convent wall, scattering schoolgirls.

'Who's she?' I asked without enthusiasm. Mona had begun to try to educate me and I was discovering that it wasn't much fun.

'Rosa Luxemburg, the great socialist thinker and martyr. If you read that you'll begin to understand something about why your grandmother decided that you should all become Catholics.'

'But she shouldn't have, should she?'

Since we had turned shortly after my tenth birthday I had been happy in my new identity, in so far as I thought about it at all. Not any more, though, not since Mona had started filling in the spaces left blank by Buba. 'It was a betrayal, wasn't it?'

'Jesus – who am I to say that? All I can say is that integration didn't do the Jews any good, ever. Read Rosa Luxemburg's life. Your grandmother was only thinking of you, Belle, I'm sure of that. It's harder to understand than to judge but it's more worthwhile in the end.'

I sighed. 'I wish I felt more Jewish.'

'You don't look Jewish either. You know the one about the Chinese Jews meeting in Peking. "Funny, you don't look Jlewish." Go on, go and read that. As of yet there are no discernible dents in your ignorance, Belle Meyers.'

Now I propped myself up on my pillow and began to read. I was still reading when Mutti came up to bed and chased me to the bathroom. When I had got undressed and under the eiderdown I took up my book again. I must have fallen asleep with it for when I awoke next morning my bedside light still burned and the book, more distressed than ever, was lodged under my arm.

A socialist, that's what I was going to be. Not a Catholic nor a Jew but a socialist. I would turn again for the last time, I would embrace the rational like Rosa Luxemburg and solve my identity crisis by joining the brotherhood of man.

I believed now that I could begin to understand Buba. She and my grandfather had turned their backs on the ghetto, moving away from its shadows, turning towards the twentieth century and away from the medievalism of long beards and gabardines.

Then they realized when they got caught up in the greater horrors of the thirties and forties that not being a Jew was not enough. Buba had decided that we would have to have a completely new identity. She had mistakenly thought that by us becoming Catholics I would never suffer as others had suffered over the centuries. She wanted above all to secure my safety and in order for this to happen I had to disappear, to sink without trace and to re-emerge a proper little Irish granddaughter.

And what about my father, the laughing soldier boy? Suddenly I saw him in a new heroic light.

It couldn't have been easy for a German soldier to court and marry a Jewish girl in the thirties. Mutti's beauty notwithstanding, her crimson heart lips, her straight seams, her lovely languid neck as she threw back her head, cigarette poised, awaiting the flick of his lighter, my father must have been an exceptional man. Loyal and loving and brave as a lion. A socialist, perhaps.

Most probably a socialist. Like me. Although would a socialist have joined the army? I would have to ask Mona about that.

As I lay there thinking about this I heard her bedroom door open and listened as she shuffled past on her way to the bathroom. She always shuffled in her slippers which had grown too wide with age but which she refused to relinquish. The bathroom door banged and the plumbing began to grumble. Suddenly I was engulfed by a huge wave of love for my little Buba. She had become a Catholic for me, for my sake. Hitler had made no distinction between the assimilated and the unassimilated Jew. How could I ever be safe unless I stopped being a Jew, unless I was reborn?

Little Buba. I would protect her. I would put my arms round her and let her know that no harm would ever come to her. If the midnight knock came to our door I would answer it *as Gaeilge* with a crucifix in my hand, my hammer-and-sickle petticoat hidden but ready to be produced if that was what was called for.

At breakfast I hugged her the way I used to when I was a little girl. Then I turned to Mutti and asked, 'Any bacon? I'd love a couple of rashers before I go to school.'

I looked slyly at Buba and smiled at her smile. A little Irish granddaughter complete.

I stuck my head inside my desk as the others began to file out. Olive Tierney warned me that I would be late for basketball but I told her that I wasn't going, that I'd got a sick note.

I was mitching. I intended to go on mitching for as long as I could for I had decided that there was no room for basketball in the life of the socialist intellectual.

'Well?' enquired Mona from the rostrum. 'What are you doing skulking down there?'

'The book, I've read it.'

'Good. Look, Belle, I can't stay. I've got to take Ma to have her corns done and I'm late as it is. Walk me to my car.'

She thrust a bundle of copy books at me and sped from the room. 'I'm delighted you read it,' she said over her shoulder. 'She was some woman, what.'

'I want to be a socialist,' I said as I ran out after her.

We crossed the tarmacadam at speed.

'Did you hear what I said?'

She took the copy books from me and put them on the roof of the car as she rooted in her bag for her keys. She looked at me sceptically. 'I suppose your heart's in the right place.'

'Please Mona, I'm serious.'

She sighed. 'It's not that easy, Belle, it's dangerous being a socialist in this country and I don't want people coming along and saying that I've been corrupting my pupils. I've enough on my plate as it is.'

'Please, nobody need know.'

'You could do some more reading, prepare yourself – '

'I'll do that anyway.'

Behind us from the redbrick building uncertain soprano voices rose in the chorus of a hymn. 'Hail, Queen of Heaven.'

I wanted to be away from all that, to be out in the big world seeking to mesh all disparate peoples into the one brotherhood. Not Jew and Gentile, not Black and White, but all one inclusive family, with the exception of Olive Tierney. Even socialists had to draw the line somewhere.

Mona McCarthy sighed again. 'I'll see what I can do. I'm not promising anything but I'll see what I can do.'

She got into the Beetle and banged the door after her. I hammered on the window.

'Belle – I really have to go.'

'But tell me, how do I become a socialist, how does it happen?' I was thinking of the rite I had undergone seven years ago when Eileen Joyce had poured stagnant water down my neck.

Mona turned on the ignition. 'Socialism is a political philosophy. If you are attracted to that philosophy, if you believe in it, then you seek out a political party and you join. But you're too young.'

I clamped my hands on to the roof of the car. 'I'm nearly eighteen, how can you say I'm too young? And I'm very mature for my age, you said so yourself. And I'm a Jew.'

This was my trump card. Mona McCarthy, a spinster school-mistress approaching middle age, took all the guilt of generations of white, Christian despots on her frail shoulders.

Mona began to push my hands away. 'My mother will be dead by the time I get home. Let go, Belle, and I'll bring you along to the next party meeting and pass you off as an eighteen-year-old student. Now, get off.'

*   *   *

102

It was pouring. I knew that my hair would be ruined by this stage, frizzed beyond reparation. My shoes squelched and my stockings were clinging in wet wrinkles to my legs.

'Do we have to go round again?' I asked Mona as we turned into the south side of the square for the third time.

'I've told you, we've got to make sure that we're not followed. You don't think Special Branch will have taken the night off just because it's raining, do you?'

In the months to come I was to learn that paranoia was the only thing that kept the members of the Socialist Workers Party together, or so it seemed to me as I sat and listened to them quarrelling endlessly over matters doctrinal, stuffed into the small, fumy room over the lock-up garage.

Round the deserted square we slopped once more. If Special Branch was here it must be roosting in the trees.

'OK, that's enough,' Mona said. 'Come on and keep that hood up.' She pulled me across the road and up a narrow lane. 'Now, remember what I said. Stay quiet, I'll answer all the questions and don't mind Heslin. If he seems hostile, the hostility is aimed at me, not you. He's an unregenerate bloody Stalinist and he only came with us as a tactical move. He thinks I don't know that but I've got his card marked all right.'

Our party had broken away from the Socialist Workers League because of their Stalinist tendencies. Mona called Stalin Uncle Joe in the same tones of contempt that she called de Valera Dev. She had no time for Lenin either because of the manner in which he interpreted Karl Marx who held the position of God the Father.

'Watch those steps,' Mona said, 'they're very steep. And remember Heslin won't ask you your age if he suspects you're too young, he'll ask you for your date of birth. So be prepared.'

My first impression as we pushed the door inwards was that we had come to the wrong meeting, everyone was so old. Rows of elderly male faces turned to look at us as we stood on the threshold. A man sitting behind a table at the front of the room barked, 'You're late,' and then returned his attention to the ancients. 'So I think Comrade Hilliard should be in no doubt where we stand on that one. Just remember Lenin's advice: "Sex isn't worth a drink of water."'

I perked up at the frank use of the word sex. And hearing someone referred to as comrade gave a flavour of dangerous foreign glamour to the proceedings.

The comrade at the table pointed a finger at me. 'Sit,' he said.

I shuffled towards a space on the front bench but Mona shoved me towards the back. She went and sat beside the man at the table.

I saw now as I sat down that the sexes were divided here, the same as at Mass. My two companions neither moved nor acknowledged me, so that I was forced to sit in between them. Their eyes were fixed not on their knitting but on the Comrade Chairman's face.

That's what Mona was calling him as she apologized for our lateness. I guessed that he was also Heslin, the tactician with the Stalinist tendencies.

I don't know what I had been expecting, soul-stirring stuff about the revolution and the rights of man, perhaps.

What I got, or what I could hear over the coughing and creaking of chairs and bodies, was dull procedural stuff laced with references to the rule book. Nobody said anything without prefacing their remarks with 'Section this, sub-section that'.

By the time my name was brought up under Any Other Business I had begun to wonder what business I had here. I watched as I was proposed by Mona, seconded by a man in front of me and accepted by a unanimous show of hands from the assembled comrades. I felt little enthusiasm. Perhaps

Mona had been right and I was too young for serious politics.

Comrade Chairman banged the table with the bowl of his pipe and told us we could go. The man sitting in front of me, the one who had seconded Mona's proposal, turned to smile at me through round glasses. From behind the distorting lenses his eyes swam out at me, crazily enlarged.

'Pleased to meet you,' he said, shaking my hand.

The Mesdames Defarges looked at me for the first time, then dismissed me to start prodding with their needles at two men in front, telling them that there would be no pub tonight.

The man in front said, 'Don't stir now till some of this lot clears.'

Up at the table I could see Mona gesticulating angrily towards the Comrade Chairman who stared at her stolidly, arms crossed, neck thrust forward.

There had been too many bodies pressed into the room and the air was rank. I began to enumerate the reasons I would offer to Mona for not attending the next meeting. And the one after.

My new companion said, 'You're Belle, aren't you? Mona told me all about you.'

I nodded.

'It was a good turn-out tonight, Belle; they must have come to give you a proper welcome.' He looked round the emptying room. 'I thought Max'd be here, he said he was coming. Do you know Max, do you?'

'Max?'

'I thought you might know him, you both being Jewish like.'

'Is it the Max – '

'Waterman, about your age. At Trinity like you.'

There couldn't be two such Maxes. I was being rewarded after all for turning my back on frivolity. 'Thank you,' I whispered behind my hand to the Holy Ghost, lapsing back into religion momentarily.

'We've always had Jews in the Party but it's only natural, isn't it?'

'I see you've met George,' Mona said, coming up to us.

'Yes.'

I was to learn that although George McNab held to the orthodoxy that religion was the opium of the people, he had a soft spot for Judaism and Jews.

'You have to understand,' he would expound from time to time, 'Jews is different. Considering what they've been through they've a pefect right to hold on to their clap-trap. And anyway, it's not such a dangerous class of clap-trap as the rest.'

Mona refused George's offer of a drink, saying that it was too late.

On the way home in the car I decided to make doubly sure.

'You remember the night of the debate,' I asked, 'the night we won the Cup?'

'What about it?' She was squinting through cigarette smoke out on to the wet road.

'Do you remember you took us to the Coffee Inn afterwards and we met this fellow there, Max?'

'He was supposed to be here tonight.'

'Then it's the same Max?'

'That's how I met him, through the Party. He leaves periodically when he gets disgusted with Heslin and then he comes back to us. I keep on telling him that reform has to come from within and that leaving just gives the upper hand to Heslin. What made you think of him anyway?'

'Oh I was just wondering.'

POLITICS AND PASSION   He didn't come to the next meeting nor to the one after that. I didn't mind so much for by now I, too, had become a socialist. Heart and soul I was devoted to the cause, even if I still lagged behind in understanding. I was a romantic socialist and I no longer saw my comrades as old men but as paladins who struggled against the forces of obscurantism and repression. And they weren't all that old. Many of them seemed infinitely younger than Olive Tierney and other of my dull classmates, as they leaped to their feet passionately to denounce some wrong.

I had found companions, soulmates. They took me to the pub after meetings and slipped me the odd sip from their glasses when Mona wasn't looking. I learned that the life of a socialist in Dublin was one of heroic struggle. Not only was there Special Branch to contend with but there was the Archbishop whose spies scoured the city looking for Reds whom he could make an example of.

And not only could you be thrown out of your job by the Boss Class but you could be expelled from your own union by the votes of misguided and divided brethren. Danger lurked at every turn, which was why before every meeting the room was scanned for strangers who might be hiding in corners.

At home I was deceiving Buba with ease, so much so that I felt ashamed. 'Don't study too hard,' she'd say as she waved me off to a Party meeting. 'Remember your health is more important.'

I had to be vigilant, though, and I could never tell her the truth as long as family life was infiltrated by a clerical spy. If Father Jack ever found out what was going on I had no doubt that Mona would lose her job and I would be sent to some sort of correction camp run by the Archbishop.

When I came home from a Party meeting to find Father Jack sitting motionless, his chair in the shadows against the wall, I felt a shiver of fear run down my spine.

He would watch me as I self-consciously placed my books on the table, then flick his eyelids up towards Buba.

'She's studying very late, isn't she, Dr Meyers?'

Buba would nod proudly. 'I tell her – too much hard work is not a good thing either. I have to watch all the time and see that she does not lose weight, that she does not become too tired.'

The lizard-like eyes would be turned on me, the fleshy lips drawn inwards in consideration. 'Not a good thing to have a young girl out so late at night. Moderation in all things, Belle – that's the prescription for a happy, decent life. And you should put your trust in God. Get up an hour earlier and be on time to attend daily Mass. That, I assure you, would benefit you more in the long run. Remember, Belle, you are an intelligent young girl but there is always the danger of the sin of pride.'

Buba would intervene then. 'Not pride, Father Jack. It is because she has not got the pride that she feels she has to work so hard.'

I'd smile at him. 'And anyway, Father Jack, I really should do both – Mass and study. God helps those who help themselves. Isn't that what they say?'

Father Jack and I were mortal enemies, and enemies, like lovers, share insights. He knew something was going on but he didn't know what. Luckily for me his imagination didn't stretch to the idea of me being involved in godless politics. He didn't see politics as an occasion of sin into which seventeen-year-old virgins might fall. His view of young women accorded with Comrade Heslin's. They both believed that we were weak-headed, prone to sins of the flesh and a danger to men because we got between them and their destiny.

He worried away, getting nowhere because my guard was up.

'Out so late every night and looking well on it. If I didn't know better, Dr Meyers, I'd say there was a young man on the horizon somewhere.'

'A boyfriend? Me?' Each separate note of laughter was polished with insincerity. 'If you know any likely candidates I wish you'd introduce them, Father Jack — I'd be delighted.'

And Buba would smile from one to the other of us, delighted with this good-natured banter between her dear friend and her darling granddaughter.

And I thought how much I would enjoy handing Father Jack over to George McNab when the revolution came.

George and I had become friends. He was predisposed towards me because I was a Jew and Mona's protégé. I found him restful, dreamy and diffident, a good man to walk around the square with or sit beside in pubs.

He drank in moderation except on occasion when he broke out, changing from stout to whiskey and undergoing a startling change in personality. He had wispy baby curls and a fine pale skin and you knew the metamorphosis had begun when the curls began to quiver and the pale cheeks deepen to pink.

He would bang his glass down on the table and, rolling his enlarged eyes round the bar, would demand that any priests present come forth and make themselves known.

'Come forth, ye whited sepulchres,' he would proclaim. 'Give us another whiskey there — '

'Now, George, you've had enough.'

'Come forth and face the Irish nation you have wronged, destroyed, enslaved to Rome. Come forth for there will be no place to hide your stinking bones once the revolution comes. When the revolution comes it will be my pleasure to see that a priest swings from every lamp post on Stephen's Green. My duty and my pleasure.'

No priest ever did come forth. If there was one present I

couldn't imagine him taking George's ferocity seriously, with the blushing cheeks and bobbing curls.

Next day George would be contrite. Looking out at me earnestly from behind the thick lens he would say, 'I hope I said nothing untoward last night, Belle, nothing to offend you in any way.'

And I would reassure him that he had been a perfect gentleman.

About a week before Christmas Mona said, 'What are you doing for Christmas?'

'Nothing. The same as usual. Father Jack will be there of course and Buba will want us to go to Midnight Mass.'

'Would you like to go to a party at the New Year?' She asked this with such an air of embarrassment that I wondered if at last I was going to meet the famous brother.

'I'd love to go, I've never been to a party in my life.'

'The thing is,' she laughed carelessly, 'it's long dresses and dinner jackets. Ridiculous, isn't it, but Cyril has these delusions of grandeur.'

'Cyril?'

'Cyril English.'

I'd heard of him. He owned the building where we held our meetings and was spoken of with a mixture of pride and embarrassment. George McNab had told me that he was the richest man in Dublin and that he had made his fortune in the Argentine.

I had asked George if he was a member of the Party.

'Sort of but he couldn't be seen at a meeting, not with his business connections. Cyril's sound, though, Belle, in spite of his money. He hasn't been corrupted and he's a bloody good employer.'

'What is his business?'

'Oh importing something or other from the Argentine.'

I thought of gun running, or white slavery, perhaps.

'Have you got a long dress?' Mona asked me now.

'No, but I haven't got a short one either, not a party dress. I'll have to buy something.'

When I told Buba about the long dress she clapped her hands. 'It is a ball – how lovely to be going to a ball.'

'I don't think so, Buba, just a party.'

'A ball, I tell you. I went to balls myself and I know. We will get you a wonderful frock so that you will be the belle of the ball.' She laughed, deepening the pouchy folds around her eyes. 'See how your old Buba can still make jokes.'

Buba and Mutti and I went shopping for the dress. They argued over what suited me and I let them get on with it for I wasn't too sure of what I wanted, only what I didn't want.

Finally they chose a turquoise satin. The satin felt cool and slithery like the feel of the inkwell on my desk at school. It shimmered when I nudged it and clung to my body as I lowered it over my head.

I looked with delight at the stranger in the shop mirror. A tall, elegant young woman looked back at me with graceful shoulders and a lovely neck. Was that really me? Could clothes bring about such transformations?

Buba and Mutti were more critical.

'I don't think so,' Buba said. 'For such a dress you need the bigger bosoms.'

The dress was strapless, the boned bodice having been designed for the well-endowed.

'I love it,' I said. 'Can't we stuff something down?'

The shop assistant who had been standing by making admiring noises said, 'Cotton wool sometimes does the trick,' and produced some from behind her back like a conjurer.

111

The three of them pushed and pulled until they were satisfied.

'Just remember to keep it tucked inside,' Buba advised. 'Tufts appearing will make it look like snow on the tops of mountains.'

On the night of the party I was ready at six although I was not being picked up until eight.

Buba assured me that I would be the most beautiful girl there. 'But tell me again, who is it that is giving this fine ball?'

'You know as much as I do, Buba. Their name is Mr and Mrs English and like I said, they're friends of Miss McCarthy.' I thought it would be prudent to supply a wife although I didn't know if one existed.

'And Miss McCarthy is kindly inviting the debaters?'

'She wants to show us off.'

'And where do they live?'

'In Dundrum.'

Buba was reassured. 'I know that place. Big, fine houses up there in their own grounds. Erika, our little Belle is coming into society. That is what I always wished for her, that she would take her place among the first ranks of Irish society.'

Buba was right – it was a ball. Well, at least there was dancing.

Cyril English's property was bounded on one side by the high wall of the hospital for the criminally insane.

'I don't know whether it's to keep them in or Cyril out,' Mona said as the Beetle grumbled up the last half-mile of hill. 'Wait till you see the driveway – potholes as deep as bogholes. Cyril can never be persuaded to spend a penny on the utilitarian.'

He was waiting to greet us, standing on the front steps with a glass in his hand. 'I was getting a bit edgy there.' He spoke with a pronounced Dublin accent. 'There's a bit of a shortage of women.'

Mona introduced me.

'Well worth waiting for, a flower, a jewel.' He turned back to Mona. 'As for yourself, Mona, "Age cannot wither . . ."'

Mona jabbed him with her handbag. 'You're a right bastard, Cyril,' she said good-humouredly.

And I followed her into the hall thinking that she looked more withered than usual in the peculiar rustly black dress that billowed around her ankles.

The entrance hall was square and dimly lit. At the far end music was coming from a room and I saw some people dancing by. Most noise, however, a sort of erupting rumble, came from our left where bodies were spilling out through an open door.

Cyril yanked some of these aside. 'Show some respect for the ladies.'

I peered inside.

A bar had been set up at the far end of the room. Between us and it serried rows of dinner jackets stood, immovable. Cyril put his head down and charged, advising us to wait.

I saw many faces familiar from Party meetings. There were others I had never seen, elderly lechers, I decided, as bloodshot eyes slid the length of my turquoise dress. A smell of mothballs rose and mingled with cigar smoke. There were no women.

Cyril, who had managed to burrow a way through to the bar, now passed us back drinks, two whiskies, one of which Mona returned with a request for lemonade.

'Doesn't Cyril have a wife?' I asked Mona.

'He's reputed to have but I think he keeps her locked away in an attic. I've never seen her at one of these affairs at any rate.'

Cyril returned to us, breathless. 'It's not civilized in there,' he said. 'Why don't you two go on into the ballroom.'

Wait till I told Buba – a ballroom.

It was pretty crowded too. Although only a dozen or so couples were foxtrotting, the walls were lined with hungry-looking men standing like runners waiting for the off.

We made our way into a window alcove which gave us some protection from the crush. Not for long, though. Two men reached Mona from different angles, each one catching a hand.

She looked from one to the other. 'Dermot first, I think,' she said to a square-shaped man with a thick grey fringe. 'Then I'll give you a twirl, Henry.'

Henry's chin collapsed inwards as he let go her hand reluctantly. Making a quick recovery he turned to me but he was foiled again. Moist, plump fingers were already pressing into my bare shoulder, propelling me towards the dancing.

We shuffled towards the floor where my partner cleared a space for us with his elbows. 'Now,' he said, taking a firm grip of my waist, 'I'm a bit jarred, to tell you the truth, but it won't affect my dancing.'

He was elderly but game and he smelled pleasantly of peppermint. And he was a good dancer too, except when it came to turning. Here he did a sort of three-pointer, reversing, going forward, then reversing again. After a series of collisions he extricated us and we headed down the room at speed. 'God,' he said, looking up at me, 'you're a great dancer. You're the best dancer in the room and' – he broke off to crane round at our fellow dancers – 'the youngest.' He cackled and swung me on to the floor once more. We were off again as the tempo of the music changed to something slower.

'Youth, youth,' came his voice from somewhere under my chin and sounding tearful.

'Overrated,' I replied to cheer him up.

It seemed to do the trick for his head came up and he gave me a brownish smile. "'And dance with Amaryllis in the shade,'" he breathed on a minty exhalation.

'Milton,' I said, keeping my end up.

'I don't care if you *are* Milton, I'm going to call you Amaryllis. I've always wanted to dance with Amaryllis in the shade and it's happening tonight. You beautiful creature.' He held me from him and squinted at me in a manner that suggested he was seeing two of me.

I was beginning to enjoy myself.

I danced with George McNab and then with Cyril English. Mona rustled by twice with different partners and deep in conversation with each.

Cyril grabbed me again as I was going out to get a lemonade. 'Later, later,' he implored. 'I love this song, you must dance this one with me.'

He gripped me tightly and we moved off. 'You, you are the one,' he sang into my ear, accompanying the pianist.

I stumbled and he tightened his grip further. I was more worried about the bones of my bodice than my virtue, for Cyril's embrace, though robust, was absent-minded.

Then above the music and general noise I heard a shout. 'Amaryllis. English.'

Cyril skidded into the grand piano, chivalrously twirling me aside so that I was protected from the impact.

Over Cyril's shoulder I saw my first partner of the evening elbowing his way towards us, pawing the ground as he approached.

'The bowsie,' Cyril said, placing himself between me and my admirer.

The Amaryllis man had undone his cummerbund and he reached up now to swish the end of it across Cyril's face. 'Unhand her, dog.' He tried to push Cyril aside. 'Has this man been importuning you, Amaryllis? Has he been importuning you with lewd suggestions?'

Cyril pushed him, then grabbed him by his starched shirt as he was about to fall. 'You drunken sod, you don't even know who this girl is. This is my guest, my friend. Her name is Belle – nobody you'd know in a thousand years. You're so drunk you can't even tell between a decent girl and one of your pick-ups. Off you go and find your Amar – whatever you call her. And let you clear off, the two of you.'

I realized that Cyril wasn't completely sober either.

My admirer raised his fists and began to dance round in front of Cyril. Other guests approached in the hope of seeing a proper fight.

As I watched I felt a pressure on my elbow as someone took my arm and drew me backwards. 'Mona sent me to rescue you if you're Belle, and you must be. You're the only one here who's under fifty and sober.'

Max, standing beside me. I smiled up at him. He didn't recognize me, which didn't surprise me for I had emerged tonight a turquoise swan who bore little resemblance to the schoolgirl duckling he had met nine months ago in the Coffee Inn. Men were fighting over me tonight.

Graciously I extended one of my lily whites, raising my eyelids slowly, not in the manner of Father Jack, I hoped, but in the siren fashion of Kim Novak. 'How *are* you . . .'

He took my hand, held on to it. 'Come on, through here. English gets impossible when he reaches this stage.'

A wide mouth, thick arched eyebrows over troubled eyes. Marvellous, opaline skin.

I forgot my status as a newly fledged beauty as I looked at the real thing. He turned and began to lead me through the crush of bodies, all bearing down on us as word spread about the fight.

Mona was sitting by herself in the hall under a suit of armour. 'Good boy,' she said to Max. 'Come on, Belle, we're going. Once that lot start it's time to pack up.'

I heard her but the voice seemed to come from a great distance.

He was looking at me, seeing me. 'Won't you stay for a drink?' he asked.

I tried to say yes but I couldn't speak.

Mona shook me. 'Wake up, Belle, and thanks, Max, but we can't stay. We're off, this minute.'

'I could leave Belle home.' He was still holding my hand.

'Don't be daft.'

'Will I see you at the next meeting then?' He was looking at me, addressing his question to me. Then with a note of anxiety, 'You are a member, aren't you?'

'You will and she is,' said Mona, and pulling the heavy door open she pushed me through.

I ran after her, picking up the skirt of my dress. Frosty grass crunched under our feet and the air bit into our faces.

'We could have stayed for a drink,' I suggested. 'It's not that late.'

Mona ignored this and lit a cigarette as she waited for the engine to warm up.

'Did Max have a big row with Heslin? Is that why he's stayed away so long?'

'Everybody has rows with Heslin, Max is just too damn sensitive. Now shut up and let me drive. The roads are going to be bloody impossible.'

We slithered down the avenue and out on to the main road. As we turned left I saw the lights of the city coming up to meet us. Up here we were in darkness except for the distant stars. Mona cursed the dark and the frost. 'I don't know whether it's a good thing or a bad that I had that last whiskey.' As she manoeuvred us out of a skid she added, 'Maybe a good thing after all.'

I drew my knees up inside my turquoise dress and tucked Mutti's beaver jacket round me, wearing it like a blanket. The village of Dundrum was asleep as we slid through but down in Rathmines people were still up and lights shone, mimicking the stars. I had never been out at this hour before.

It had happened and from tonight my life was changed. I could feel the inevitability of what would happen next, of currents sweeping me onwards involuntarily.

My life was changed. I shivered, feeling in the midst of all my excitement and delight a moment of regret for my old life. For Buba and the old certainties. For nights by the fire, my head on her knee as I waited for Mutti to bring in the hot chocolate. There was no way back to all that.

'Listen, Belle.' Mona's voice came out of the dark without warning. 'I want you to be very careful with Max.'

'What do you mean? What's wrong with him?'

'Nothing. He's a great fellow and he's a good friend of mine. But he's also a heart-breaker. And you're young.'

I was thoroughly sick of that phrase.

'And you've no idea how moody he can be. He's so complex. If there are no problems there he'll go looking for them. Nothing is ever simple with Max and I don't want you falling for him. He's the last person in the world for a sweet girl like you to get involved with. He's so – dark, sometimes.'

She didn't realize that everything she was telling me about him made him the more desirable. Who wanted the mundane, the quotidian? At nearly eighteen my greatest fear was that life would turn out to be too simple, too sunny. I welcomed the dark, the brooding, the complex.

'And God, he's so damn serious.'

'I'm serious,' I said, insulted.

'Not like that. Look, Belle, you are young and you need protecting. We can look after ourselves, Max and I, but you're the one who needs protecting. Just take it easy, that's all I'm saying.'

Before the year was out I was to discover that I wasn't the only one in need of protection.

I've come out here to clear my head, to shake myself free from the viscosity of all those clogging emotions.

They are so potent, these emotions, that my body is duped into a sudden surge of happiness and I look without recognition at the ageing face that stares at me from the mirror. I puzzle over its appearance, its obscuring of my own bright features, transformed now by love so that they glow with something akin to beauty.

I turn away and shake my head and force my fingers to feel the groove etched between my eyebrows. Then I grab my secateurs and come out here where the air is tinged with green and nature joins in the game, sending up shoots of renewal at such a pace that it would have me believe that growing old, withering and death are the illusions.

I should have started pruning the roses a week ago for I like to have the task complete by Patrick's Day. It is the task by which I define the end of winter tranquillity and I like to take it leisurely and enjoy it.

I cut into the new growth with savage delight, relishing the clean snap of the steel blades as they meet. Curly new leaves look up at me from around my feet and I prick my finger on a thorn.

'Any more trouble from you,' I warn, 'and it's the pudding-basin cut.'

I've never known what to do about roses. I used to grow them in the mixed border but they took up too much room and dominated all the lesser beauties. Five years ago I decided on a rose garden but I'm not satisfied with it, least of all on a day like this when the bald patches between the bushes are so much in evidence. I've underplanted with violas and dianthus but it is too early for them to make an appearance.

I suppose I should think ahead to June when this rectangle of ground will be transformed. My complacent beauties sleep the winter away on a bed dug thirty inches deep and enriched with the choicest farmyard manure but they do reward me in the summer when they begin to stretch and yawn, then put themselves on display to the oohs and aahs of patients, staff and visitors.

Special pilgrimages are made from the hospital to visit these beauties. Nurses and patients and young interns stand and stare at *Gloire de Dijon* as she climbs a west wall, wandering nonchalantly, scenting the air, exciting her audience with a suggestion of the slattern. They reach out to touch *Tuscany*, they ask how *Rosa mundi* does it, where she gets those stripes.

It is the rose garden that will save all the rest, so I should accept the bald patches with a good grace and remind myself of my own off days. And weeks. And months.

I had finished pruning all the bushes which grow in front of the Irish yews when I saw Anto walking up the incline towards the hospital. With that loose stride and those silver curls I couldn't help admiring him but I felt no desire. I've let him go, he means nothing to me any more. If he were the father of my children I might feel differently about him but he's just a man I used to know. I've let him go.

Not so my gardens. How could I ever have thought of letting go here? Thirty years of digging and cutting and hoeing and planting, of calloused hands, an aching back, of sweat and exhaustion, of hand-rearing and mass murder, of still births and triumphant coming of age. I have fought against slug and aphid and mealy bug; I have waged war on the codling moth and rust and black spot; I have felt my heart stop when I thought I recognized the black shoelaces of the honey fungus.

I have borne no children but I am not a barren woman. And a mother does not turn her back on her children, ever.

LONESOMENESS My memory is like a screen on a computer. When I push certain buttons coherent print comes on to the screen and I can read it without difficulty. Another button and I get nothing but the white glow of panic. Another, what I'm getting now, throws up print but bathed in fuzzy grey so that I must peer and peer before it will give up its sense.

The difficulty starts when Max takes my hand in Cyril English's house. As I try to remember, the grey shadows appear though they are still faint, a suggestion. They gather density as I come home now and find Buba waiting for me to hear all about the ball. I don't want to look too closely because of the sensations that are beginning to gather behind the wall of my chest. I know those sensations for they have followed me throughout my life. They can be evoked by the ordinary, indeed banal: a dog barking in the stretches of the night, the whistle of a distant train. I am particularly vulnerable at moments of happiness. Space opens up round me as fences and boundaries are knocked down. The world begins to expand, leaving me empty, desolate. I name the feeling, make my lips say the word – lonesome.

A queer, old-fashioned word, the sound evoking the meaning. Words. The meaning of words. Belle – suggesting optimism and confidence. It was Mona who first made me think about the meaning of words. With Mona there were lots of first times.

Lonesome people fear change above all else. As I look at Max's beautiful face I know that I love him, that I will forsake all others for him. I will start out on a new journey with him and I am afraid. I want to retreat to the familiar. I am lonesome.

But the journey is delayed because Buba becomes ill. I say good-night to her but she holds on to my hand outside her bedroom door. We whisper so as not to disturb Mutti who has not stayed up to hear about the ball.

'But it was a good night, Liebchen?'

'Wonderful.'

'And you danced?'

'All night long. Every single dance.'

'This is what I hope. An Irish Catholic girl like you. So clever, so pretty. You go to university soon, and after you marry anyone you like in the whole of Ireland.'

Would she settle for dark fathomless eyes and an opaline skin or are her sights set on a Catholic princeling?

'And you meet more people and they introduce you to others and soon all the time you are going to balls. Soon Erika must take you into town to buy new clothes. A girl like you.'

I don't know if the sort of people Buba has in mind exist in Dublin, but if they do I'm luckily not going to meet them through Mona or Cyril English.

I give Buba a hug because she is being deceived yet again. 'I'm falling down with the tiredness, Buba.'

'Yes, Liebchen. Bed. Tomorrow we have a goose for New Year's Day and Father Jack is coming. Erika is getting up early to stuff the bird and have the fire ready but you must sleep late. The beauty sleep it is called.'

I kiss her, put my arms round her again and smell her familiar scent of cigars mixed with lily of the valley face powder. I think I will stay with Buba for ever.

Night is scattered by the arrival of snow. The reflected brilliance seeps into my bedroom so that I wake early trying to figure out what is different. I twitch at the curtain. 1956 has emerged in purity. Everything is transformed outside, landmarks obliterated in a new, uniform white. Above, the sky is opaque and swollen. There is more snow to come.

'Look, Mutti,' I say as my door opens and she comes in. 'Snow.'

She doesn't even glance at the window as she places a small tin tray on my knees.

'Tea, to wake you up.'

She pours it from a china pot decorated with delicately painted Chinese figures. She looks pale under her make-up as if she hasn't slept very well. Her hair is brushed but not yet rolled, kept back from her face with combs. As she talks I notice a fleck of lipstick on a tooth.

'Your Buba is not well. I am saying that she must stay in bed but she gives me a fight as usual. You must help me to persuade her, she does not look well.'

By the time I go to her room she does not want to get up. She looks feverish, her hair wispy and damp round her forehead. For the first time I realize that she is old: a frail old woman shrunk inside her long-sleeved, high-throated nightdress.

'We must get a doctor, Buba, now, at once.' It is clearly my fault, keeping her out of bed so late last night, sitting in her dressing gown after the fire had gone out.

'No doctor.' Her voice is also shrunk. 'No foolish Irish doctor to fuss around me. I know, I think, it is pleurisy. Once I had it before during a cold winter.'

She sends Mutti to the surgery and me to the kitchen with careful instructions. Sleep, she says, is the most important thing, sleep and peace so that the body may heal itself.

I am afraid that she will die. In the kitchen I get down on my knees and pray to the Holy Ghost, reminding him of my past devotion. I apologize for neglecting him over the years

123

but promise, swear, that I will be faithful to him evermore if he will save Buba.

The house feels strange and deserted. I wander round at a loose end. The sitting-room grate has not been cleaned out; in the kitchen the goose lies half stuffed on the table alongside some yeast frothing in a blue bowl. When Father Jack knocks at the door I answer it and explain what has happened. He doesn't want to come in, stands on the doorstep and says he will pray for Buba and to send up his best wishes, his very best.

I go outside and kick at the snow, which turns out to be nothing more wonderful than frozen water. I fear that I am being punished, that Buba is ill because of all my deceit during the year.

Once Buba said to me, 'You cannot understand the evil of communism. On this little island nobody can because they have not seen. What do they know of what goes on in the big world? But I know because I have seen.'

And I wilfully went off and joined a communist party, for that's what it is, whatever it calls itself. And I might have been excused if I had done it out of conviction but my motive is suspect. Why had I joined — a need for excitement? A desire to be in Mona McCarthy's company?

As I wander round snow begins to fall again, covering over the scuff-marks I have made. Flakes fall on my upturned face, swirling from every direction.

Pure as the driven snow is the ideal held out to us at school. Mona and I often laughed about it, Mona confessing, with what I suddenly realize is bitterness, that she never had an option.

I am about to strike a deal with the Holy Ghost, offering him life-long purity in return for Buba's recovery, when Mutti opens the window and shouts at me to come in.

Buba has slept and already her condition seems less critical.

She wags a finger at me and warns me that there is no room for two patients in the house.

I dry my hair with a towel that Mutti hands me and say that I will go downstairs and start sorting out the tasks which have to be done. As I close the bedroom door I hear Buba's murmur: *gut girl, such a gut girl.*

There won't be snow this year, it is too late. There are vicious frosts, though, like the one last night. I woke up feeling cold and conscious of the stillness: not a breath of wind. When I went outside I found that the big lawn had been turned into a lake of silver. I avoided walking on it and took the long way round to break the pewter surface of the pond. Under the beeches I found little clumps of aconites. All very beautiful, or so the RTE man thought. He arrived this afternoon to talk about the film he is going to shoot. He makes it sound like *Gone with the Wind.*

This is our last chance to save the gardens. As I told Anto, he should have nobbled his friend-the-minister before the elections. Now it's too late and the new coalition is full of self-righteousness and fiscal rectitude. I can't see them worrying over a garden. The Eastern Health Board has more or less told Anto that they have to sell the land, that they need the money, so that leaves us with a fight on our hands. Shields says we should enlist the help of local people, that it would be an amenity on their doorsteps if the gardens were saved and opened to the public.

I've really been touched by the enthusiasm of so many people. Shields now – who would have thought she'd give a damn? When I tactlessly said this to her she told me to fuck off. 'You're such a stuck-up cow. I wouldn't lift a finger to save them gardens except that I know they're nothing to do with you. You're just the hired labour. Remember that, "Poems are made by fools like me but only God can make a tree." Think about that when you're giving yourself airs and graces and come down off your high horse.'

She's been losing her rag a lot lately. I think she's upset by all that's happening and she's dreading Anto's departure. She's drinking more too. When I bought her the hip flask it was only because she was always going on about the one Marilyn Monroe had in Some Like It Hot. I bought her a red garter too but I didn't expect her to hike up the skirt of her uniform in broad daylight in view of the patients, pull out the flask and start swigging vodka.

'You need to watch it, Shields,' I said to her.

She rounded on me. 'Why do I need to watch it? What fucking difference does it make now? They've taken my job away from me – I'll not work again.'

She's right of course. Maybe neither of us will work again. In the meantime I have a meet with Mervyn tomorrow a.m.

That's the way Mervyn talks but he's a nice boy with all the sweetness of youth. I'd almost forgotten that quality, I so seldom meet young people. I listened to the way he laughed, with no underlying sourness. I'm not used to that sound although recently it's been coming at me from another direction. Travelling down through the years and I hear my own laughter, as sweet as my young girl's breath. Not nostalgia, though, but truth. That's what this is all about, trying to come to some sort of truth.

CAPSULES OF HAPPINESS I am coming to a period of my past that is complete and separate as I recall it. Wrapped round, cut off, nothing reaches it from outside, there is no past or future, so totally is it sealed inside its capsule. Happiness is what's inside. It is a capsule of happiness.

Buba got to the stage where her life was no longer in danger but where she still had to take care. The weeks of her convalescence began and my life was suspended, willingly suspended.

I told Mona that I wouldn't be able to attend any more Party meetings for a while.

'I should think not – your place is at your grandmother's bedside. And I wouldn't worry about the Party. I don't imagine anything will have changed very much by the time you get back.'

I rushed home from school every day not only to help Mutti but to be with Buba. To sit in her room, just to be there.

She never complained nor made demands. She never asked for anything but smiled at me, her eyes following me around the room as I tidied and dusted. As she got better I used to make jokes, telling her she was the best patient she ever had.

I liked to linger at the dressing table, smelling the cut-glass perfume bottle and the powder bowl with its giant puff. I would re-arrange her trinkets and her silver-backed brush and comb and take up the photograph of the man with the heavy, Lord Kitchener moustache and examine it. My grandfather.

There was another photograph on the dressing table. In it I am holding Mutti's hand and I have a ribbon round my hair. Mutti is wearing one of those strange saucer-like 1940 hats, pulled down over one ear. Her jacket is tight-fitting with aggressive shoulder pads. She is smiling into the camera, expectant, beautiful.

I knew the history of this photograph. How we were snapped crossing O'Connell Bridge, the day after our arrival in Ireland.

'Where are you, Buba?'

Mutti answered. 'Your Buba never likes to have her photograph taken. I remember how she put up her hand when she saw the man raise his camera and then pushed us forward to be snapped again.'

As she grew stronger I brushed Buba's hair and made it into two thin plaits. When she was young, she told me, she used to wear them in a coronet round her head. She said that she had never had Mutti's beauty but that boys admired her hair. By the time that she was eighteen she could sit on it. One of her admirers had begged a lock to take with him to the front in 1916. He had not come back and Buba had never again given away a lock of her hair, deeming it unlucky.

From time to time Father Jack called. He never came over the threshold but stood on the doorstep to enquire after Buba. He seemed embarrassed, moving from one foot to the other, reluctant to go and refusing to come in but letting in the cold winter air as he stood there. I think he was afraid that we might invite him up to Buba's bedroom.

Nobody else called. Buba's locum had his own key and kept himself to himself. The house was even quieter than before for we lived upstairs now and away from the gramophone.

It was as if all three of us were recovering from an illness. We ate little meals, we pottered, we napped. So sleepy and quiet the house seemed that if I sat down and closed my eyes I found myself drifting towards sleep.

So restful, so novel, so tranquil to live in the present, especially for an eighteen year old. I became even more detached from my school life, indifferent to all except Mona whom I had put on hold, offering her smiles in the meantime but scurrying away from her if she tried to engage me in conversation.

As for Max, it was not his time yet. I never questioned my love for him or the inevitability of my going to him, but all that lay in a complex future.

Loving Buba was so simple, so familiar. I sat lazily brushing her hair or reading from a book of poems by Alfred Lord

Tennyson which Mutti had produced from somewhere with the totally unexpected information that he was Buba's favourite poet. 'In English.'

'And in German?'

'So long ago I don't remember.'

We ate our meals in Buba's room, Mutti and I sitting beside the bed, each of us with our own tray. I remember them as picnic meals, light and snatched. They heralded the end of the formal meal in our house and Mutti never went back to the rigid formula of three courses followed by coffee, much to the dismay of Father Jack.

I think we only ever had those sort of meals because of Buba. Heavily and aromatically nostalgic they reminded her of her girlhood home. She used to describe to me family dinners with her parents and her three brothers and herself sitting in the stiff dining room being served by maids wearing little white caps.

Mutti had tried to evoke this atmosphere, at least through the food. Potato dumplings had steamed on our kitchen table; joints of meat glossy with gravy, vegetables coated with velouté sauce and then browned under the grill. There was always sauerkraut and pots of grainy mustard which were served with little wooden spoons. And thick floury soups to start and puddings afterwards. Apple strudel or steamed chocolate pudding or some creamy torte.

Now Buba decided that she was too old for all of this and that, much to her surprise, she actually liked the lighter food that Mutti brought up on trays.

'Gut food,' she would say, eyeing the grilled fish or steamed, still crunchy carrots. Mutti would smile and watch with pride as the fork moved between plate and mouth.

'And our Belle is coming to the age when she will put on weight if she eats the big meals. Healthier this way, Erika. Better for all of us.'

As the days grew longer and milder Buba decided that it was time to start coming downstairs in the afternoons. She was worried about the well-being of her patients and the competence of the locum. She hadn't been able to find a woman doctor and she was sure that this raw male presence in the surgery would be an affront to all her female patients.

All I had noticed about him was his extreme shyness. He had red hair and very white skin which blushed a dark red if he met either Mutti or me in the hall. It was a novel experience for me, more used to blushing than being blushed at, but I felt sorry for him and wondered what on earth had possessed him to become a doctor. How did he ever manage to land a stethoscope on a bare female chest, never mind anything more intimate?

When Buba was fully recovered and back in her surgery Mutti said to me, 'You have been a good girl, so devoted to your grandmother. But now it is time to go back to your own life. I want to see you going out with your friends again.'

I found myself reluctant to do so. I clung to the silent, dreamy house, to the calm rhythm of life with my grandmother and my mother. It was as if I knew that this would never be repeated, not the calm unshadowed ease of those afternoons, not the presence of those two beloved women, not the wordless communion. Other periods would follow, more passionate, more exhilarating, but never again would I experience the steady, certain heartbeat of those days, their endometrial peace.

Now when I think about them I feel my jaw unclench, the skin on my forehead relax. My body uncurls, my breathing slows and I smile to myself as I feel again the pile of Buba's white candlewick bedspread. I rub my fingers against it as I read from Alfred Lord Tennyson and the light fades outside. Then Mutti brings in tea and toasted tea cakes. I bite into the spicy bun and butter runs down my chin. My grandmother looks at me from across the room and I feel myself the centre of a loving, multipetalled family that death has not yet begun to strip. I am safe, protected for years to come.

The dog in the next-door garden starts a sudden barking. Buba sighs, a buttery, pleasure-laden sigh, and says, 'That I should have the delight of listening to my little granddaughter reading Alfred Lord Tennyson and each sound so perfect. It is so gut, so beautiful.'

And I have to agree with her.

LOVE AND POLITICS I had withdrawn from life and now when I returned to it I was surprised to find that it had run on without me.

One Monday after school towards the end of the summer term I approached Mona.

'I was thinking of going to a meeting tonight. There's one on, I suppose?'

She placed a hand on my shoulder. 'How's your grandmother?'

'Oh she's fine.'

'I didn't want to harass you with endless enquiries.'

'No, she's pefectly recovered.'

'Then come tonight. Belle, you've no idea what's been going on – I'd say Heslin is at this minute kneeling in front of a photograph of Uncle Joe praying for strength.'

'What's happened?'

'What hasn't? The world is changing and for the better. Look – I can't stop. I'll pick you up at the end of your road at about half-seven.'

The meeting was packed. There were all the usuals, faces I didn't know and others that I hadn't seen since the night of

Cyril English's party. I caught a glimpse of Max sitting in the front before the weight of bodies forced me onwards down to the back of the room. I squeezed on to the end of a bench and any standing room behind was soon filled up.

Heslin rose to his feet. He looked bad-tempered, his head thrust forward, his unlovely neck exposed, goose-pimpled and red.

'There was no need for this meeting,' he began without preamble. 'I don't hold with it and neither does anyone who calls themselves a communist.'

'A Stalinist you mean,' someone shouted from behind me.

'Bloody fascist,' somebody else replied.

Heslin, eyes bulging dangerously, banged the table for order. Above the general uproar I heard Max's voice ask, 'Why don't you use your shoe?'

To me it seemed a pretty senseless remark but not to the rest of the assembly, half of whom it delighted while the rest were incensed.

George McNab who had been standing behind me pushed me off the bench and stood on it. 'Lads, comrades.' A shower of saliva rained down on my head and I moved over to the wall.

Nobody was paying any attention to George and his appeals for order. Underneath him heads and eyes rolled, backs were straightened, fists thumped into palms. The comrades were preparing for a showdown. And I still didn't know what it was all about.

Up at the table Heslin was sitting with his head in his hands. Mona whispered something to him. He nodded and she jumped up on to the table in front of him. She stood there, one hand on her hip, one leg thrust forward slightly. She had good legs, long for her general size, slim but shapely. I think she was quite vain about them for although she never bothered much about clothes she chose her stockings and shoes with care and she always wore stilettos.

Within ten seconds all attention was focused on Mona. Tension was not so much dissipated as re-directed. Again the reaction was mixed. The sight of Mona's legs clad in sheerest nylon evoked extremes of emotion from simple lust to righteous disapproval. But they were all mesmerized. From my vantage point halfway along the wall I looked across at the upturned faces. Mouths were slack with surprise, lips glistened with desire or pussed in disgust. Hands that had been getting ready to smash in someone's face now found themselves raised to no purpose and were self-consciously stuffed into pockets.

Mona stood and surveyed like a general or an evangelical preacher, sure of herself and her timing. She waited, her body still but her eyes moving around the room, those green cat's eyes, determined to seek out and subjugate any opposition.

Eventually she began to speak. 'Comrades, fellow socialists.' Eyes began to move upwards reluctantly, to dwell on her face and leave the legs alone. 'We know why this meeting was called. It is a serious day for socialism. It is a time for serious debate, thoughtful debate, not this disgraceful carry-on that we have just witnessed. I am really surprised by the lack of maturity so many comrades have displayed here tonight – I expected more of you. If you behave like schoolboys then that is how you will be treated.'

I could feel the mood in the room changing and I knew that her tone was wrong. These men were *not* schoolboys and they were not going to be lectured at. The rustling and muttering increased so that she had to raise her voice, which made her performance seem less effective.

'We have followed the Rule Book which has allowed us to convene this meeting and now we must decide tonight whether or not to issue a statement to the press about the situation in the Soviet Union. Comrade Khrushchev has – '

'Comrade Khrushchev is a bollix.'

The spontaneous laughter that greeted this remark was really only a release of tension but it infuriated Mona. She began to lecture them again, sounding more than ever like an irate schoolmistress. 'That's enough, that really is enough. This sort of infantile behaviour should have no place within this room. I've better things to do with my time, I can tell you, than to stand here – '

'Then why don't you sit down like a good girl.'

It was the 'like a good girl' that did it. I knew that above all else Mona hated the way some of the comrades patronized her because of her sex. She screamed out in fury, raising her arms to beat the air over her head with her fists. The movement of the arms unbalanced her body and she swayed for a moment, then crashed forward on to the floor.

Hemmed in by bodies I couldn't reach her but Max was up and at her side in an instant. I watched as he bent over her, we all did in sudden silence. He helped her to her feet and then to a chair. Then he turned and stared down the room. He was alight, beautiful, full of anger. His voice however was cold with contempt. 'If this proves anything, it proves how necessary this meeting was tonight. We all know now that it was these sort of bullyboy tactics which Stalin used for years and much worse of course. Khrushchev – '

'Go home, Jewboy.'

The phrase seemed to be almost whispered although I heard it clearly, as did everyone in the room. Max, his mouth open, had stopped in midsentence. There was an expression of shock on the faces around me, everyone staring towards Max. For seconds nothing happened as we remained held in tableau. Then the room exploded. Everyone was on his feet and I lost sight of Mona. Seats were knocked over or thrust aside. A man in front of me rolled up his sleeves and spat into the palm of one hand. I could see George McNab banging a folded chair on the floor, calling for order. But it was too late for order. Fights erupted like brush fires here and there, bodies locked in combat or rolling on the ground. A cap flew through the air, followed by a book which landed at my feet. I picked it up and saw that it was a collection of essays by August Bebel. An approved missile?

I was worried about Mona who would surely need to be rescued. As two adjacent fights opened up a path for me I scrambled through to the front. I looked around for Mona and caught sight of her on the other side of the table near the door. She beckoned me forward, then told me to hold on. I did and watched with disbelief as she calmly walked up to a man I didn't know and elbowed him in the groin.

He roared out in pain and she, turning her back on him, smiled at me with seraphic sweetness. 'That's the bastard who called Max a Jewboy. Come on, let's get out of here.'

She dragged me after her through the door and we ran down the steps.

'What about Max?' I asked as we reached the street.

'He can take care of himself and anyway, to give that lot their due,' she nodded back towards the meeting, 'he'll have more people on his side than against him.'

As we sat into the car and Mona slammed into gear I noticed her excitement. I had imagined that she would have been upset but she was more animated than I had seen her ever. Currents of energy were running off her as we rattled down Baggot Street.

'I didn't think you'd find anti-Semitism among socialists.'

'And you think that Heslin and his friends are socialists? God love your innocence. Crypto-Stalinists and not so crypto some of them. They're on the run now, though, at last we've got them on the run. After Khrushchev's denouncement none of them will sleep easy in their beds at night.'

She told me then what it was all about. That Khrushchev had come out and condemned Stalin and the cult of the personality, that this had set off reactions throughout the socialist world and in socialist parties throughout the West, or as we referred to it, the capitalist world.

'The effect is only beginning,' Mona said. 'It's like a giant tidal wave that is going to engulf us all.'

'Then we'll all drown,' I said sourly, thinking more of Max and me than of the onward march of socialism.

'Only the Stalinists, I hope. Remember we have the Soviet Union on our side. God – Khrushchev, he's like a breath of fresh air. And once something like this starts it gains its own momentum.'

We were gathering momentum inside the Beetle. Mona swerved out from behind a bus and gave a clenched-fist salute to a driver who blew his horn at her.

'Do you remember what Rosa Luxemburg said about seizing the moment? That's what we have to do now. Socialism has been on the wrong road for years but now things can change. Can't you feel it, Belle? Can't you feel it in your blood?'

I was considering my feelings when she yelled out, 'Spontaneous revolution!'

I waited but she said no more. Did she mean spontaneous revolution here, in Ireland? I didn't know if I was quite ready for that.

'Come on, let's go and have a drink.'

We stopped opposite Mooney's and crossed a deserted street into a deserted bar. In the snug at the back she ordered a hot whiskey for herself and lemonade for me.

'I think I'll have a vodka,' I said. If I was old enough to die for the revolution then I was old enough to drink alcohol.

'You'll have no such thing. What is the world coming to with schoolgirls ordering vodka.'

Spontaneous revolution, I felt like telling her, but I knew that she would not hear. She was distracted, feverish, eyes whisking towards the door, one hand playing with a beer mat while the other one clenched a cigarette.

'I hope Max is all right.' She stubbed out a cigarette which she'd only taken a puff or two from.

'You said – '

'I know, but he's a long time coming.'

'I didn't know – '

'We've been meeting here since the hoo-ha started. It's safer than the other place. No chance of bumping into Heslin and his cronies.'

George McNab led the way, head erect, puffy and blackening eye on proud display. Behind him Max was unblemished but looking sullen. His lips pouted. They needed to be kissed into a smile was my frivolous and incorrect reaction.

He sat beside me and took my hand. It seemed the most natural thing, as if we had seen each other yesterday, as if we were already lovers. Perhaps the fever of imminent revolution would speed up all aspects of life.

'Why so miserable?' Mona asked him. 'Look at poor old George here and he's still smiling.'

Max had begun to stroke the palm of my hand. I forced myself to keep my eyes open, to ignore what was happening in my body.

'You are fools if you think that tonight's carry-on is anything to celebrate.'

I drew his hand on to my lap. I placed my hand on top of his so that his fingers were now stroking my thigh.

'And you're a fool if you can't see what an opportunity is being handed to us.'

'Just what I told him, Mona, but you can't talk to him.'

I moved my leg closer to his while my mind, which had separated from my body, was startled by such a display of brazenness.

'This is the break-up of socialism as we know it. This is just the beginning – '

'Jesus God Almighty. Stalin was nearly as big an anti-Semite as Hitler. What are you talking about, Max? Are you gone mad?'

The rhythm of the stroking was becoming hypnotic. I stopped struggling, closed my eyes, then bent my head so that nobody would see.

'If it wasn't for Stalin Hitler would be ruling over a Europe-wide Reich today. I know what goes on in Russia, I know that Khrushchev is right, but what's going to happen if we start quarrelling among ourselves?'

Go on, Max, go on. Don't move your hand away, keep on.

'Look at that poor child, she's fallen asleep. Belle.'

I let her shake me, keeping my eyes closed as I pretended sleep. I wanted to punch her silly hands away, to shake her off and return to bliss.

'Come on, Belle, time to go.'

'I'll see her home.'

'No you won't.'

'Yes he will.'

We walked home together through the pale summer evening. He held my hand and told me that he was afraid.

'I'm a physical coward, Belle. I've never told that to anyone before but I am. I hated what went on there tonight.'

'Being called a Jewboy.'

138

'What? Lord no, that doesn't bother me. After all, I've no illusions on that score. I just hate all this violence that's inside so many of them. Even Mona. It's as if they enjoy being hurt and inflicting pain. It makes me feel sick, it always did, even at school.'

My Max. My lover, my limb, but no unmitigated source of joy. His troubled view of the world became mine and the old simplicities and certainties were left behind. The world became an agoraphobic space as Buba's walls came tumbling down.

In the shadows of a shop doorway he put his arms around me and began to smooth back my hair, smiling now, forgetting about all the violence out there. 'I won't be seeing you for a while.'

My heart lurched painfully against my ribcage.

'Trinity's been closed for a fortnight and I've got to go and make some money. A cousin of mine in Manchester has offered me a job for the summer. But I'll write and you write back.'

Whatever tenuous hold I had on reality grows thinner and more brittle as I poke around in the past. Today when Mervyn called I brought him in and handed him a bottle of Mexican beer as I had been instructed to do by Shields. I sat down opposite him, to listen to his plans about the film, but I found that I was hearing nothing. I was watching his body and his face and his smile; I was smelling his young man's smell and I was desiring him. Someone young enough to be my son and I wanted him in bed with me. I could imagine myself opening the buttons of his shirt . . .

It could simply be hunger but it is more likely my body reviving with all those memories of Max. I can recall the texture of passion although I cannot taste again the flavour of Mutti's apple strudel. Isn't that strange?

I took us for a brisk walk around the gardens. The

139

boy found it hard to keep up, which was good for my vanity.

'This'll look quite different in June,' I assured him.

'We'll have to shoot before then.'

'No, it has to be June. The roses, the peonies – '

'But Anto won't be here.'

That cooled my ardour more effectively than the biting east wind. 'What's he got to do with it?'

'I wouldn't have got involved if it wasn't for him.'

He spent the next ten minutes explaining Anto to me. I must realize, he told me, how unique a person he was, how unusual, how amazing, how – how good.

'A saint,' I suggested.

'It's not a word that is in my vocabulary but yes, you could call him a saint.'

I'd forgotten about the conceit of young men and I'd forgotten about my own middle-aged crustiness. I might still lust after a lovely young body but I was no longer prepared to put up with the rest of the nonsense that went with it.

He smiled at me, a shade too complacently, so I told him that as I was the gardener it was either a June shoot or forget it.

'I'll have to think about it.'

'You do that.'

It will be such a relief to get back to the past again, away from child producers and ageing saints.

WAITING That summer I remember as one of endless waiting. The cool temperature did nothing to help swallow up time, leaving me full of energy at the end of the day while darkness evaded somehow the sharp, glassy hours of the night.

Buba was busy and purposeful again and no longer needed

me. Mutti withdrew once more behind her matt reflective eyes and stickily painted mouth. The intimacy that had so pleased me while we three camped together in Buba's bedroom had evaporated.

Max was gone, Mona went. She told me she was going walking in the Alps with a friend. I wondered who the friend was, jealous that I had been left behind.

I put on my mac over my summer dress and went walking through Dublin's empty streets. Dublin families who could afford to had emptied out on to the little seaside towns along the east coast, where the adults grimly walked the length of the beige strands under low grey skies.

I discovered the National Gallery and wandered its echoing corridors, staring up at gloomy landscapes and depictions of ancient battles.

In our house Father Jack was back. I avoided him as much as I could, now that I had a life to hide from him.

Mutti said to me, 'Your eighteenth birthday. I would like to cook you a special meal and you must ask some friends to share with you.'

Self-pity swept through me. Friends – I had none, I had been deserted by all.

'No one?' Mutti questioned. 'No one at all?'

Buba signalled to her over my head, then turned to me.

'Could we not ask the good Father Jack? Our oldest friend, our benefactor, he must come to celebrate your birthday.'

He arrived bearing gifts. A box of Black Magic chocolates and a biography of Blessed Maria Goretti.

He placed the book in the middle of the table, shoving aside the salt cellar. He pointed with a long, yellow finger. 'We must all pray for her canonization. The Church needs saints like her in this godless age. She chose to die, Belle, rather than be defiled by a man. Sure she's a saint in all but name, she has to be.'

I stared at the bright colours of the dust jacket. A young girl with improbably blonde hair, considering that she was an Italian, knelt, her hands clasped before her in prayer. She wore a blue dress and over her head, as if falling from the sky, hung sprays of pink roses.

There didn't seem any adequate reply so we sat down and waited for Mutti to bring in the soup. She had made pea soup because she knew how much I liked it. So did Father Jack who cheered up now, pushing his spoon into the creamy, green depths.

'Well, Belle.' I jumped at his voice. 'Do you know what it is, I've got hold of this idea that you've been avoiding me lately.' His fleshy lips were shiny with soup and he dabbed at them, then pushed them into the stuff of his napkin as if he were implanting a kiss on its starched surface.

He looked up at me from under a jauntily raised eyebrow. 'Oh I know all about young ladies like yourself when you start avoiding the likes of me. It usually means there's a boyfriend on the horizon. Would I be right there now?'

'I don't know what gave you such an idea, Father Jack.'

'Ah come on now, child – I'm not as green as I look.'

Buba laughed. 'A nice Irish boy – I would like that. But first things first, Father Jack. First the exams and then the boyfriends.'

I rose to help Mutti, getting the potato pudding from the oven as she carried in the large oval meat dish. Buba pushed apple sauce and pepper towards Father Jack.

He rubbed his hands. 'You're doing us proud, Erika. One of my favourites, Wiener schnitzel, and nobody can cook it like you.'

He cut through the thin meat, scattering breadcrumbs, not waiting for anybody else to be served. He was always served first by Mutti.

He chewed, swallowed noisily, licked his lips. 'I've got a question for all of you now. Can anybody tell me, is it really veal they give us in this country or do they try to pawn us off with pork?' He raised a loaded fork to his mouth, then lowered it. 'That's what somebody told me once, that when you go to buy veal in an Irish butcher's what you get is flattened pork. And us poor goms none the wiser.'

He bent his head over his plate once more and began to scoop up potato pudding with his upturned fork. Already he was eyeing the meat dish in the middle of the table where two escalopes of veal remained.

'Not that I'd turn up my nose at a decent bit of Irish pork, no more than anyone here. Am I right, Dr Meyers? A bit of Irish pork is good enough for us – what? Our friends now, though,' he gave a snigger, 'our friends down in Clanbrassil Street, they'd be getting into a right old tizzy at the thought of a bit of decent Irish pork.'

Mutti looked at him coldly. 'I assure you, Father Jack, that this is veal. I can certainly tell the difference and so I imagine can the kosher butchers in Clanbrassil Street. And kosher meat is specially chosen and killed, surely you know that?'

'Well indeed.' For a moment his venom showed, then he flicked his eyelids down again and smiled at his plate. 'You'd know these things far better than I would, Erika. You and Dr Meyers – not like Belle and myself. We'd be none the wiser, would we, Belle? But then again, we wouldn't mind. And when you find that nice boy your granny was talking about, sure he wouldn't mind either. An Irish husband would enjoy a bit of Irish pork every bit as much as a Wiener schnitzel, especially if his wife turns out to be as good a cook as her mother.'

His head came up as he spoke and he gave me a long, steady, almost benign look. He knew. This conversation had not been about telling the difference between pork and veal, it had been orchestrated so that I would know that he knew.

I wasn't fooled by the mildness of his look; when Father Jack appeared mild he was at his most dangerous. He would save me from the perfidious Jew.

That's what they all were in the eyes of the Catholic Church. The Second World War and the gas ovens had not changed that, so that every Good Friday still prayers were offered for the conversion of the perfidious Jews. I had been counted among them, and Buba and Mutti, until rescued by Father Jack. He would fight to hold on to me, fight for the salvation of my immortal soul.

'Husbands,' Buba shook her head. 'Really, Father Jack, I am surprised that you talk of such things. Have I not said that first there is the exams and then I hope that there is the university for our little Belle. Time enough then for the talk of husbands.'

Father Jack speared the remaining pieces of veal on to the serving fork and held them up to the table. 'Nobody else for these then? Well, we don't want them to go to waste.' He turned to smile at Buba. 'We all hope the same thing for our dear Belle and with God's help it will all come true. Don't I pray every night that one day we'll all see Belle ready to step into her grandmother's shoes, to take up the burden of serving the Irish people? And then a happy marriage. Belle O'Brien, maybe, or Belle Murphy.' He laughed, nodding towards me, then towards Buba. 'And then the Meyers family will have settled down in Ireland, truly become part and parcel of the Irish nation.'

It was the last birthday I was ever to spend at home although what worried me as we sat there waiting for Mutti to bring in the cake was that I would be trapped there at that table for ever. Between Buba and Father Jack with no means of escape.

With Father Jack's return to our house I knew that I would

have to get out. I was almost grateful to him, for his constant presence would make it easier for me. Buba would only get what she deserved. She was the one who wanted him around, nobody else did. Then if it turned out that his presence drove others away she had nobody to blame but herself. I could leave when the time came with a clear conscience.

LOVE AND REVOLUTION   Just as we were going back to school the weather began to improve. It grew milder with long sunny afternoons and still clear nights.

I was in sixth year with my Children of Mary medal on a blue ribbon around my neck. A symbol of purity, I intended to hand it back to the nuns as soon as Max made love to me.

Mona returned a day late, without explanation. She smiled at the class, loaded us with homework and said to me, 'I want to see you after school, Belle. If you can wait for me outside the staff room.'

Olive Tierney gave me a dirty look.

Mona was waiting for me impatiently when I finally escaped from Sister Benedict and French irregular verbs.

'You took your time.'

'I was kept back – '

'Never mind. You're looking great, filled out. You're a young woman now, Belle.'

I blushed with pleasure. She was looking marvellous, a sort of rosy brown colour and bright clear eyes.

'Come and have a coffee with me in Roberts,' she said as we sat into the Beetle. 'I'm meeting Max there at half-four.'

'He's home?'

'He called round last night but I wasn't in. So much is happening, I've been trying to catch up since I got back.

145

That's the worst of getting away from it all. When something does happen you end up knowing nothing about it.'

The rat. How long had he been home? He hadn't bothered to get in touch, which must mean he didn't care. Had he met someone else in Manchester during the summer?

'I brought you a present – somewhere there on the back seat. Poke around, it's wrapped in black tissue paper, very chic.'

A square of deep-pink silk, hand-stitched around the edges. Vaporous, tender, I crushed it in my hand and held it to my cheek. Women friends stood by you, women friends were real friends. Women friends were not out for what they could get.

'What's happened anyway?'

Mona laughed. 'Nothing's changed, I see. When are you going to start living in this world, Belle? You mean to tell me you are unaware of what has been going on in Hungary over the summer?'

'Yes.'

'Light us a fag there while I try to fill some of the holes in your education.'

Apparently while I had morosely wandered the streets of Dublin things had been hotting up in Eastern Europe, particularly in Hungary and Poland. There had been student unrest in both countries and talk of police brutality at demonstrations. Worst of all was Khrushchev's role. He had started the whole thing with his condemnation of Stalin but now he appeared to be backpedalling.

'And Heslin is still at it. I heard last night that he wants us to condemn all the unrest as the work of fascist infiltrators. I ask you. I want to organize enough support so that we can kick him out once and for all. Let him go back where he belongs to the League and all the rest of the Stalinists.'

We parked at the top of Grafton Street. The street was crowded with shoppers and it was only when we were outside the café window that I saw Max standing inside.

He was leaning on the counter staring moodily into space. Once I had thought that to myself or said it under my breath I knew that there was no point in trying to harden my heart. Moodily, not vacantly nor morosely. Moodily. Interesting, beautiful people stared moodily, not like the rest of us who would have to make do with some mundane adverb. I had forgotten that beauty, framed now in Robert Roberts' window. I grasped the frame as my knees began to wobble, as if the kneecaps might detach themselves and float off into space. Mona banged the glass, then bustled in the door, pulling me after her.

I hung back, not defiant or sulky but overcome by shyness.

'Belle.' He took my hand, smiled at me, no longer moody. 'I've missed you.'

'Hello, Max.' For a moment I didn't recognize my own voice, emerging as it did in a tiny squeak.

Still holding my hand he led me towards the counter at the back of the café. We sat up at it on high stools. Mona followed and lifted herself up, sighing theatrically. 'I hope you two aren't going to spend the whole time making cow's eyes at each other. I'm all in favour of romance but there's a time and a place.'

We both laughed, I delighted at Mona's recognition of the romance.

'Have you contacted the people I told you to yet?' Mona asked while signalling the waitress in sign language to bring us three coffees.

'I don't think it's a very good idea.'

'What!'

'I mean isolating ourselves. Heslin will go back to the League and take others with him.'

'And good riddance.'

Max shook his head. 'You don't know what the mood is, Mona, you've been away, remember. We could be left very much out on a limb – '

I could see Mona gathering wind, expanding her chest to launch an attack. Before she could say anything however our attention was drawn by a shouted call from the door. The café was between rushes, one of those moments of calm which occur in such places no matter how busy the day. So we heard the cry and saw the girl. 'Maximilia-a-n.' The last syllable was extended.

Anyone who was in the café turned to look but she seemed unaffected by the attention she was getting. She walked slowly, tall, blonde and very sure of herself.

She sauntered to the counter and inserted herself between Max and Mona, turning her back on Mona. I looked at her face, large-featured and handsome. She was ignoring me also although she had glanced down indifferently at my hand still held by Max.

'So, Maximilian. You are back with us again.'

Max said nothing but I could feel his fingers tighten round mine.

'Things are beginning to happen – yes? I had a letter from a cousin in Poland, very excited about the possibilities for freedom there.'

She paused as if waiting for him to say something. When he didn't she continued, 'Not yet in my poor country of course but soon even there I hope. Freedom is in the air, Max, it is contagious.'

We watched her as she walked away, just as slowly as she had approached. At the door she turned and gave Max a little wave and a nasty smile.

'Jesus,' said Mona pulling on a cigarette, 'who's Lady Muck?'

Max slammed an open hand down on the counter. His anger seemed to be directed at Mona. 'Good. Now maybe you can see what is happening, now maybe you'll understand what I've been telling you about. She's a White Russian, one of that gang in Trinity. She's delighted by what's going on – of course she is. Meeting me here has made her day. She'll go off and tell her fascist friends how we're on the run in Ireland too.'

They were old enemies apparently, used to spitting venom at one another across the lecture theatre.

'Apart from being a fascist,' Max explained, 'Marina's also a bitch. She just likes needling people. She's gone out with half the rich guys in Trinity, she gets what she can out of them and then she drops them. A bitch. I need hardly add that she's anti-Semitic – oh nothing blatant, she's too sophisticated for that, but lots of little digs.'

He pushed his coffee cup away from him and ran his fingers through his hair in a distracted fashion. He had forgotten about me and how glad he was to see me again.

'So what do you think now, Mona? Is that the sort of person you want to be associated with? Because you will be if you start siding with the students and against the Soviet Union. Every bigot, every fascist, every loony, you'll be lined up with them, against – against our brothers.'

Now it was Mona's turn to bang the table. Not only had they forgotten all about me, they had also forgotten about everybody else in the café. People were turning to look at them, attracted by the raised voices and flailing hands. In a political argument Mona and Max always sounded much fiercer than either of them was. It had to do with their volatility, their indifference to everything outside the ideas that possessed them.

'Brothers – are you mad? How can you be so stupid, how can you reduce everything to such simplicities? You're in there, Max, there's no excuse for you. What's happening in Hungary and Poland is a genuine movement of the people against Stalinist governments. Don't you see – '

'You don't see what it's going to look like here. Wait till the newspapers get going, wait till the Catholic Church gets in on the act. You want to be lined up on the same side as the bishops, applauding their encyclicals when they start condemning – '

'Don't try to teach me anything about the bloody Catholic Church – I've been there before, Max. Remember that.'

Then Max made one of those sweet, unexpected gestures which always surprised me. They shouldn't have, for in their unexpectedness and their sweetness they were typical of him. He reached across and kissed Mona's cheek.

'I'm sorry,' he said. 'Of course you have. I get carried away with an idea and I forget everything else.'

'Well,' said Mona, managing to look both deflated and embarrassed. She drew furiously on her fag. 'We might as well have another cup of coffee then.'

My Max. He was as changeable as an Irish summer's day.

We left Roberts together after Mona had hurried off on some errand for her mother.

'Would you like to see my rooms? I've moved into Trinity.'

We strolled down Grafton Street hand in hand. I thought that lack of self-consciousness must be a by-product of love – I didn't care who saw me, who recognized my state.

As we approached Trinity Max stopped and looked at me critically. 'Better take off the blazer, and the tie. If the Archbishop hears that a schoolgirl in a convent uniform was seen entering the Front Gate he won't rest till he finds out who she is.'

I didn't know whether he was serious or not but I bundled my blazer under my arm, the crest concealed.

We moved under the shadows of the great wooden door. Every time I passed this door in the back of Buba's car she would say to me, 'One day in there, Belle, you to study medicine.'

We moved through and out into a vast cobbled expanse. It was empty for term had not yet begun.

Max said, 'I live up there,' pointing to one of the grey buildings that lined the square.

I turned at the tone of his voice and saw that happiness had drained from him and he looked suddenly grey as the buildings all around us.

We walked up three flights of stone stairs, each step dipping in the middle, worn away by hundreds of years of tripping, scurrying, plodding feet. Max plodded ahead of me, shoulders hunched.

'My humble abode,' he said, pushing a heavy door inwards. The room smelled of toast. Light imploded into it through two tall windows. I looked through one of them. The sky here seemed less grey than that which hung over Dublin. It was more luminous, pearly.

'It's like living in the sky,' I said.

As I turned back to the room my eye was caught by a poster that was pinned on a wall over the fireplace. I stared at it. 'What is it?' Anger and chaos poured from it, boiling over the edges and streaming into the room. Used as I was to the calm remove of art in the National Gallery, I found myself drawn into the poster, upset by it even though I could make little sense of the jumbled animal and human heads and moons and other painted symbols.

Max came and stood beside me. 'Don't you recognize it?'

I shook my head.

'Guernica.'

'What's Guernica?'

'Picasso. The Spanish Civil War, the bombing of the Basque

town by the Germans. Don't you know any of that? God, you're a ferocious little ignoramus.'

He pushed me down on to a bed and began to kiss me. I kissed him back and put my arms around him and pulled him as close to me as I could. I didn't care if I were an ignoramus, I had my whole life to work on that but I had only now for this new pleasure, now in this high, cold room.

'You're a wonderful girl,' said Max, coming up for air. I pulled him back.

'No, wait.'

'Why?'

'Because I'm responsible for you and I promised Mona you'd be home for your tea.'

We both laughed at this mundanity.

I held him from me at arm's length. I wanted to examine him so that I would be able to recall him inch by inch when I lay alone in bed, thinking about him. I ran my fingers over his hands with their too-long nails, along the arch of his black eyebrows, on the curve of his full short upper lip. I rubbed his skin, the colour and glint of sand under a summer sky. He was so beautiful.

'You stop that, witch.'

He dragged me off the bed and we stood together in front of the poster. He nodded towards it. 'I'm surprised Mona hasn't given you one already, she does usually to all her friends. I had Lenin up there but she made me take him down.'

'Why?'

'Surely you know what she thinks of Lenin? Not quite the demon Stalin is, but getting there.'

We stood in front of the poster, staring at it.

'I don't like it,' I said. 'It upsets me.'

'So it should. Great art always upsets, unsettles anyway. And Franco's still over there in Spain, remember that.'

He walked up to the poster and tapped it with a finger. 'Look at it, Belle. Look at the pain and destruction and the sheer senselessness of it all. That's fascism, that's what we have to fight and Mona knows that. She's the real revolutionary, not me, I'm just playing at being one. I really want things to remain as they are so that I can go along to Party meetings and make a few speeches and go on a few marches. Anything else and I'm running scared. A spoilt Yiddish boy indulged by loving parents and flirting with socialism for a few years before he takes up some respectable profession.'

There was a disgust in his voice which suggested a serious dislike, as if he had thought long and hard about it. Then his mood changed again and he was clowning around the room. 'That's me, a real mama's boy. You must meet my mama. She'll approve of you once you let her see that you love me too. And my young sister can join in. Lots of female admiration, that's what this fragile male ego needs.'

By the time we had walked through College Park to Lincoln Place I knew I was going to be very late for tea.

'We'll get you a taxi, come on.'

'I can't afford one.'

'I can. Come on.'

He waited with me at the taxi rank, not saying anything, just holding my hand. I wanted to touch him with my free hand, to finger all his surfaces from silk of eyelash to stubble of beard.

I sat into the back of the taxi and closed my eyes. He hadn't arranged another meeting, just said he'd see me at the Party premises next week. I'd die if I didn't see him before then. I tried to conjure him up then but for some strange reason I couldn't find his face as violent fragments of the Picasso poster flashed scarlet behind my closed eyelids and Buba's voice said, 'Another war – never,

Belle. That is why we come to Ireland where there will be no wars.'

I thought of those words today when I heard of another five people shot dead by a gunman in Belfast. Except of course that nobody calls that a war, only the IRA.

I was having lunch with Shields in the Bunch of Grapes, our local, when the news came on the radio. Shields paid no attention, she never does, and Dessie just turned the transistor off. It's an old-fashioned pub this, no sound system, just a transistor.

'Nothing but animals up there,' Dessie said when he brought me my coffee. 'All the bloody same.'

Perhaps he's right. It's what Buba used to say about the communists and Mona about the fascists. I reserve my spleen for psychiatrists.

Shields said, 'He's going to have a party for us, a farewell do.' She emptied her glass, screwing up her little blue eyes in pleasure as the vodka hit the back of her throat.

'Who's going to have a party?' I asked.

'Anto. Didn't you get your invite?'

'No.'

She cackled. 'Maybe you won't – on account of you not being a professional like. I'd say she might think that unskilled labour would bring down the tone. You know the wife, very hoity-toity.'

Dessie came over to empty the ashtray. 'Are yis all right, girls?'

Calling us girls was Dessie's attempt at flattery. He sat down beside us. 'Any more news from up above?' He nodded towards the hospital.

'Any day now we'll all be off,' Shields answered.

Gloomily he flicked a dirty cloth round the table, disturbing ash and putting an empty crisp packet to flight. 'I don't know what we'll do once it goes, nobody does around here. Sure whatever we say about you lot, you spent a bit of money in the area.'

Shields made a face at him. 'Nice to know when you're appreciated.'

'No, God's truth. I can see them pulling down the hospital and building some of them luxury apartments. People who live in them sorts of places wouldn't be doing their shopping round here. Nor their drinking.'

We watched as he ambled off again, flicking his cloth as he went.

'It's amazing, that,' said Shields. 'When I started working up there they didn't even want to serve people who worked in the hospital. I think they were afraid we'd bring madness in with us on the soles of our shoes. It was hard-going in those days. I remember mothers warning their children not to play anywhere near the Mental in case any of the lunatics broke out. And even then Anto was talking about integrating into the community. That man was before his time, I'm telling you.'

I had been one of the lunatics in those days, securely locked up so as not to endanger or infect.

Shields finished her drink. 'Well, are you going to the party then or not?'

'I haven't been invited.'

'Seriously, though.'

'We'll see.'

He must think it doesn't matter now that he's going. Too late for either wife or mistress to make a scene.

I'm going to miss this neighbourhood. It's old and settled and unfashionable, just like myself. But even if I could stay on in the lodge I wouldn't. Too lonely, too haunted.

I'm going to miss Shields – and one or two of the others.

155

Mates can be more of a help through life than friends. You invest less in them and they're there at the end of the day to share a joke and a drink. Or a takeaway after the pubs close.

Shields and I usually came down here on a Saturday night for a few drinks. We've been doing it for over twenty years. Before that I used to keep my Saturday evenings free for Anto. With a married man you can't plan in advance, but you had to be prepared to grab the opportunity when it arose.

There's been little change in the neighbourhood over the years. There's been little crime either, most of the population being both elderly and poor. Sometimes the kids come in from the suburbs to visit their grannies and the grannies show them off and the kids glower and chew gum and puff smoke in your face. Otherwise we don't have any blow-ins.

Most of the houses are lived in by women, the men having died or buggered off years ago. Shields maintains that this is its main drawback and that if the hospital had been situated in a different part of town she would have been spotted by some man, picked up here in the Bunch of Grapes as she flashed a bit of thigh getting on a high stool.

'I'm going to miss this neighbourhood,' I said to Shields.

She had stood up and was looking at herself in one of Dessie's smeared mirrors. 'I'm definitely getting a new dress for the party and I'll have to do something about my hair.' She sighed as she began to pull at the hennaed locks. 'When Anto is off in Romania I want him to remember me at my best.'

LOVING AND LEAVING Now that I was in sixth year Buba was expecting me to put in some hard work. I knew that I could get by on a minimum. Once I matriculated I would be accepted into any of the medical schools and you had to try really hard to fail Matric. Buba, coming from Germany, didn't know this and I didn't inform her. It was handy to be able to disappear out the door with a martyred expression and a vague comment about study.

Buba seemed to have forgotten that she had ever been ill. She was back to her full quota of cigars per day and she was working even longer hours in the surgery as more and more patients sought her out.

Father Jack, wiping cake crumbs from his lips, said, 'You won't feel it now, Dr Meyers, till you have a partner to help you out in your practice. And the National University of Ireland turns out the best doctors in the world.'

I smiled at him. 'Trinity, Father Jack. I'm not going to UCD.'

He stared at me, then flicked his eyelids upwards towards Buba. 'What's this nonsense?'

Buba looked confused. 'Trinity College – the best, I've always thought. So old, so many famous people.'

'Not allowed, dear lady, especially not where medicine is concerned. The Archbishop does not allow Catholics to attend a Protestant university. And no need to now, thank God, when we have our own.'

We'll see about that, I said to myself.

'And it's not just the study side of things, there's also the people Belle will meet. Company keeping, Dr Meyers.' He stretched over and tapped Buba's hand. 'We must avoid not only sin but all occasions of sin. At least if a lad comes from a good, Catholic background.'

Company keeping. Outside on a still October night, pressed against one of Trinity's ancient stone walls, I kept company.

Beans on toast in his rooms. Eaten sitting on the bed though apart, no coming together of flesh. Propped up on pillows he looked at me, a look of passionate intensity. Not for me, though, for the cause.

Hours and hours of talk as our tea grew cold in our mugs and the last of the beans congealed on our plates. Mona had been right and what was going on in Hungary was the beginning of a genuine workers' revolt. Of course as usual the Irish were firmly grasping the wrong end of the stick, convinced that it was all about saving Catholicism and reinstating Cardinal Mindszenty.

Fresh tea, more talk.

'I'll have to go, Max.'

Distractedly he looks for his jacket, then still talking hurries me down the stairs.

Then he suddenly seems to remember who I am as I stumble against him on the cobbles.

'Belle,' he says and pushes me into the shadow of an elm against the smooth stone still warm from the daylong sun. He kisses my neck, then draws his fingers down over my left breast. I shiver and pull him to me but he is the pleasure master and he holds back and repeats the exercise slowly. And repeats and repeats.

'I can't bear it, Max,' I gasp. 'I'll die if I go on feeling like this. Too much.'

He stops and plants a schoolboy kiss on my cheek. 'OK,' he says, 'but this is only the beginning.'

It was to prove the beginning of many things, including my sentimental and political education.

Max was my tutor, wakening me up in body and mind. In the late afternoons, straight from school, I went to his rooms and we made love in his narrow, lumpy bed. Then over beans and toast (I don't remember any other food) we explored Marxist politics.

Being less doctrinaire than Mona he was a better teacher.

He too had doubts and he always answered my often naive questions with patience and consideration. I was never an intellectual Marxist – since being let down by the Holy Ghost I was sceptical of all religions – but energized by love-making I committed all my excess emotions to the cause.

People talk of the fifties as a period of unrelieved grey; to me those years were very heaven. Swanking around Stephen's Green, arms linked with Mona and Max, I felt myself to be part of a worldwide revolutionary movement. Beset by dangers, Stalinists, Special Branch and the Archbishop's spies, I knew that I was living dangerously. Ironically enough, the one real danger I was in, getting pregnant, I discounted.

Within the Party we had failed in our efforts to oust Heslin. With Catholic Ireland up in arms over the treatment of Cardinal Mindszenty there was much sympathy for his position. For most members of the Socialist Workers Party the Catholic Church would always be a greater source of evil than Stalin.

When they couldn't see that what was happening in Eastern Europe was the spontaneous revolution that Rosa Luxemburg had talked about, Mona wanted to go in and knock their heads together. Max preached caution.

'Our position is a delicate one, Mona, and it merely reflects what's going on all over – even inside the Soviet Union. Why do you think Khrushchev is being so cautious? He can't be having it all his own way with the Politburo full of Stalinists. An upheaval like that upsets everybody. You can hardly expect members of the Party to be overjoyed at the prospect of lining up with priests and reactionaries.'

'We're a Marxist party, these are Marxists who are being bludgeoned by police. Rationally there is only one position we can hold.'

Max laughed. 'There was nothing very rational about tonight, was there?'

'That's because we have them running scared.'

I didn't agree with Mona. We had been thrown out of the meeting because people were generally fed up with us: with Mona's disruptive hopping up and down on points of order, with Max's insistence on reading out a statement made by Trotsky's widow on Stalinists in the Soviet Union, and with my noisy encouragement of the other two. I thought we were losing the battle of hearts and minds within the Party, and the shriller we got the more impatient the others became with us.

Now we walked along Baggot Street in the rain because Mona's car was in the garage getting a new clutch. We crossed over the bridge and made our way up the quieter bank of the canal where golden leaves still clung to the trees, dripping on the heads of lovers, indifferent as we were to the downpour.

I took Max's hand. 'When do the Poznan trials begin?' I asked.

'Next week – Wednesday or Thursday.'

Max had answered me without comment but Mona stopped to give me a hug. 'And to think that you were just another convent girl this time last year. I'm really proud of you, Belle.'

I was proud of myself. Every time I used a word like *dialectic* I listened to myself with pride. Eventually I supposed I would cease to be self-conscious about my socialism and take it for granted like Mona and Max.

When I got home Mutti and Buba were still up, absorbed by the pages of a newspaper which they had divided between them. I had never seen a newspaper in our house before.

Mutti smiled at me and beckoned me to her. 'I got it specially because of the photographs. Everyone is talking about the new fashion. What do you think, Belle?'

Two pages of the paper were spread out on the sofa beside her. I looked at the photographs of mannequins wearing

160

dresses and coats with long, full skirts. The headline read, 'Dior's New Look'.

Mutti shook her head. 'OK for the tall ones like you, I think. Not on me. On me I would look a frump.'

Buba, taking the cigar from her mouth and waving it at Mutti, said, 'Erika, you know we should buy these newspapers. Always I have thought them boring but now I learn something good from them. In West Germany, as they call it, the communists have been outlawed. Good news I think that.'

I wondered if they had been Stalinists, in which case I would agree with her.

They stayed up after I had gone to bed, poring over the newspaper. They were like children, pointing out interesting bits to one another, laughing, arguing over what they read.

It must have been her experience of newspaper reading that led Buba to go out the following week and buy a wireless.

It was a wine-coloured Bakelite set shaped like the cover on a Singer sewing machine. Buba decided that she wanted it in the kitchen and Mutti brought down a table from her bedroom on which to place it. But somehow or other they never caught the habit of listening to it.

Buba soon lost interest in news bulletins. Mutti listened for some time to the Saturday-night play from Athlone but she lost interest, saying that they were too Irish, and most of the time she couldn't understand them because she didn't know the background. In the end I was the only one who ever turned the set on.

They returned to the sitting room and Schubert on the wind-up gramophone.

I was suffering from exhaustion, out at impromptu meetings held in Max's rooms, getting in around ten or later. Mona would leave me off at the door and Buba or Mutti would stare after the car, then turn their attention to me. I was pale, they told me, with rings under my eyes. I said that I had no option if I wanted to get a scholarship. Mona was coaching me and she knew how much work I had to put in.

Mutti would rush to make me chocolate, Buba would smile and nod but the worry remained in her little black eyes, dulling their sheen.

And I would go to bed guilty and resentful, which brought on another wave of guilt.

In the meantime, halfway across Europe, things were reaching a crisis: young men and women not much older than I were being handed down savage sentences for their part in the Poznan riots. There were workers' strikes in East Germany (always referred to by us as the GDR) and in Budapest there were huge anti-Russian demonstrations.

Now either before or after Party meetings we held our own meetings. We had become a tendency within the Party as we tried to steer it on a true socialist course between the Stalinists on one side and the capitalists on the other. And we were beginning to pick up a following. George McNab came to our meetings and some friends of Max and an older man who seldom said anything but listened with concentrated intensity.

Max's room was getting dirtier – there was no time to clean up after these gatherings. The air always smelled of cigarette smoke and spilt stout. There was no time for anything now except these meetings.

Mona was sitting on cushions on the floor, her legs folded neatly under her. She could sit like this throughout a meeting, never getting cramp or pins and needles as I had done on the one occasion I had tried it.

'God,' she said, 'I'd give anything to be over there now, just as it's all beginning. I wish I had the courage just to go. Give up the good, pensionable job and just walk out and into history.'

We were silent, taken by this image, until George McNab said, 'I don't know so much, Mona, there's work to be done here.'

She flicked a sweet wrapper at him. She had been eating sweets in an effort to cut down on the fags which were giving her a perpetual cough. 'Work but no glory, George. I want a bit of glory before it's too late.'

'And another thing,' said George, levering the top off a beer bottle with a penny. Max didn't have a bottle opener and there was never any time to buy one. 'Another thing, there's a rumour going round that the Hungarian government is going to release Mindszenty. Now that's going to be difficult for us, comrades. How do we explain our position, our support for the rebels, and not be mistaken for Catholic extremists?'

These were the sorts of dilemmas we discussed every night. We had begun to get on one another's nerves. The lack of action, the endless talk, the late nights, the smoky rooms, the amount of beer sunk, all contributed to our irritability. Well – theirs really. I was still dazzled by it all. I was smoking now and drinking, for Mona had become too preoccupied to keep an eye on me. I had a lover and I was part of a revolutionary movement which was setting Europe alight. Every morning as I pulled my gymslip over my head I marvelled at the turn my life had taken.

Max asked, 'Can anyone throw any light on the meeting between Khrushchev and Tito? What does it signify, d'you think? What had the Irish Times to say about it? I didn't get a paper today.'

Mona groaned. 'Grow up, Max. What does it matter what the Irish Times says about it? I know more about the situation than they do.' She swallowed a sweet she had been chewing and lit a cigarette. 'Khrushchev is look-ing for support – what do you think? He needs all the support he can get, he's quite likely to be shafted by the Politburo.'

I was dying for a cup of tea and I knew it would help waken me up. I forced myself to listen, to keep my eyes open and not to yawn. Mona got annoyed when anybody yawned, particularly if she held the floor.

I straightened my back and locked my eyes on to her as she sat on the cushion gesticulating. She was saying something about the CP in Italy, that they had issued a statement saying that socialism should be allowed to develop differently in every country. We should do the same, said Mona, issue a statement agreeing with them.

I thought of all the statements issuing from rooms like this all over Europe. Or perhaps grander rooms in other countries where socialism had a stronger hold.

Mona spread her arms, threw back her head. In spite of all the late nights and the drinking and the smoke-filled rooms she had never looked better. I could imagine her heart racing inside her chest, pumping out the blood which coursed around her body, bringing that glow to her face. Sometimes in the morning, standing on the rostrum in school, she looked quite old, the rosy brown of her summer in the Alps yellowing, turning her cheeks to the colour of an old newspaper. Then I noticed too the deepening fan of those little lines around her eyes and new lines beginning to cut a path around her mouth. At night, though, she was transformed by passion and excitement. With her thin little body and her glowing face and as she prodded and pushed us and harangued us, she seemed the youngest person in the room.

Sometimes I wondered what would happen to her when all this was over, when things were settled one way or the other in Hungary and Poland and beyond. I couldn't see her returning to the old life of preparing school debates or listening to Heslin's uninspired pronouncements. A struggle can go on too long and Mona's had been going on since she was a schoolgirl and her brother had gone to fight in Spain. This time round something had to happen.

'Look at you.' She whacked me out of my half-sleep, landing a blow with her small fist on my shoulder. 'You youngsters, you've no stamina.'

'A cup of tea,' I said.

'No tea. Bed and put that cigarette out. You're going to the dogs, Belle Meyers, it must be the company you keep.'

In Poland Gomulka was released from jail and Soviet warships steamed into Polish waters. There were more anti-Russian demonstrations in Budapest, with students demanding a new government under Nagy.

Father Jack came to visit and told us that Ireland must start praying. 'All the priests of the diocese have been asked by his Lordship to offer prayers next Sunday for Cardinal Mindszenty. The Hungarian government has declared a state of emergency and the poor Cardinal – God help us all.'

Buba tapped ash from her cigar and nodded her head. 'This thing does not surprise me. Always the communists are so ruthless. In Ireland people do not realize how ruthless they are.'

I brought in coffee from the kitchen. Mutti had disappeared upstairs, claiming a headache. I thought that she had just had too much of Father Jack who, these days, seemed to call oftener and stay longer.

He rubbed his yellow hands and darted a hooded eye towards the horseshoe of apple strudel. 'Goodness me, Erika has been busy.'

Buba smiled. 'Not Erika, Belle has become the pastry chef and a very good one too.'

165

He looked at me sceptically then began to help himself, shovelling the delicate pastry on to a plate.

'And where does she find the time with all her other interests.' It was not a question, more a statement of disapproval.

He took a forkful of the strudel, tidied his mouth by flicking a crumb from his moist lower lip with the tip of a red, pointed tongue. 'Excellent pastry.' He chewed and swallowed, gulping down coffee and strudel together.

'I hope you're not overdoing it, Belle; we all know how hard you've been studying.' (I could hear the inverted commas round the studying.) 'And then there's the debating and so forth. Though' – the eyelids were folded back for a second and I met a thoughtful blue gaze – 'less of that in sixth year, I suppose. That teacher of yours busy with her teaching, I suppose?'

I nodded, not wanting to speak, not wanting to help him ferret out any more information.

'Well.' He held out his cup for more coffee. 'Well, I hope you will have time to attend a Holy Hour next Sunday afternoon. I'm arranging a Holy Hour when prayers will be said for the release of Cardinal Mindszenty. As your grandmother said, communism is a terrible scourge and we need to be on our guard always against its corrupting influence. Especially in this city.' He turned to Buba. 'Do you know, Dr Meyers, that I have it on good authority that Dublin has become a hotbed for godless communism. All over the place, all sorts of respectable people infected. Even schoolteachers.'

The hoods were lifted and the eyes stared directly into mine.

I could feel myself grow red as I pretended to busy myself with the sugar and milk.

I knew that man so well, I knew what he was up to. What worried me now was that he could read me with equal ease, in which case it was probably I who had given Mona away.

166

As I have said we communicated as lovers do, wordlessly. The strength of our mutual dislike meant that we listened to each other, gave each other the sort of attention that lovers share. But despite my dislike of him I was now beginning to think that there was something of the sportsman in him. He gave me chances, warnings, as if he knew that I needed a bit of help to make it a fair fight. He was telling me now that he knew about Mona, giving me a chance to pass on this information so that the quarry would be warned before the hunter moved in for the kill.

Next morning I was outside the staff-room door at a quarter to nine. I waited and waited, watching the hands of the clock at the end of the corridor pass the point where I would be late for Assembly. At last I heard footsteps rushing up the terrazzo steps. She came running into sight, discarding her coat as she moved.

'Belle, I've no time to talk, I'm late as it is. What are you doing here anyway?'

'I've come to warn you. They're on to you, Mona. You'll have to do something or you'll lose your job.'

She stared at me, not seeming to understand what I was saying.

'Mona, you're not listening. Father Jack – '

She shook herself free from my arm. 'Too late to worry about the Father Jacks of this world – haven't you heard the news?'

'What news?'

'Nonsense and more nonsense. Those bloody kids in Budapest have opened fire on the Russian tanks. Can you imagine the stupidity of it? God knows what will happen now. This is the excuse they've been waiting for in Russia, now anything can happen.'

She told me to spend as much time listening to the wireless as I could. When I got home I tuned into the Home Service and a cool English voice reassured me. Skirmishing in Budapest, it said, making Budapest sound like Bath struggling to contain Teddyboy high spirits.

All afternoon I listened to news bulletins, sometimes switching to Athlone which didn't even seem to know about the riots. Then Buba came in from the surgery and asked me to find some nice music as all the talking was giving her a headache.

But next morning when I came down to breakfast it was she who had news for me. 'They've released the Cardinal,' she said. 'It must be all those prayers that Father Jack told us about.'

Father Jack obviously thought that the Cardinal's release was entirely his doing. That very evening he called to see us, dancing into the kitchen in front of Mutti, waving his long yellow hands in the air. 'Thanks be to God and His Holy Mother. Such news, such wonderful news. I knew our prayers would be answered.'

I had never seen him so animated before, not even when Buba had offered our souls to him in a job lot. His horrid lips spread in a moist, pink smile as he looked around him in triumph. 'A great day for the Catholic Church. A great day.' He squeezed my arm and shook Buba's hand. He was like a mummy come to life, dragging his raggedy limbs round the kitchen in a parody of joy.

I wondered if I should be pleased. Mindszenty was nothing to us but the students had wanted him released. So this must mean that the government was acceding to the students' demands.

'Praise the Lord,' sang Father Jack, waving his yellow hands as Buba clapped her little fat ones and Mutti looked at both of them as if they were mad.

'I think what is happening in Hungary has a lot more to do with than the Cardinal,' she said.

Father Jack smiled at her kindly. 'Do you know, Erika, I could do with a cup of coffee. A cup of your excellent coffee wouldn't go amiss.'

*   *   *

Things were happening so fast that I couldn't keep up.

When I asked Mona about Mindszenty she said, 'Oh that's only a side show, naturally Nagy let him out.'

'Nagy?'

'Nagy, yes, the Prime Minister.'

'But when – '

'Oh Belle, for heaven's sake. Wake up, will you.'

She was giving me a lift home from school, hunched over the wheel, bad-tempered and blowing out smoke like a dragon. I didn't ask any more questions. I sat beside her in silence and tried to ignore her driving, which always scared me when I had nothing to distract me.

She swung wide round a corner and we missed an oncoming lorry by inches.

'I wish those fellows would mind where they're going,' Mona said, her voice irritable but mild. 'I don't want to get myself killed just now – too ironic.'

She told me then as we drove along an empty suburban road. In a square, girls from a Protestant school were playing hockey, their voices lifted then lost on the wind.

She was going to Hungary to fight for socialism as her brother had gone to Spain twenty years before. I watched the girls as they flashed past behind the railings. In our school we played basketball, which was deemed a more ladylike sport.

'I have to go, you must see that, Belle. The latest reports from Budapest talk about thousands dead. I can't just sit here.'

It must be some sort of disease her family suffered from, rushing off to fight in foreign countries.

'It's going to be tricky, though. I don't want Heslin to know until I'm in but I'll have to tell de Lourdes.'

I stared out the window, humming to myself.

'Belle, come on now, you're the first one I've told. Except for Ma, of course. She doesn't know whether she's coming or going. Who'll do her shopping, she wants to know, and then – when can she tell everybody that her daughter's gone off to fight for Cardinal Mindszenty.'

As we cleared a corner and came out from the shadows of a terrace of tall buildings a shaft of low October sunshine hit the windscreen and filled the interior of the car with merciless golden light.

As I looked at Mona's profile in cruel relief I was reminded of her words about her brother: what happens to old revolutionaries, the ones who botch it up and don't get killed?

I had a premonition that Mona McCarthy would not botch it up.

'Aren't you going to say anything, Belle?' she asked, pulling down a sun shield.

'What do you want me to say?'

'You could at least wish me luck.'

But the words gagged in my throat and I turned my head away so that she wouldn't see my tears.

Her exit was less than glorious, more farce than tragedy.

Mother de Lourdes had been sworn to secrecy but she was so bursting with pride that she had to mark the occasion in some fashion.

So on the morning of Mona's departure, when she hadn't come into school but when not a word had been said about her absence, the school was informed at Assembly that a candle-lit procession would process to the Lourdes grotto at twelve noon, headed by the Children of Mary.

By twelve o'clock it was raining steadily but Mother de Lourdes was undaunted. Someone had made little paper shields for the candles which de Lourdes said would protect them from the rain, especially if we held them at an angle against the prevailing wind.

We set off in twos to walk round the grounds, down as far as the basketball pitch and on to the grotto, then back again and round again until we had five decades of the rosary completed.

There were mutinous mumblings as we set off in the rain. Within seconds most of the candles had been extinguished except for half a dozen which had set fire to the paper shields. Screams replaced the murmurs as girls fell out, flaming torches in their hands. Mother de Lourdes, not at all worried about the safety of her pupils, urged the rest of us to gather round the flaming torches that we might relight our extinguished candles.

Luckily one of the other nuns intervened and with some reluctance de Lourdes gave the command — candles out. Then we set out, quick march, to slosh around the grounds. From behind our general's voice reached us thinly as she started the rosary.

By the time we finally assembled at the grotto we were soaked through. In order to be seen Mother de Lourdes had hoisted herself up on a shelf beside the statue of the Blessed Virgin. 'Sing,' she ordered, giving us a note. '"Hail, Queen of Heaven."'

'"Hail, Queen of Heaven,"' we bellowed back.

De Lourdes beamed down on us as if she, not the wan creature by her side, were the real queen of heaven.

When we had finished the hymn she beckoned us forward conspiratorially and told us in a stage whisper which carried surprisingly well that we must all pray for a Special Intention. She couldn't tell us what it was, she could only tell us that it concerned someone we all loved and respected. And we must pray every morning and every night for this Intention and it would be a good idea too to offer up little acts of mortification for the same Intention.

By late afternoon a rumour had swept the school: Miss McCarthy was pregnant. There was much comment too on de Lourdes' decency and it was generally agreed, even by girls who had begun to sneeze, that the procession had been a good idea.

Mona had arranged that Max was to have the Beetle while she was away. Then she asked us both if we would take her to the North Wall where she was catching the boat to Liverpool.

'Then you could go on to the meeting and tell Heslin that I'm sick. Tell him that I've got something that'll keep me in bed for a while. That way he won't be suspicious and I'll be across the border before he can alert any of his pals.'

We picked her up at half-six. She was waiting at the end of her road with a small attaché case and a brown-paper parcel. She sat in beside Max and threw the suitcase into the back. I caught it. It was lighter than the case I brought to school every day.

'Ma insisted on making me sandwiches.' Mona held up the brown-paper parcel. 'Sandwiches and a slice of brack. Not a very glorious start to my revolutionary career, is it?'

But neither Max nor I had the heart for jokes.

We drove through empty streets. As we approached the Liffey a wind came up, blowing leaves and sweet papers against the windscreen. The river was high and choppy; it would be a rough crossing that night.

Halfway down the Quays Max drew up outside a pub.

'We'll walk from here,' he said. 'It can get very crowded further down, we'd be quicker walking.'

He took Mona's little case and set off, not waiting for us. Mona took my arm. The streets down here were cobbled and difficult to walk on.

I supposed that this was where I had arrived first into Ireland but I didn't remember anything about this desolate spot. Grey water gave way to grey warehousing so that the river was no longer visible. The other side of the road was lined with boarded-up buildings. Most of them looked derelict. On a corner a pub threw out sudden light and the sound of voices raised in drunken song. Beyond there was another sound, less defined, low, like the grumble of distant traffic but without traffic's distinctive whine. As I peered along the badly lit quay I saw at the end a great crowd of people. It was from them the sound was coming, their mutterings and stirrings merging into one general throb.

'What on earth?' I pointed.

'Emigrants, poor devils – they're all waiting for the boat.'

I thought that half of Ireland must be leaving and as I watched the couples, the groups, the solo travellers, it seemed to me as if the air over their heads was sodden and heavy with sorrow. They stood patiently like animals, expecting nothing more than this wait in the cold wind. Whole families were waiting to board. I watched one, four little children with the fifth, a baby, in its mother's arms. The children clung to one another, forming a fragile chain, the mother protected the baby inside the curve of her arms and the father looked round him angrily, from time to time cuffing one of the children who looked back at him dumbly.

It was the lack of animation that struck me, the passivity. One little group of youths was making an effort, shoving and jostling, swearing with bravado. They had red, country faces and wiry hair tamed with Brylcreem. When they saw me watching them they became even more boisterous but still they didn't hide the panic in their eyes. They looked younger than me.

Some wild-looking men pushed in front of me, speaking Irish. They used their powerfully muscled shoulders to cut a path through the crowd. Soon those shoulders would be put to different uses, digging English roads and laying English sewer pipes.

'Mother Ireland,' said Mona looking around her. 'And people wonder why I'm a socialist.'

She wouldn't let us wait to the last, shooing us off as soon as they started taking passengers on board.

We drove in silence across the city to the meeting. It was packed and we were late. As we pushed in at the back people turned to look at us, without any sign of friendliness, I thought. There was a sudden silence in the room which suggested that we had been the object of their discussion just previously. Or perhaps I was imagining things.

'You're late, comrades,' Heslin barked out. 'And Comrade McCarthy — is she not gracing us with her presence tonight? Other fish to fry, I suppose.'

The attack was swifter and more venomous than either of us had expected and beside me Max opened his mouth to say something, then shut it again. 'No, no,' he finally got out. 'She's sick.'

Heslin raised one eyebrow and stared at him in silence. So did the rest of the room.

'Yes. Sick,' repeated Max in desperation. 'She's got — gout.'

This was greeted by seconds of stunned silence before laughter engulfed the comrades. It started as a ragged titter and then grew until the whole room was filled with roars and howls of mirth. Even Heslin at the top table was wiping tears from his eyes.

'Gout. Gout.' The word echoed round the room.

Poor Max. He tried to say something else but Heslin told him to sit down.

The mood in the room had changed, whatever tension that had been there was dissipated now by the laughter as people turned to smile at Max and me. But Max was not noticing.

'What on earth possessed you?' I asked him as we drove away afterwards. Luckily we had been at the back of the room and had found it easy to escape as Heslin was drawing proceedings to a close.

'I don't know. I was trying to think of something that would keep her at home for a long time but that didn't sound life-threatening.'

'But gout. Not high on the list of acceptable socialist diseases. She'll never forgive you, Max.'

'I know.'

And for the first time since Mona had told me she was going I found myself laughing – healing, releasing laughter in which Max had soon joined.

'She won't be much good to them in Budapest with that gout,' I said.

'I don't know. They might think she was Rosa Luxemburg reincarnated when they see her hobbling around.'

And so we joked and laughed and the more we did so the more ludicrous it seemed that Mona was heading off to a place where real guns were tearing holes in real flesh.

We kissed good-night like lovers anywhere and death and revolution were no more than words in a newspaper headline.

'Those poor students,' Mutti said to me next morning as she sleepily poured herself a cup of coffee.

'What students?'

'In Budapest. They've given up. They've laid down their arms and it's all over.'

The timing was a personal disaster for Mona or for her cover as we all in love and anger and fear and frustration started to blab.

175

'But Mona, Miss McCarthy, she's gone out there to join them,' said I.

'I can tell you of that Special Intention now, girls,' said Mother de Lourdes. 'It was for Miss McCarthy, our colleague and teacher, who had gone off to fight for Catholicism and freedom in Hungary. Too late as it turns out, but we must still pray for her safe return and that God will put some mercy in the ravening hearts of those communist beasts.'

'I hope you're happy now,' said Max to Heslin. 'It's a great day for socialism when revolutionary workers in Hungary are defeated by Russian tanks. I'm only sorry I didn't go with Mona. Even if she was too late at least she had some guts.'

We were all wrong, as it turned out. She wasn't too late. Whatever deal Nagy had done with the Russians which enabled him to get the students to lay down their arms broke down and Nagy withdrew Hungary from the Warsaw Pact.

Hungary was now a neutral country, he declared, as Russian troops began to mobilize and move towards the Hungarian border. Nagy appealed to the UN and next day the Russian tanks attacked. Nagy was deposed and replaced by a new, pro-Russian government.

And where was Mona? Nobody had heard from her, nobody had any idea where she was. She had got on that Liverpool boat and been swallowed up.

For the first two days we had expected her home. Then as time went by and the fighting in Budapest was resumed with renewed ferocity we began to think that she must have got in.

She had left me her wireless and I listened to it in my room as down in the kitchen Mutti and Buba listened. At last they had been drawn into the Great World as they waited anxiously to hear how things were going on the continent that they thought they had left behind. Mona had become that poor, good teacher whom Buba shook her head over as she lit a cigar.

All of Ireland was now interested in the fate of Hungary and all of Ireland, or nearly all, sided with the students.

Max said to me, 'Will we chance going to a meeting? Things must be getting pretty tough for them just now and I'm fed up to the teeth hearing about Catholic Hungary.'

But our way was barred at the top of the steps as we tried to get into the room. Two men stood side by side. One of them, Jack Furlong, had been a friend, or so I thought. Now he spat on the floor, inches from my feet, and told us to wait for Comrade Heslin.

Heslin approached us without bombast. His voice was low, conversational, as he told us that we had been expelled from the Party. No room for traitors, he said pleasantly, at a time of siege.

We learned later that the premises had been attacked earlier in the day: windows were broken and the door forced and a group from the Legion of Mary had performed an act of exorcism, purifying the premises by saying the rosary and sprinkling holy water.

Back on the street Max and I looked at one another. It was raining. It was always raining that November, while in Budapest snow fell steadily day by day.

'We could go to the pictures,' Max said.

And we headed off for the Astor where we sat in the dark holding hands and watching Ingmar Bergman as he bared his reassuringly depressive soul.

I couldn't go to school; I couldn't face all the endless speculation about Mona and, worse still, the relentless praying for her safe return.

I asked Buba if I could have a few days off. She smiled and nodded and said that I was working too hard anyway.

I stayed in bed the next morning, trying to get Radio Free

Europe on Mona's wireless. Max said that he had got it on the Long Wave but on that waveband I got nothing but static.

At eleven Mutti brought me a cup of coffee. She looked into my face, then took my chin and turned my head towards the weak November light. 'Go out and get some air,' she said. 'Now, before the rain comes.'

It was falling in slanting, stinging arrows when I got off the bus opposite Trinity. I heard the conductor say to a woman in front of me that there was snow in the sky.

I crossed the cobbles in Front Square with my head bent against the rain. There was music coming from some of the rooms on Max's staircase but his was empty, the door open.

I looked around. There was grey ash in the grate and unwashed dishes on the table. And there was something different about the room. It took me some seconds to realize that the *Guernica* poster had gone.

I stepped backwards and my foot crunched on something. Broken glass. When I looked at the floor I saw shards spread over a wide area. A book with its spine broken was lying in a corner.

'Max,' I called, not expecting an answer, and I didn't get one.

As I was making my way back across the cobbles I saw a group gathered outside the Chapel. There was shouting and two people unfurling a banner. One of them looked like the girl, the Russian, who had accosted Max in Robert Roberts, but from this distance I couldn't be sure.

A girl came towards me, wheeling a bike.

'What's going on?' I asked, pointing towards the group.

'It's the White Russians,' she replied. 'They've been on a commie hunt and now they're organizing a march.'

'Did they find any?'

'Any what?'

'Commies.'

She shrugged. 'It doesn't look like it or they'd have strung them up after what's happened in Budapest.'

'In Budapest?'

'Russian tanks have killed women and children.'

And she moved off, wheeling her bicycle.

Where would I find Max? I didn't know where to start looking. I wandered round Trinity hoping I might see some friend or acquaintance of his, then I walked up Grafton Street. The cafés were full of students but no sign of Max.

Worried and wet I caught the bus home. I was just turning into my road when I heard a familiar rattle behind me. The Beetle drew up.

'Hop in, water rat.' He was smiling, unmarked, when I had been imagining him bruised and beaten by White Russian staves.

He laughed at me. 'They're just a bunch of thugs.'

'But you've left your door open.'

'There's nothing worth stealing now they've taken the poster and some books. Luckily most of my books are still at home, I hadn't brought them into College yet so they've escaped the bonfire.'

'They had a bonfire?'

'A ritual burning in College Park. But the rain put it out and they were forced to clean up their mess. Marina was outraged. What are College servants for, she wanted to know.'

Max had decided to return home until things cooled down. 'With Heslin after me because I've betrayed the working class and the White Russians out to skin my communist hide I've no option but to return to the ghetto.'

But he seemed cheerful, more so than at any time since Mona had left.

'Come to tea on Sunday?'

'In your house? Your family – '

'They won't bite you, in fact they're dying to meet you. Only don't start talking about Mass and confession, they think you're still a nice Jewish girl.'

By Sunday Max's good humour had evaporated. He was picking me up on the main road and as I waited for him I wondered how I would introduce him to my family. Because I had kept our relationship hidden I had created a problem where none need have existed. And I didn't know why I had done this. Was I naturally secretive or was it because he was spun into the web of lies surrounding Mona and the Party? I realized that I had become a habitual liar, inventing one to cover another. Tonight I was supposed to be having tea with Olive Tierney.

He was hunched over the wheel, jaw and hands clenched.

'Mona's been in touch,' he said and I was washed by a wave of sorrow and fear as he said it and I breathed in the familiar smell, her smell, a mixture of cigarettes and chalk.

'How?'

'A telegram to her mother, from Vienna. She was crossing into Hungary that night, before the fall of Nagy. Otherwise I don't think she'd have got in.'

I thought of Russian tanks. 'I wish she hadn't.'

He turned to look at me, his mouth bitter, as if he were tasting lemons. 'She's better off there than here – at least she's doing something. I can't stand this hanging around, this waiting. It's driving me crazy.'

His angry energy filled the car like static electricity. I kept quiet as he put his foot on the accelerator, forcing a speed out of the poor little car that it was quite unused to. When we stopped outside a bay-fronted house he took my hand and said, 'Remember, Belle, no matter what happens, I love you.'

And these words, sounding like some sort of final pronouncement, instead of cheering me up filled me with foreboding.

The family had gathered to greet me in a stiff and chilly front room. I saw at once where Max's beauty came from as I looked at his mother who took my hand gravely and welcomed me without a smile. She appraised me then handed me over to her husband who greeted me with more effusion, squeezing my hand, smiling up at me reassuringly.

We ate in the kitchen, where Max's grandmother sat in a basket chair beside the range. She looked at me then asked, 'Who's the shiksa?'

'Don't mind Bobba,' the mother said, showing me a place next to her at the table.

I was disappointed by the Watermans or rather by my response to them. I had thought that there would have been some sort of recognition on my part of our shared heritage. This family was like any Irish family I had ever visited. Apart from the father's skull cap and the old granny by the range there was nothing Jewish about them.

The meal could have come out of any Irish kitchen: fried plaice and chips and white, sliced pan. I realized that this family, despite its religion, was Irish in a way we never could be, despite Buba's best efforts.

Poor old Buba, she'd got it all hopelessly wrong and no matter how much holy water was poured on our heads we would remain foreigners for ever.

As the meal progressed Mrs Waterman became more relaxed. The two little girls smiled at me shyly and passed me plates of food. The father asked me about my school and my plans for next year. Despite this there was a background tension which I sensed had nothing to do with me. It could be coming from Max who sat silently at the end of the table. From time to time he smiled at me but he made no effort to join in the conversation.

When we had finished Mrs Waterman's stodgy apple pie Mr Waterman said, addressing his son for the first time, 'Could you come up and help me with your Bobba's bed, the headboard seems to have come loose.'

As soon as the door had closed Mrs Waterman whipped round the table, gathering plates. 'Belle,' she said, 'the girls will mind Bobba and if you'd come in and give me a hand with the dishes.'

We stacked the dishes on a tin tray on the wooden draining board. Mrs Waterman filled an enamel basin with boiling water and said, 'It's a nuisance having only the one sink. I'm sure in your house you have two.'

She must have noticed my blank face. 'For the milk and meat meals.' Then she added, sounding doubtful, 'Your mother does keep kosher?'

'Oh of course – my mind was just a blank there for a minute.'

She washed and I dried. She plunged her hands into the scalding water without seeming to notice as they turned a bright pink.

'This was just an excuse, not that I'm not glad of the help. But we're not able to say a word to him, he won't listen to us. We were wondering, his daddy and me, have you had a word with him?'

'What about?'

'This foolishness about going to Hungary.'

My mouth was suddenly dry. When I tried to speak no sound came out.

'He's been so unhappy since Mona went. He's ashamed, I think, of letting her go on her own. I always knew she was a bit cracked but you can't tell him that. He won't hear a word against her.'

When I found my voice I said, 'Max isn't going to Hungary.'

'He talks of nothing else.'

'But he wouldn't get in. How could he get across the border?'

'Oh our Max can do anything he sets his mind to.' She rinsed out the basin and began to dry her swollen pink fingers on a roller towel behind the door. 'Look, love, if you could only have a word. He'd listen to you, I know he would.'

I would have no words with him. As soon as I sat into the car for the homeward journey I began to chatter, not giving him a chance to talk in case he told me something I couldn't bear to hear. I told him how much I liked his family, how he resembled his mother, how interesting his grandmother was. I went on and on, filling the car with the sound of my voice, unaware in my anxiety that he was making no effort to interrupt me. It was only as I was standing on the pavement looking after the tail lights of the Beetle that I realized that he hadn't even opened his mouth to say goodbye. Just smiled and touched my arm and shot off into the dark.

Next morning when I came downstairs there was a postcard from Vienna waiting for me. I looked at the view of St Stephen's Cathedral, then slowly turned to the back. Mona had written, 'Sitting in coffee houses eating cream cakes is not to be recommended but very enjoyable none the less.'

It had been posted six days ago.

Buba came in as I was propping it up on the mantelpiece using Mutti's little glass bowl where she kept her lipsticks as a support.

She looked at the photograph. 'I have always loved that city, where I had my honeymoon. I think I had forgotten that, so long ago. And where your father came from, Liebchen. From Vienna.'

Mutti, bringing in coffee, said, 'I hate it.' Her hair was still clamped in the dozen metal curlers she managed to sleep in at night. 'A city of the dead, dead emperors, dead composers. Dreary, dreary. A horrible place.'

I checked my pencil case and my books. I was going back to school – I couldn't stay away for ever.

Mutti poured coffee. 'I hope your teacher is all right.'

'You mean Miss McCarthy? Why? What's happened?'

'The news is not good. It says that the fighting is over, the students are fighting no more. Poor things, how they held out this long is surprising.'

My first thought was, then Max won't be going. I couldn't help a lightening in my heart even as my second thought was for Mona and how she would get out.

'Communism is the worst evil in the world,' Buba said as I kissed her goodbye. 'It will destroy those poor people and nobody will help.'

I had arranged to meet Max after school. We met in parks now for they offered us privacy and anonymity. Max didn't want to go back to his rooms in College and we were bound to meet one or other of our detractors in the pubs and cafés around.

It was typical November weather, still and mild. Too grey, though, to entice people into parks where fallen leaves lay congealed in sticky clumps. We chose a seat behind some sort of berried tree. Little birds foraged noisily over our heads, seeming incongruously purposeful in this dead season.

Max looked ghastly. His lovely skin was grey as the November day and drawn tight over the bones of his face.

He didn't greet me, just took my hand and said, 'The students have surrendered.'

'I know, Mutti told me. I suppose it's all over now.'

'Oh the workers are continuing with the general strike – until the Soviet army leaves.'

He reached up to pull off a branch, scattering damp leaves over our heads. He began to strip the branch of its yellow berries. 'Mona,' he said. 'What's going to happen? What happens to a foreigner in those circumstances?'

'Better for a foreigner, surely. I mean, wouldn't the Russians be more chary of dealing with a Westerner?'

He threw the branch from him. 'I should have gone. I'll never forgive myself if anything happens to her.'

'Nothing will happen to her.'

'That woman had more guts than the rest of us put together.'

'Has,' I corrected him.

Fear dulled his eyes. He reached out and touched the wood of the bench we were sitting on. 'Has,' he repeated.

The revolution had failed. In my bedroom I listened to the Home Service on Mona's radio, listening in terror to descriptions of streets in Budapest being swept by Russian tanks, of basements being raided and dead bodies slung on army jeeps.

In our sitting room Father Jack denounced godless communism and the weakness of Western governments who had ignored the appeals of the students.

In school we prayed for Miss McCarthy's safe return and were given a replacement history teacher, a woman who wore costumes under her gown and walked up and down the classroom banging out important dates with a ruler. Even Olive Tierney's eyes began to glaze over.

With nowhere to make love, I began to wonder if Max and I ever had or if I was just imagining things. His sadness seeped into me so that I was unable to say positive things about the future when Mona would be back to tell us about her adventures.

The Russians began to deport Hungarians and the Irish

Independent reported that 10,000 people had demonstrated against the deportations, choking the streets of Budapest with their impotent fury. Had Mona been among the demonstrators?

The most difficult thing was having no news. Max kept in touch with the mother, who was surviving only because her son had moved back home.

'Where is she?' Max asked again and again. 'Why doesn't she get in touch with someone?'

Walking through Stephen's Green one afternoon we bumped into George McNab. He told us that the New Left bookshop had been ransacked and that Heslin had cancelled all meetings until things calmed down.

'Anyway,' George added, 'he's thinking of amalgamating with the League. Special Branch is beginning to harass people, calling at houses, the usual. Heslin maintains that our only hope is to stick together, the lot of us, until this blows over. Any news of Mona?'

'None.'

'Shocking. Just shocking.'

It was at moments such as this that we especially missed her. I could imagine her pleasure at George's news, her squawk of delight that Heslin was acting true to form.

Half-heartedly George asked us if we'd like a drink. We refused and he seemed relieved as he waved goodbye.

'Cathal, the brother, you know,' said Max, 'he's going to London to see the Soviet ambassador and to try and find out something.'

'Has he a hope?'

'A veteran of the Spanish Civil War should have some clout, I suppose, that is, if he makes the journey. The man's a wreck, living out there in that caravan all these years. Mrs McCarthy told me he's frightened even going to the shops. Can you see him coping with boats and trains and a city like London?'

Poor Mrs McCarthy, voting Fianna Fáil all her life as Mona had told me, mystified by the passion and politics of her children.

Thinking of Mrs McCarthy I started to weep. Max heard my sniffles although I had averted my head.

He stopped and turned me towards him. I could see from his expression that he was seeing me for the first time in weeks.

He put out a hand and stroked my hair. 'You're very pale, Belle, you've rings under your eyes.'

I tried to joke. 'Thanks a lot – you know how to fill a girl with confidence.'

'I haven't noticed because I've been so self-absorbed. Come on,' he took my arm. 'Let's stop all the moaning and do something. Would you like to go and see a play? There's one on in the Pike that should cheer us up – someone told me it's the most depressing thing they've seen in years.'

'Who's it by?'

'Can't remember but I like the title. It's called *Waiting for Godot*.'

At home they had stopped questioning my comings and goings. I knew they had misgivings about me and were being careful not to push me.

Buba watched me with anxious eyes. Mutti fed me delicacies and told me not to worry. That I must learn not to worry or I would never get through life.

One Saturday afternoon Mutti asked me if I'd like to go into town to do some shopping. We had never done this before and there was a shyness between us as we sat together on the bus.

We went first to Todd Burns, a shop we both knew because it was where I bought my uniforms. Mutti didn't like their coats, however. 'Let's go and see what they have in Switzers. A smarter shop, I think.'

We walked across town and took the lift up to Switzers' coat department. Mutti moved surely along the rails, taking down some garments and passing by others.

'Try this,' she said.

I dumped my school gabardine on the floor and tried on the green Topper. It had a tiny check pattern and was made of very fine wool. There was one button under the collar and it was cut wide in the back, falling in folds to my hips.

Mutti looked at me critically. 'The colour is right but – too sophisticated, perhaps.'

The shop assistant, a girl of my own age, smiled. 'They're all wearing them,' she said, 'all the girls. And look at the value – 59/11. You can't beat that.'

'I love it,' I said, doing a pirouette in front of the mirror.

'Then we take it.' Mutti smiled at me.

On the way past Charles Wayre we stopped to look at the furs in the window.

'That beaver lamb,' said Mutti pointing. 'So stylish.'

'Let's go in and you can try it.' I wanted her to have something too.

She looked at it critically. 'Fourteen guineas and I like the way it buttons.'

'Come on then.'

She shook her head and turned away. 'But no – where would I wear such a coat? Nowhere.'

It was true. Hanging up in her wardrobe were clothes that I had never seen her wear, cocktail dresses and little fussy jackets. Mutti's only social outings were to the cinema, and to the cinema in Dublin you wore a warm overcoat.

Going home we sat on the top of the bus so that she could smoke.

'I enjoyed our outing,' she said.

'Do you like living in Dublin?'

188

She shrugged. 'It's a life.'

I had spent so little time thinking about her and what she was like. If I thought of my family it was Buba who came to mind.

As if she could read my thoughts she said now, 'I know how close you are to your grandmother.'

I was embarrassed. 'To both of you.'

'No, I do not resent it, I know there is a special bond between you two. But sometimes she does not see. I think that she is so sure of the world that she does not look and so she does not see.'

I didn't really want to discuss Buba with Mutti. These were not the sort of conversations we had in our family and it was too late now to change that. For years they had kept their secrets to themselves; now I had my own. There was nothing vengeful about this, it was just life.

'She sees you as a little girl still. I think maybe too she forgets what it is to be young. I remember, though – for me it is not all that long.'

I found nothing poignant in those words or if I did I blocked it out. The parcel on my lap was heavy. I scratched at a corner of the brown paper until I had torn it open. I felt the material, caressing the richness of the nap.

'If you wish to tell me things, Belle,' Mutti said, 'if you wish that I advise you, I always listen. At your age you must enjoy yourself, that is natural, but be careful. Men can break your heart.' She turned away to stub out her cigarette then put her gloves back on. With one gloved finger she tapped the parcel on my knee and laughed. 'Such a lovely colour, that green. Always I have liked it but never worn it because of superstition. For me I think green brings bad luck.'

And I felt sorry for Mutti then who had been brought up in such old, superstitious ways.

*   *   *

The UN passed a resolution condemning the deportation to Russia of the Hungarians involved in the revolution.

We sat listening to the wireless in Max's rooms in Trinity, driven back to them through indifference and colder weather.

Inside it was cold too. A chill had settled over the bed and armchairs so that despite the coal fires that Max burned we couldn't get warm.

Making love might have warmed us up but we didn't seem to go in much for that any more.

I took his hand and tried to warm it between both of mine. 'At least it's something,' I said. 'Now that the UN have spoken others may begin to take notice.'

His face was sad, eyes quenched, lovely skin dull. 'Too late,' he said. 'It's too late for anything now.'

'Let's go out,' I said. 'Let's go somewhere and have a coffee.'

He looked up at the blank, starless sky. 'It's raining. There's no point in getting wet.'

It had been raining for three days now while in Budapest snow would be falling, concealing bloodstains on road and pavement.

The wireless had stopped talking about Hungary and had moved on to Suez. We were not listening but left it on, too indifferent to stretch out a hand and turn it off.

'Then I'm going.'

'Don't go.' He held on to my hand. 'Don't go. I want to tell you something.'

I knew what he was going to say before he said it. I didn't need to listen to the words. I watched his lips moving and then I put my hand over them to stop him, to stop the sounds.

He wrenched my hand away and continued with his crazy

talk. I grabbed him, holding on to him, digging my nails into the tweedy material of his jacket.

Words rained down on my head. Mona. Responsibility. Find. Coward. Rescue. Cowardly.

'Go then. Go. Go. If she means more to you than I do, go.'

I ran out into the rain, clumsily rushing across the slick surface of the cobbles, stumbling, then turning on my ankle.

I hobbled on, welcoming the pain. Now it was my words that were inside my head, those shameful words. I hadn't meant them, I had used them to keep in those other words that I had wanted to throw at him. Coward, yes, coward. And now it is too late to go. You can do no good now so accept the fact of your cowardice and don't compound it with idiocy. Mona is either safe now or dead. Either way she is beyond your help.

I was standing at the bus stop in Nassau Street when he came up. He handed me my school attaché case. 'You forgot this.'

'Thanks.'

'Don't sulk.'

'I'm not – '

He pulled me against him and raised my face to kiss my mouth. It was like the kisses we used to share and I put my arms around his neck, indifferent to the people standing at the wall, sheltering from the rain. I clung to him, trying to fit my body to his, despite the soggy layers of clothes that intervened. It seemed important that I would be able to recall the contours of his body, its lean maleness.

'Go,' I said. 'Go and find her.'

'I'll be back.'

'You'll be back.'

I woke up fighting for breath. Sometimes this happened when in my sleep I had ended up with my face buried in the pillows.

The panic would persist for some minutes after waking and I would just lie quietly and breathe shallowly until it began to recede. Now as I tried this it got worse. The sensation of choking increased until I knew that some real terror lurked in my sleep-fogged consciousness. I sat up as my alarm clock went off. Just another school day then. Another – Max. That was it. Max was going. Off on a wild goose chase to appease his conscience. I hated him this morning.

I washed and put on my uniform and went downstairs to breakfast.

The other two were chirpy when I got to the kitchen. Even Mutti, who usually never came to until after her first fag, was bright and buzzy like a day-old chick. I wondered how they got like that, how they could have left hope and love behind and still smile over the coffee cups as they looked at me.

'A stain on your tie,' Mutti said.

Buba scooped unmelted sugar from the bottom of her cup. 'This morning I go into town on business so I drive you to school. Such rain – I have never seen such rain. Everybody has coughs and bad chests. Certain things I have run out of so I must make this journey.'

Inside the Wolseley we kept the windows closed. The wipers made little impression on the sheets of rain that slid down the windscreen and Buba squinted and clucked her tongue disapprovingly. 'So many cyclists,' she said. 'Where do they come from, all these Dublin cyclists?'

'They can't stay home just because it's raining.'

I was appraised by an angled black look as we pulled up at lights. Buba shook her head. 'It happens like that so fast. It was just the same with Erika. One day they are little children, next, looking at you chin to chin – full-grown women. My little granddaughter has grown up while I have taken my eyes off her for a second. I begin to feel old.'

The lights changed and as if to defy her decrepitude Buba shot off at speed, merrily spraying the poor cyclists who waited patiently, one foot on the pedal, the other resting on the ground.

Dropping me at the school gates Buba said, 'Try to be early this evening, *Liebchen*, Father Jack is coming to tea. That man, he is so fond of you, you know.'

I did know. Ever since Mona had gone off to fight godless communism the shadow of her halo had fallen on me. Now when I saw Father Jack he greeted me with nods and plump, pink smiles. I preferred his malevolence, our old partnership of mutual dislike.

'I'll do my best,' I said, 'but I can't make any promises.'

The unfocused day was endless, seeming to get stuck in chunks as I waited for the bell to go at the end of a class, looking again and again at my watch, shaking it and putting it to my ear to see if it had stopped.

The windows in the classroom steamed up and the smell of damp serge clogged the air. Was this what the rest of my life was going to be like, sitting waiting for time to pass?

Not if I had any say in it, not while there was still time for me to catch Max. Two could look for Mona more effectively than one. And today, sitting in school, his plan didn't seem so daft. Mona was alive: when I looked at the floorboards she had walked across, when I saw the blackboard she had pounded, when I smelled the chalky air into which she had breathed out such passion, I knew that Mona would not be so easily snuffed out.

I returned home full of resilience and good humour, determined to outsmile Father Jack and to outsmart him.

But he wasn't there.

'No,' said Buba. 'Like everyone else he's caught this wretched chest infection. And you, look at how wet you are. You too want to be sick, is that it? Go and change – into a dressing gown now that Father Jack is not coming.'

Mutti had made sauerbraten with red cabbage. The meat was tender and sharp, the cabbage slightly sweet. I asked for second helpings and Mutti smiled and Buba nodded approvingly.

Our kitchen at the back of the house got the prevailing winds and on a night like this with rain being hurled against the window and the sound of dustbin lids being blown in some back yard, it lost its cosiness. We would have coffee in the sitting room, Buba decided, where the fire was bright and the gramophone waiting.

Mutti had made vanilla biscuits, crisp fragrant rounds of pale gold.

I crunched one slowly, then asked, 'Do I have any money of my own?'

The two women stared at me, uncomprehendingly.

'I mean, did I ever have anything left to me, by my father, for example?'

Mutti sniggered, Buba looked cross but with her, not me.

'You don't need money, Liebchen,' she said. 'And if you do, you come to me. I am always – '

'Listen,' Mutti interrupted. 'Listen.'

The sound of the doorbell was distorted, somehow, the timbre of its ring changed by its journey through the thick, silent darkness of the house.

I noticed the other two stare at one another, their faces pale. I felt my heartbeat quicken.

In other houses, I imagined, a ring at the door at half-seven at night would not be a cause for alarm. But nobody ever rang our doorbell at night. Since Buba had stopped taking night calls, Father Jack or I were the only ones who ever came after dark.

The bell rang again, a longer peal.

'Father Jack after all,' Buba said. 'Maybe he was not feeling so bad and changed his mind.'

None of us believed that.

'Go, Erika, go and answer it. Look through the glass, that would be best. Such a night for anyone to be out.'

We listened as Mutti's slippers flip-flopped up the stairs, splashing against the linoleum.

'But Buba – Father Jack.' I had remembered something. 'He never comes to the upstairs door.'

Buba took my hand. 'A patient then, who forgets that I do not come out at night.'

There was a sound of voices from the upstairs hall, Mutti's raised in anxiety. Then footsteps again, but clattering this time, harsh.

Mutti pushed into the kitchen. 'He says this fellow, that he is your friend, Belle.'

He looked round him, blinking in the light. His wet hair sticking to his skull made the bones of his face stand out. His eyes bulged in their swollen sockets.

'Max,' I said.

He must have heard the relief in my voice. Maybe it sounded like joy to him although all it was was relief that he was still here, alive, even if something else was clearly wrong.

'Max,' he said, copying my tone. 'Max. Isn't it wonderful we've saved Max. Wonderful, wonderful Max.'

He flung out his hand in a clumsy, angry gesture and catching a coffee cup with the cuff of his sleeve, he sent it crashing on to the ground.

'Young man.' Little Buba went up to him and, standing on her toes, stared up into his face. 'I do not know who you are but you had better behave. Behave, sit.' And she pushed him towards a chair.

Suddenly he covered his face with his hands and began to

cry. The harsh sound didn't seem to come from his throat but from somewhere deeper inside him. I could imagine it surging up from his belly, tearing at the soft flesh of his gullet.

'Don't,' I said. 'Please don't.' And placed my hand on his head.

He grabbed it, held on to it, crushing it. 'She died,' he said. 'She's dead now. Mona died.'

I had known of course before he spoke. I think I had known from that first ring of the doorbell. When I had prayed silently, let it be . . . so that it is not . . .

Perhaps it had been joy that he had seen on my face after all.

Buba took charge. She began to issue orders. 'Coffee, Erika, and bring the sugar with you. Belle, a towel and a rug, the one in the surgery. Hurry, please.'

I ran through the house, fearing ghosts bent on vengeance. When I came back Buba was holding a cup up to his mouth. His teeth chattered against the white china, sounding like the beginnings of a jig.

'You must drink all, all,' Buba said as he turned his head aside. 'You will get pneumonia if you do not drink this. You are soaked through and frozen. Now, to the last drop.'

A brown dribble ran down his chin. I wiped it with the back of my hand, feeling the coarse stubble of his beard. He pushed my hand away and his body tensed, seeking an escape.

'Max,' Buba said. 'Max. Listen to me.'

He looked up at her, threads of blood showing in the blue whiteness of his eyes.

'Do you have a family?'

He nodded.

'Then you have to go to them. I will take you because you cannot go alone. Have you got a car?'

He jerked his head backwards, slapping it into the high,

wooden back of the chair. 'No. No car. I can – never again. I won't be ever able to again.'

Buba soothed him. 'Of course not, I'm going to drive you to your home. I just wanted to know if you had left a car some place, just to know it's safe.'

Buba was able to manage him so well. She managed all of us that night, issuing orders which we obeyed, glad to be told what to do.

While she went round to get the car out, I wrote down Max's address and Mutti plotted a route for Buba to take through the dark, wet suburbs.

'I do not want to get lost,' Buba told her. 'This boy should be in bed soon as possible, out of these wet clothes and into bed.'

'Max.' She turned to him. 'Stand up, Max. Come on. I cannot carry you. Up.'

He stood and stumbled after her towards the door. Then he turned. 'What about – Belle?'

As I went to move towards him Buba signalled me back. 'Tomorrow, Belle, you will see Belle tomorrow. Now, tonight, home to your family.'

When they had gone Mutti gave me coffee. It tasted unpleasant and fumy with alcohol.

'Brandy,' Mutti explained. 'You too have had a shock, remember. We all have.'

She lit a cigarette and then, for the first time in her life, offered me one. With her little finger she removed a thread of tobacco from her tongue. I suddenly noticed how awful she looked, her bright hair and lips gaudy and brash against the pallor of her skin.

'Your boyfriend?'

I nodded.

'Oh God.'

She began to unroll her hair, as if getting ready for bed.

As she removed each pin she placed it in a neat row on the arm of her chair. Her hair fell round her shoulders in blonde waves like some elderly doll's.

'I thought – in Ireland,' she said. 'We both did.'

'What about Ireland? What did you think?'

'Poor Belle. Poor little Belle.'

I was relieved when Buba bustled in. Mutti was behaving so strangely, as if I were the one to be pitied, but not because Mona was dead but for some reason that I knew nothing about.

The feel of things changed once Buba returned. She began to pull us together with her sensible, solid presence, castigating me for the mess of unwashed cups and Mutti for letting the fire go out.

She spoke of Mona without embarrassment. Poor young woman, she said, such a wasted life. So much to offer the young girls she taught, all the work she did with them, the interest she had in them. Now all brought to nought.

Then she told us that we must think about what we were going to wear at the funeral. Funerals were important occasions, she said, and must be marked by formality and respect.

When I lay in bed later that night I cried for the first time for Mona. I remembered how she had dazzled us that first day when she had walked into the sleepy classroom, changing all our lives, but mine more than most.

I turned on my light and got out of bed. From the jumble of books on top of my chest of drawers I picked up a shabby blue-and-white-covered Penguin. Then I got back into bed, turned over my pillow so that the wet side was underneath and went to sleep with *A Life of Rosa Luxemburg* clutched in my hand. Despite the fact that it had been in my bedroom for over a year it still smelled of Mona.

*   *   *

In those days nothing much seemed to happen in Ireland so it was not surprising that Mona's death caused a stir. Few people agreed with Buba, seeing it as a waste. For the Right and the Left it was a glorious death as both sides vied with one another to claim her as an official martyr.

When Max didn't call again I became worried. At home Buba was avoiding any reference to him, which was strange considering how curious she was usually about my friends. Perhaps she was being tactful because Max had also been a friend of Mona's.

I called round to Trinity and waited for an hour, sitting on the stone staircase outside his door with my school gabardine folded underneath me.

I didn't recognize his step, heavy and fumbling like an old man's.

'Belle.' There was nothing in his voice. He spoke my name without surprise and without interest. He held the door open for me, then followed me into the room and sat at the table.

In the corner the bed was unmade. Grey ashes spilled out of the grate and there was a saucepan on the table with what looked like a coating of burnt beans stuck to the bottom.

'Do you want a coffee?'

I shook my head. 'How was she killed?'

There were different versions in different newspapers: buried under rubble, blown up by a bomb, shot in the back. All agreed it had been done by the communists.

'A sniper. An accident, apparently, just a casualty of war.'

He had taken a bottle of whiskey from a cupboard and now began to pour some into a smeared tumbler. 'She was on her way home, they were going to get her out but they had to get her a coat. A bloody badly made Hungarian coat so that she wouldn't look conspicuous. The streets were clear, so Cathal has been told. They came up from the cellar where they were hiding, she had only walked a few yards when a sniper picked her off. They left her then, of course, the bastards, just ran off. Scared for their own skins, I suppose. A Russian tank picked her up and dumped her with a load of other bodies somewhere. It was only by chance that somebody reckoned she was a foreigner so they took her to a morgue, and when Cathal started making enquiries – do you want a drink?'

'No thanks.'

He splashed some more whiskey into the glass. His hand which grasped the bottle was grimy and so was the cuff above it.

I stretched out my hand to take his but he pushed it away. 'Don't,' he said. 'I can't manage that sort of thing now.'

Probably he meant to be cruel to ensure that I left.

I was halfway across Front Square when he came running after me. He caught my arm.

'Go back, Max, it's raining.'

He held on to me, pushing his face into mine. I caught a whiff of sour breath. 'I've got to tell you something, listen to me. On the last day, Mona begged me to go with her.'

'I don't believe you. Why should she want you with her? She thought of you as a boy.'

'Oh it was just a great adventure for Mona – she wasn't a coward. And she knew I spoke a bit of Polish, she thought that might be useful.'

'Don't blame yourself, Max.'

'Who else should I blame? I was too much of a coward and I let her die alone.'

He turned and began to run back in the direction of his room.

Over the grey streets and squares of Dublin a hum of guilty secretive mutterings now hung as a shamefaced pleasure was woven, not from the fact of Mona's death but from the excitement that it generated.

In school, we hung out the bunting. Mother de Lourdes festooned the building with papal flags and Irish tricolours to honour 'our own Irish, Catholic martyr'.

People told of how they knew somebody who knew her. Father Jack said that while Ireland produced young women of her calibre then Ireland need have no worries.

Among the commies and the socialists and the Trots a tremendous battle was in progress as they heaved her name back and forth between them, claiming her as their own. Possession being nine tenths of the law, it was inevitable that Heslin was going to win. She had been a paid-up member of the Socialist Workers Party and if he had expelled her, well, the biggest quarrels always arose in the closest knit families.

As I was getting dressed for the funeral Mutti came into my bedroom. She was wearing a grey costume and a small hat made of black feathers. She pointed to the green topper hanging in my wardrobe. 'Wear it. It is quite dark enough for such a time, quite respectful. And your Buba has said a hat.'

She sat down on my bed and lit a cigarette. She was looking out the window and not at me but I still felt self-conscious with her sitting there. Mutti and I did not have that sort of a relationship and I wondered why she was here.

'That boy,' she said at last, 'the one who called when – on that night. Is it serious between you?'

The bitter liquid that flowed into my mouth flavoured my laughter. 'Max? Good Lord, no. What gave you that idea? He was just very emotional that night, well naturally, I was too. But there's nothing between us, nothing at all.'

She stubbed out her cigarette against my fire grate and came over to tweak the collar of my topper so that it lay flat. 'That is better. Good. I suppose he will be there today, that is why I ask. So's I know how to behave.'

'Well, now you know, Mutti, you don't have to behave in any way.'

If you can talk about funerals being successful then Mona's was a success. All of Dublin was there, which made for some difficult moments. It was the sort of social occasion where you didn't want to miss anything but where certain eyes had to be avoided at all costs. So the congregation craned and ducked and murmured, pointing out to each other the famous and the infamous.

A bishop sat at the high altar, his face the same shade of royal purple as his robes. Behind him a row of lesser clerics gossiped and ogled, lacking the bishop's piety or sophistication. Heslin arrived like a Mafia boss, surrounded by heavies, or as many heavies as he could muster from among the ranks of the Socialist Workers Party. Defiantly they marched up the aisle and defiantly they took their seats without genuflecting.

Then I saw Cyril English. He came in on his own, reduced by Mona's death as none of the others were. Without his swagger he seemed small inside his Crombie overcoat, and old, his drinker's nose backlit in a sudden shaft of sunlight from a tall window.

Up in the organ loft a choir from school began to sing and I took my place with the other sixth-years to form a guard of honour to accompany the coffin up the aisle.

It was pushed in on some sort of wheels, too heavy because of its lead lining to be hoisted on to shoulders.

And it was draped in the Starry Plough, the flag of James Connolly's Citizen Army.

A cold starry night at Baggot Street Bridge. We three had stood on the lock looking up at the sky. Mona had pointed upwards and said, 'Look, can you see it, Belle – the Plough. Now, if either of you are around when I die I want you to remember one thing. I want my coffin draped with the Starry Plough. Will you remember that or will I have to put it in my will?'

Had Max remembered?

The undertaker's men pushed slowly and we kept pace on either side but we were still going too fast for the chief mourners coming behind. The men stopped to let them catch up and the congregation waited to see if they could make it.

A tiny, frail couple, they supported one another across the huge length of red-and-blue tiles. Baby steps faltered, then tried again, and above their faltering limbs their shocked faces flinched from the sudden exposure. It was a long journey, longer than from Dublin to Budapest, longer than from Dublin to Jarama. The longest journey.

We waited at the top of the main aisle.

'The famous brother,' Olive Tierney whispered in my ear. 'He looks older than the mother.'

Old revolutionaries who muck it up.

For the first time in weeks I found myself smiling. Good for you, Mona McCarthy. And I gave her a quick and surreptitious clenched-fist salute.

The sun was shining when we came out into the churchyard. Buba and Mutti were not going to Glasnevin because they hated burials. Neither was I, although the nuns had arranged transport for any girl who wished to go. I had said my goodbyes.

'Where is the poor mother?' Buba asked, shaking back a bunch of cherries which dangled from the brim of her black hat. 'I must go and offer her my words of sympathy.'

'Over there,' Mutti pointed.

I hung back. I had nothing to say to that poor woman who wouldn't even hear the words anyway.

I pushed my way to where our car was parked just outside the railings. A young man was standing there, an ordinary young man with a reddish nose and putty-coloured skin.

'Belle.'

It was my darling but so transfigured by grief that I would have walked past him.

We sat on the running board, away from the crowds. We held hands and closed our eyes and raised our faces to the sun.

'I'm sorry, Belle.'

'Sh'sh.'

'And you've been mourning too. I'm just very selfish, I'm afraid, I just can't seem to get past myself. Can you forgive me?'

The sun or something was melting all the ice inside me and I had to send him away so that I could weep or laugh or do whatever it was I was going to do alone.

'Will you call to see me, Max, soon, tomorrow, will you call?'

'I'll call, of course I'll call.'

As we drove away from the church Buba said, 'I really do not know how they are going to manage without her.'

And I caught a glimpse of the brother lodged in a crevice of the building like a wounded animal at bay. An old animal, though, too old to be dangerous as he raised moth-eaten paws to deflect the curious.

Max didn't call. I waited and waited, hearing phantom footsteps on our steps, seeing phantom shadows through the red glass of the front door, but he never came.

I went once to his rooms in Trinity and they seemed abandoned. I put my eye to the keyhole and the space inside came at me, sterile and pure, stripped even of memories.

I thought of calling to his home but I was too afraid in case I found out that I, too, had been abandoned.

The days unrolled in flat, endless succession and I saw them stretching out for ever to the end of my life.

Then it was the Christmas holidays and Buba rubbed her hands together and lit an after-lunch cigar.

'Erika, you have not made the cake this year and now it is too late. What has come over you? Now we will have to buy one and they are never so nice.'

I jumped up, seeing an excuse to get away. 'Will I go and look in Fergusons? They always have really nice cakes.'

I went out into the mild, damp afternoon where daylight was already on the wane. I walked slowly, wanting to make my absence as long as possible, looking around me at the familiar road which I travelled to and from school, hurrying along with unseeing eyes.

Today I dawdled. Mutti had said that our neighbourhood was going downhill fast and I could see now that she was right. Many of the bigger houses had been turned into flats and front gardens were now sprouting dustbins, not roses. Gates had been removed and occasionally railings, and inside dirty windows curtains hung askew.

Mutti had advised Buba to sell as soon as she retired or even sooner, for patients would follow her wherever she went. Mutti suggested a smaller house near the sea – Blackrock or Sandycove.

If they moved I wouldn't go with them. Out to the sea to walk along some beach in the sad hours of twilight, returning home to silence and the sort of order that was an old people's order, smelling of decay.

But where would I go?

I turned into the main road, passing the butcher's and the hardware shop. Outside Fergusons the door opened on a waft of hot, spicy air and a woman rushed at me. 'Look, love, your eyesight is better than mine. Is that a 15b?'

I turned to look at the bus making its way towards us. 'Yes, it is.'

The 15b, Max's bus. It was an omen, it must have been sent along at that moment, just like the woman, to tell me something. To tell me to go and find him.

I waited behind the woman and fingered the coppers in my pocket, wondering if I had enough.

When the conductor came round he asked me, 'Aren't you full fare?'

'I'm still at school.'

He looked at me sceptically but took my proffered pennies.

As the bus trundled off to the newer suburbs I began to think that I had been rash to embark on what might well lead to a slap in the face. Max mightn't want me.

I pulled myself together. If Max didn't want me then the sooner I found out the better.

I got off at the terminus, the only passenger to alight. Nobody was around, no cat or dog even. I walked towards Max's house and no curtains twitched as I passed by, no light shone from fanlight or front room although by now the grey afternoon was thickening to black. A single, solitary Ford Prefect marred the empty symmetry of the road. A ladder leant against a gable, the only other evidence of human habitation. Nobody to see me tremble or hear the noisy gusting of my breath.

I came to Number 45, passed by, turned back and rushed at the gate before I could change my mind. It squeaked, loud and discordant like an orchestra tuning up, but the sound brought nobody to the shiny, wine-coloured door. I pressed the bell. It was either one of those whose ring you couldn't hear or it was broken. I lifted the knocker to be on the safe side.

I waited. Nobody in. I turned in relief to scurry down the path.

'Yes?'

Mrs Waterman looked at me, her expression mild and totally blank. Fool, fool that I was to come.

'Mrs Waterman. I just – I wondered – is Max in?'

'Max?' She raised beige eyebrows. 'Max?'

'Yes, I'm – '

Suddenly she smiled. 'Don't tell me – wait. I'm such a featherhead. Belle, that's it. Belle. Funny how I didn't recognize you there for a second. Come on in, child.'

I followed her down a cold, dimly lit hall into the kitchen. This room was warm and cosy with a smell of baking. On the table a tray of scones was waiting to go into the oven and the oil cloth was scattered with flour.

I sat in the chair she pointed towards. 'Is Max not at home, Mrs Waterman?'

'Well of course he's not at home. Don't you know – ' She stopped and put her hands up to cover her mouth. Her eyes twinkled at me with a mixture of mischief and shame, the expression of a naughty child. 'He'll kill me,' she said. 'He'll just kill me when he finds this one out.'

She reached up to the mantelpiece and took down a brass letter rack. She emptied the letters and cards from it on to the floury table and began to sort through them, talking all the time.

'I'm on my own, Bobba's in bed with a chill but you'll wait and have a cup of tea with me. Now where did I put it? I know it was here somewhere, I can see myself putting it away carefully until I had a chance to post it. If I wasn't so careful – ha!' She pounced and held up a blue envelope triumphantly. 'I knew it was here somewhere.' She handed it to me. 'He went off in such a hurry and I promised that I'd post it straight away and then it just went out of my head. If you hadn't called . . .'

I looked at my name on the envelope, my hand trembling in my lap. Whatever I had expected it wasn't this.

'Open it there while I make us a cup of tea.'

I put it in my pocket.

'Of course he didn't want to go but luckily Estelle was over at the time and between us we persuaded him to go back with her. He knows people over there, he's made friends since the summer and he needed a change from Dublin.'

'He's gone to Manchester?'

'Isn't that what I'm saying.' She lit the gas under the kettle and came back to sit beside me. 'He got so depressed we couldn't do anything with him here. And then he seemed to blame himself for her death. I never wanted him to get involved in those politics but his father said, let him alone, he'll grow out of it. Poor Mona didn't, though – did she? We were very fond of her here but I sometimes used to think that she was leading Max astray with all that silly talk about revolutions.'

She got up to check on the oven, opening the door a crack and adjusting the heat. From the dresser she took down two blue-and-white cups and saucers and, wiping the flour from a corner of the table, set them in front of us. 'A nice cup of tea, that's what you need, and a scone. I can see from the look of you you've no need to slim. No, Max was always hard to rear, boys are, they say. He was always that delicate and then moody. But we never saw him this bad – never. So when Estelle was here, it seemed like a godsend. He'll miss out on his Trinity course but that's not important where health is involved.' She stopped talking to look around the kitchen. In a whisper she continued, 'His father's family – a history of nerves there. Not his father now but uncles – couldn't keep a job even some of them. So I've always been that bit worried about Max.'

I fingered the letter in my pocket, guessing at its thickness, then trying to interpret this. Thin – a goodbye? Thick – an explanation of a goodbye?

'I should have posted that letter, I promised him faithfully

I would. Then I put it away to keep it safe and completely forgot about it. You have so much on your mind it's hard to keep track.'

Standing at the bus stop I tore open the envelope with clumsy fingers. In the pool of light thrown by the street lamp I began to read, shielding the flimsy pages against the rain which had just begun to fall.

He had never written to me before. My darling, it began. I blushed with shyness and pleasure, raced through the two pages and then started again, reading more slowly this time. On the bus I read it for a third time. It was a love letter and an explanation and an appeal. And it had been written ten days ago.

By the time I got off the bus opposite Fergusons I had made up my mind. He had given me his Manchester address so that I could write to him. I would do better than that – I would go to him. He couldn't live without me, he said, well, he didn't have to. I'd ask Buba for the money and catch the Liverpool boat tomorrow evening as Mona had.

Buba would understand; she wouldn't make any difficulties for me. Mutti had said that she had forgotten what it was like being young, but Buba loved me beyond all else and she wanted me to be happy. Life suddenly seemed so simple. I buttoned up my coat and started to run down the main road. I splashed along through the rain which was now falling steadily and rounding the corner into our road I ran full tilt into Father Jack.

He put out a hand to steady me. 'Whoa, child.'

'Father Jack. Sorry.'

'I should think so too. Where on earth have you been? Your poor grandmother is going frantic with worry.'

I had completely forgotten the time. I had gone out to look

at the Christmas cakes in Ferguson's window and I had been away for almost three hours.

'Is Buba furious?'

'She'd have a right to be, wouldn't she? You should remember, Belle, that your grandmother isn't getting any younger and have some consideration for her.'

They had gone up to the top steps to look out for my return. Mutti had her hands over her head, shielding her waves from the downpour. Beside her little Buba stood with her bun coming undone as rain fell on her indifferent head. Poor little Buba.

I ran up to them. 'I'm sorry, I'm so sorry.'

She held out her arms to me. 'Nothing, say nothing. All of us must get dry first and then we worry about the talk.'

Father Jack followed us in and downstairs to the sitting room where Mutti handed us each a towel. I had hoped he would go home for I was offering no explanations in front of him.

The fire was built up in the grate and I stood before it as Mutti took my wet coat and shoes to the kitchen to dry.

We stood around the fire drying our hair. Father Jack gave his a few dabs, patted his face with the towel then folded it and handed it to Mutti telling her that there was no need to wash it at all.

'You are a bad girl,' Buba said and wagged a finger at me, 'giving us all such a fright.'

'I know, Buba.'

'And then Erika starts talking wild talk that you have run away. "Where?" I ask. "To get married, perhaps," she says.'

Buba laughed and I laughed too. Father Jack stared at me, opening his fleshy mouth, his tongue coming out in an anticipatory lick.

That decided me. I turned my back on him and sat on the sofa facing Buba. 'I met someone outside Fergusons, a girl from school, you wouldn't know her. She asked me in for a coffee and we got talking and I never noticed the time. Then I walked up to Lees with her because she wanted to look at the dresses they've got in for Christmas. I just forgot all about the time, Buba, I'm really sorry.'

As soon as I had finished my lying tale I began to regret telling it. The more lies I told, the harder it would be for me to turn round and tell Buba that I was leaving for Manchester and could she please give me the fare. If only she weren't so easy to deceive. If only she didn't receive my lies with such eagerness.

'It's a pity you didn't think to look at your watch.' My old enemy could read me effortlessly.

I smiled at him and dared him to say any more. The days of his hegemony over me were coming to an end.

During the night something woke me. It was a cloudy, starless night and inside my bedroom the dark was solid, impenetrable. I listened to the old house shift and creak, familiar sounds which had often comforted me but which now filled me with a sense of imminent loss. Would I be gone this time tomorrow, on my way to Manchester? It seemed too soon, too soon to leave Buba.

I got up to go to the bathroom but, as I passed her door which always remained open during the night, she called softly from within.

I went and sat on her bed. I was shivering. She propped herself up on one elbow and peered into my face, trying to read my expression in the light from the landing.

'You cannot sleep? And you are cold, shivering. Come, get in beside your old Buba like you used to so long ago.'

I slipped in between the rosemary-scented sheets. Such familiar textures and smells. It would be hard to leave all that behind too. If only I could slip backwards into my old life as I had slipped into Buba's bed.

She put her arms around me and began to stroke my hair. 'I don't want to leave you ever, Buba,' I said.

We lay fitting so comfortably together, just like the old days. The contours of her little round body, so different from the spare, muscled flesh that had replaced it, were well remembered.

'Some day you will leave,' Buba said. 'And soon enough too. Eighteen. You are growing up – grown-up. A woman. Erika was married at your age and you too will meet someone some day and then you will want to leave your old Buba. You will be in such a rush away.'

She could have guessed my plans, so accurate were her predictions. Rushing off, that's what I was doing. Tomorrow I would be rushing off, rushing away from my little Buba as fast as I could.

Buba yawned. 'It is the way of the world and when it is time for you to go, then we will be sad but we will rejoice for you.'

Outside the wind had risen, driving the clouds before it so that the moon was made visible and threw a bar of silver light against the wall beyond the bed. My grandmother, I was beginning to realize, was wiser than I. The way of the world, the inevitability of time marching on.

We turned together and I put my arm around her waist. 'Don't you ever feel Jewish, Buba? Don't you ever feel you would like to go back to your roots?'

'Never. Now I am Irish through and through.'

Being a foreigner in spite of what she said, she didn't know you could be both quite comfortably. 'But you can be Jewish and still be Irish, Buba – lots of people are. Like Max, for example.'

'Max?'

'You remember, the night we heard about Mona.' I was surprised at how easy it was to say this.

'Poor Miss McCarthy, I remember.'

'And you remember the boy who came – '

'The boy with the too red lips.'

It was a strange comment but I let it pass. 'He's Jewish, Buba, Jewish and Irish. Well, he's not really religious but you know what I mean. Like you really, Buba, you and the Free Religious Declaration in Germany.'

'Not like me, I am Catholic.'

Buba's obtuseness was very irritating. 'You're in Ireland now, you're safe. Nobody's going to do anything to you because you're a Jew.'

'I am not a Jew.'

'I understand.' I tried to keep the irritation out of my voice. 'I know what you mean, Buba, and I know that you became a Catholic for my sake. But once a Jew always a Jew. Max says – '

'Nothing. You understand nothing.' Angrily she threw off my arm. 'This Max – we have nothing in common with such people. We do not come out of some ghetto where they live like in the Middle Ages. We are Europeans, civilized for generations. Now, enough talk. Just go to sleep.'

It was now my turn to be angry. I wanted to jump out of her bed but I reminded myself that I also wanted my fare to Manchester. I turned my back on her and thought how stupid she was to talk about civilization after all she had been through.

All she had been through. Mona had said, 'You'll never know what they've been through, Belle.'

Ashamed, I reached a hand behind me and touched her side. 'Good-night, Buba.'

'Good-night, Liebchen.'

But I was no nearer solving my problem. I lay awake listening to the wind and to my grandmother's tranquil breathing. The clouds returned and obscured the moon so that the slivers of light on the far wall were blotted out. Still I couldn't sleep.

Perhaps Mutti was the answer, Mutti would understand young love, remembering what it had been like. And she could help me explain things to Buba.

Next morning the bed was empty when I awoke.

In the bathroom as I brushed my teeth I could smell Mutti's rolls baking, the warm smell mingling with the sharper tang of freshly brewed coffee.

When I got down to the kitchen I found that Buba had already gone up to the surgery. Mutti smiled. 'So nice the holidays have begun. Now we can take our time at breakfast and you can enjoy these rolls.'

She placed a plateful in front of me, poured coffee for both of us, lit a cigarette. 'I hear you last night with your Buba. Whisper, whisper until I fall asleep. What was all that whispering about?'

I fingered the letter in the pocket of my dressing gown, then, making a quick decision, I took it out and handed it across to her.

She read, her lips moving as she deciphered the script. When she had finished she turned it over, smoothed out the sheets on the table, looked at them, looked up at me. 'This is what I have been thinking for some time, this is no surprise to me.'

Her reaction certainly surprised me. 'But how did you know?'

'When he called, the way you both act. Besides, I know for some time that you are preoccupied. That faraway look in the eyes. Your Buba didn't notice of course – '

'That's just it, Mutti, and I don't think she'd understand anyway.'

'Go to him.'

'What?'

'Go to him. You have his address. You are both serious. I give you the money – go to him.'

Getting my own idea flung back at me across the breakfast table gave me a shock. Understanding was one thing but shouldn't a mother be counselling caution?

'Look. He is a good young man – '

'Of course.'

'A serious young man. You love him, he loves you. You write to him and tell him your plans. If he does not write back, then we think again. If he writes back and says yes, I give you the money and when you are gone I tell your Buba.'

Things were happening too fast. I had been prepared for a battle when I would wear Mutti down and together we would approach Buba. What she was proposing would commit me now, this instant, to a certain course of action.

'A pen and paper,' Mutti said, pointing to the mantelpiece. 'Write the letter and I will post it.'

Mutti was being too eager, not giving me time to think. 'Later, I'll write it later.'

'Not too late, I hope. Love does not wait, believe me, Belle.'

I offered to do the bedrooms and spent the morning on the top floor of the house, away from both of them. I stripped beds, plumped pillows, dusted and swept with the one phrase running through my mind: love does not wait.

I looked at the photographs on Buba's dressing table and thought how quickly we all grow old. Perhaps Mutti was right but I wouldn't do it her way. I owed Buba more than that. I wouldn't behave like a coward.

Mutti and I were alone for lunch because Buba was out on a call.

'Well?' Mutti asked.

215

I shook my head. 'In my own time. Just let me be.'

'Don't leave it too long and ask me before you do anything. The money is in my bank account waiting for you. Remember that.'

We washed up in silence and as we were finishing Buba came in from the garden, having walked up from the garage.

I got her lunch from the oven but it was dried up, the gravy congealed around the edge of the plate. When I offered to get her something else she shook her head. She was preoccupied, worried about the little girl she had been called out to see who had some complication from measles. Or so Buba feared.

When we went into the sitting room to have our coffee she cheered up and lit a cigar. Mutti poured the coffee into little rose-coloured cups with faded gold bands. The cups were part of a set which had been given to Buba as a wedding present and she said that they would be mine as soon as I got married.

I drank my coffee as a ray of low winter sun came through the window behind Buba's head, gilding her so that she shone like a saint in a Russian icon.

'Did our family come from Russia originally?' I spoke idly, pleased with my image of Buba as a Russian saint.

She frowned and so did Mutti.

'What are you talking about?' she asked.

'So many Jewish families came from Russia, before they settled in Western Europe I mean. I was just wondering about ours.'

Buba looked at me with distaste. 'You are back talking the same as last night.'

'No I'm not – '

'Yes you are and I don't want it, it gives me a headache.' She threw her cigar into the fire, got up and walked out.

'Now you see what you've done. I told you, tell me before you start anything.' Mutti glared at me.

'But I was only – '

'It is always the same with you, Belle, you never listen to good advice.'

I really couldn't understand the fuss they were both making. Was I not supposed even to mention the fact that we were Jews, or had been? And I had imagined that Max's Jewishness would have made him more attractive in their eyes.

I went up to Buba's bedroom and knocked on the door.

She was sitting, writing at her dressing table, her little half-moon spectacles perched on her nose.

'I'm sorry, Buba.'

She smiled.

'I didn't mean to go on. It's just that I want you to like Max. He's very important to me.'

She took off her glasses and turned round to give me her whole attention. 'How important?'

'I love him, he loves me. We're serious about one another.'

She sighed.

'No, listen.' I took her hand between mine. It lay flaccid and unresponsive. 'It doesn't matter about him being a Jew – he doesn't really believe anything anyway. It's just his parents, you know how they'd be.'

She sighed again. 'I suppose they are orthodox?'

I thought about the old grandmother sitting by the range, the two good little girls, the mother with her two separate washing-up bowls. 'Very.'

Buba took off her glasses, folded them and placed them on the dressing table with the lenses upwards. She straightened her silver-backed brush and comb, she examined the backs of her hands. Then she looked up at me and shook her head. 'I am sorry, Belle, but it cannot be.'

'What – what do you mean?'

'It is not a question of me liking this young man. Such a family, orthodox, they will never accept you. Never.'

I laughed with relief. 'Oh Buba, you've forgotten about being Jewish, you've forgotten that all that really matters in the end is being born Jewish. A Jewish mother, that's all that matters, that makes me a Jew no matter how often I go along to Mass.'

'But you are not.'

'I'm not what? I've just told you – '

'Belle.' She put up a hand to stop me speaking. 'You are not Jewish, Erika is not. None of us. No Jewish blood in our family. We are not Jews.'

It was like I was listening to a foreign language. I heard the words, they were familiar words, but I didn't understand their meaning. I looked across at my grandmother to see if by staring into her face I might make some sense of her words. We are not Jews.

'I don't understand.'

I looked into her face. All I could see was infinite sadness. Dark, sad eyes. Suffering eyes. Jewish eyes.

'You are joking, Buba?'

'No jokes, no lies. Too late for anything but the truth.'

I tried again. I would not give up so easily. I had to fight her on this one and make her unsay what she had just said. 'You're jealous, Buba, jealous and possessive. You don't want me to leave you, you want me to stay here for ever so's I can look after you and Mutti. You don't want me to be happy.'

But she gave me a look of such pity that I had to turn away from her.

'You're just jealous,' I repeated, looking down at the garden, no longer believing what I said.

The garden had been flattened by frost. It was limp and brown. Dying. Yet in defiance of all the decay around it a lone bush bloomed sleek and glossy with a mass of pinky-white flower clusters just coming into bud. A survivor from another time, another regime.

'Do you know the name of that bush?' I asked, pointing. 'I think the flowers are scented when they come out.'

My grandmother said, 'We should not have told you lies. As a member of the family you should have been told the truth all the time but I was advised otherwise.'

'I'll go and cut some of those flowers,' I said. 'They'll open up in the heat of the house.'

Mutti stopped me at the back door. 'She's told you.'

'I'm going to get some flowers.'

'Your face, Belle, I know from your face that she's told you.'

She pulled me away from the door and pushed me into a chair at the table. 'You are in shock — she should have seen that, she is a doctor.'

'Maybe she's not. Maybe she's been pretending about that too.'

For some reason I found this funny and I began to laugh. I laughed and laughed until Mutti came up and shook me. Then she put her arms around me and drew my head into her scented bosom.

I was not used to Mutti's embrace. This seemed a strange, foreign place. Other, more familiar arms —

Max. I had forgotten about Max.

I began to cry.

Mutti patted me and even in my distress I could feel the awkwardness of her fingertips. Not like those other softer hands, those fat little arms that I had run into as a child.

'What am I going to do? I don't understand anything any more. Can you explain, Mutti?'

'I cannot explain, perhaps from shame I cannot explain. Go to Father Jack, he will tell you the whole story. Then you can decide what you must do.'

'Father Jack – what does he know?'

She laughed humourlessly. 'Oh he knows all right.'

I had phoned Father Jack and asked him if I might come and talk to him. He told me that I was the first person to phone him on the new phone in his house and that this must be a good omen.

I agreed with him. The longer I thought about what my grandmother had said the more I was sure that there must be some explanation. If we hadn't been Jews, what had we been? Not Catholics or we surely would not have gone through the charade of conversion. And if we weren't Jews why had my grandmother been so anxious for us to assimilate, so frightened and worried about the past, so unwilling to talk about it?

Apart from the shiny new telephone in the hall, Father Jack's house was as I remembered it. The corridors sweated dankly and in the library the glass eye of the stuffed pheasant leered at me as of old; around the red mahogany table the piles of religious periodicals looked unchanged.

I was old enough however to refuse Father Jack's tea and I folded my arms and waited for him to begin.

'It's all for the best, Belle,' he sighed. 'You had to know sooner or later and if you had been told years ago as I wanted, we mightn't find ourselves in the mess we're in today.'

He got up and walked across to a window where he stood looking out. There was nothing to see except a pebbledash wall and an iron fire escape clinging to it. When he turned back to the room his face was quite transformed. It looked younger, glowing as I had never seen it before.

'Ah, Belle, you should have known your family before the war. Your grandmother, your grandfather, wonderful people.' He shook his head. 'And your poor uncle.'

'My uncle?'

'They don't talk about him. It broke your poor grandmother's heart, I'm sure of that.'

'What did? What did he do?'

For a moment his face resumed its old spiteful expression. 'He died, that's what he did. TB. A killer disease in the thirties. He died and with him died a part of your grandmother. He was the apple of her eye and the best son. She's never really recovered from his death, that's why even today, she never talks about him, nor lets anybody else mention his name. That's why you've never heard of him.'

He stood up again and began to move around the room, touching objects with his long, yellow fingers. For years I had watched him in my grandmother's house, repelled by his reptilian fixedness; now he couldn't seem to sit still for a moment.

He returned to the table. 'That's how we met, how I got to know your family. Gunter and I were students together in Rome. He brought me home with him for the holidays, Germany being nearer than Ireland, and your grandmother made me so welcome. Imagine me, a raw seminarian from Kilkenny and there I was – '

'Hang on,' I interrupted. 'A seminarian. Doesn't that mean going to be a priest?'

'We both were, what else would we be doing in Rome?'

'But my grandmother told me that they were not a religious family, that they made the Free Religious Declaration or whatever it was. So that was just another lie.'

'Wrong, Belle, stop condemning. Your grandparents were not religious, neither of them. They never went to church as far as I know. They'd been born Catholics, though, and they sent Gunter to a Catholic school, not for religious reasons but because it was the best school, as is often the case.' His fleshy lips spread like pink blancmange in a smug smile. 'The mysterious ways of God, Belle, the complexity of human nature. Here you have this young boy brought up without religion and yet at sixteen years of age he decides he wants to serve God and become a priest.'

'What about my mother?'

'Erika? Not religious. Brother and sister – chalk and cheese.' With a flick of his long, yellow hand he dismissed Mutti and continued to talk about my uncle. 'Everyone loved Gunter. I don't know what it was about him unless it was just goodness. And he had such gifts – good looks, intelligence, an outgoing temperament which made him friends everywhere he went. I think his parents had hoped originally that he would follow them into medicine but once they saw how dedicated he was they were happy for him.'

His voice was breaking with emotion, I looked away in embarrassment.

He cleared his throat and continued. 'Your grandparents, especially your grandmother, they were devastated when he died. Their only son, a golden youth, in his prime. Imagine the tragedy, Belle, imagine what it did to them.'

He took out a large blue handkerchief and began to blow his nose, vigorously. When he started to speak again the tone of his voice had changed, sounding suddenly harsh. 'So you have to understand, Belle – all this talk about the Jews. God knows, I don't hate them, I never did. I pray for them, I pity them. But other people have suffered too. And – they did reject the Saviour.'

I was trying to follow him, to leap the elliptical chasms with him. I wasn't yet ready to admit to the monstrousness of what I saw beginning to emerge.

'Well, well – enough of that. He died in '34. I was ordained in Rome in '36 and I called by to see them on my way home to Ireland. Broken people and your poor grandfather already beginning to fail. I always kept in touch with them, I always remembered their kindness to me and I think that for your grandmother I was a surrogate son, because of my friendship with Gunter.'

I had often wondered about my family. I had pictured them living a stylish, assimilated life among Gentiles, my doctor grandparents and their beautiful daughter. I had read a bit about such families, I had marvelled at their innocence, the terrible poignancy that hindsight gave to their lives. Now I was being forced to think about another sort of life, lived by another sort of family.

'Your grandmother used to blame herself for letting him go to Rome, believing as she had that it was an unhealthy place. She used to say that if he had remained in Germany where she could keep an eye on him he would never have caught TB. Poor Dr Meyers – there was nothing for anybody in Germany when Gunter left. Money was useless. You got rid of it as soon as you got it. Off you'd go and buy a couple of tins of meat, something to hold on to. We used to bring things with us when we came on holidays and the Church was always good to Gunter, helping out with money and that sort of thing. The mark was worth nothing. Your grandfather was a senior surgeon in a regional hospital and he'd have been as well off cleaning the streets.'

He was on the move again, prowling around the room. Suddenly he came and stood over me, unhooding his eyes, which was always a sign that he was about to strike.

'So you can understand, Belle, it wasn't easy for anybody in those days. And Jews were rich, flaunting their wealth. Is it any wonder that people went out and joined the National Socialists?'

I backed away from him, as far as I could get. 'Do you mean to say – are you telling me that my grandparents were – that they had something to do with – '

'So dramatic, the young. What sort of a question is that to ask? I'm surprised at you, Belle.'

He stretched across the table and tapped the glass dome as if to reprimand the pheasant who continued to stare back at him with a bright and beady eye. I put my hands under the table top, well out of reach.

'I've never been a one for politics, never had the interest. Necessary, though, sometimes in extreme circumstances. I can see that.'

He laughed suddenly. 'I was going to say that religion has always been my thing, as if you didn't know. As if I wasn't a priest. What I mean is, though, your grandmother. I've always known what a remarkable woman she is and all down the years I've prayed that she might return to the Church. It would have been Gunter's dearest wish.'

He cupped his yellow hands and held them up in front of him, then opened them, as if he were releasing something into the air. 'The soul, Belle, the soul is what counts. This is a vale of tears, suffering is a part of life, but all that will pass so long as we pay attention to the soul. When the calls of the flesh are at their most deafening that is when we must pay most particular attention to the needs of the soul.

'Well.' He stood up, dismissing me. 'Now, off you go, there's a good girl. You are most precious to your grandmother, always remember what you owe her.'

I remained seated.

'Hurry, child. I've a seminarians' meeting at three.'

'But what you've said doesn't explain anything. Why did we become Jews then? Why did they pretend to me all that stuff? It doesn't make sense.'

He drew his lips inwards in a thin pink line. 'All right, five minutes. Your family, Belle, was a very respected one.' He had begun to speak more slowly as if this would help me to understand. 'They were prominent and well liked and very tolerant. They lived in a lovely flat but it was a bit on the small side, particularly after you were born and – '

'Father Jack, I thought you were in a hurry. What's all this got to do with anything?'

'I'm trying to explain, please, Belle. As I was saying, the flat was a bit on the small side but they managed as best they could. The flat next to theirs was occupied by a lawyer and his family. Jews. Oh they were quite an advanced family, although the old grandmother was rather – foreign in some of her habits. Anyway, both families got on very well, they used to play cards together sometimes on Sunday afternoon and the little girl, your age, went to school with you. Same school, same class. That's what people forget about Germany, the tolerance, the kindness. Anyway the war came and they were taken away.'

'You mean –?'

'And your family was offered their flat. It had been left just as it was and I think all your grandmother did was lock things away in the attic, personal possessions and the like. So.' He looked out the window beyond my head, yawning as he did so. I could tell that it was not a genuine yawn but the sort you make out of awkwardness and embarrassment.

'So, Father Jack?'

'So it made it easier when I was trying to get them out. They had a ready-made identity. The grandmother and the little girl of your age. It was a bit of a coincidence really when you come to think of it.'

He still wasn't making sense. 'Father Jack, Buba said you rescued them, from the *Lager*. I thought – I mean – Why did they have to have a new identity? Why were they in a camp if they, we weren't Jews?'

For a moment he too looked puzzled, then he clapped his yellow hands together. 'Child, child – is that what you were thinking? No, it wasn't a *concentration* camp – well, it was in a way. There was so much hysteria when the American troops arrived, they saw every unfortunate German as a Nazi. Your family – it was easier for me to get them out, more straightforward with those papers. Easier for your poor grandmother who had suffered so much.'

He stopped, shook his head, drew a yellow hand down over his mouth, exposing uneven and stained bottom teeth. 'And you've no idea how much difficulty it caused in the heel of the hunt – when I was trying to get you in here, I mean. The Irish government, they were cautious men and they didn't want the country overrun by Jews when the war ended. No, Belle – there's no need to look like that. It was a sensible precaution, to avoid outbreaks of anti-Semitism in the country. In fact, I would go so far as to say that they were only doing their duty. Anyway, it didn't make my job any easier. Here you all were with your new identities, that got you out of Germany fine. But when I got you as far as Ireland – well, it was a good thing I could pull a few strings where it counted.'

Now I was the one who wanted to get away. I stood up and began to edge my way round the table. I wanted to keep it between us in case, just in case I might brush against that awful yellow skin.

'Belle, what's wrong with you, child? You ask me for explanations and now here you are rushing off.'

I was already out in the corridor. He came after me, talking all the time.

'– so don't go imagining all sorts of lurid things. Just listen to your grandmother.'

I got to the door, wrenched the heavy lock backwards and was outside.

His voice followed me. 'And I'll pray for you, Belle, that you do the right thing.'

* * *

It was one of those still winter days. The good weather had brought people out and the streets were full of Christmas shoppers. Queues had formed at bus stops with fractious children and anxious mothers.

In a draper's window I stopped and looked at the two life-sized dummies with blonde wigs dressed in the New Look.

Between them a child dummy wore a red velvet dress with smocking across the chest. Had I once had a dress like that?

I moved back from the glass and as I did so I saw a face reflected back at me. Black curly hair and pretty eyes. Someone I used to know. Someone who had been quite sure of her identity in spite of praying to the Holy Ghost. Jewish in sinew and bone and skin; Jewish in temperament; Jewish in destiny, swimming through a Christian sea to be carried by a current to her Jewish lover.

I placed my hand on the glass so that the face would be blotted out.

I didn't know that girl. I knew the facts of her life or most of them but I didn't know who she was. I didn't know her reactions, her intelligence; most of all I didn't know her heart.

I didn't know anything any more. I would have to learn, going back to some beginning. I would have to learn to hear and to see again, to understand speech, to recognize touch. Then I might begin to know who I was.

Now there is a blank: a white, flat, featureless space into which all memory has vanished. A landscape that is so white it hurts the eye and the more I peer into it the less I see.

But I persist, stretching my eyelids to prevent myself from blinking. I peer and peer. A faint shadow. My body begins to tremble. I am afraid.

I am afraid of Buba. I don't want to confront her. I don't want to hear what answers she will give me, I don't want to see those beloved lips forming obscene sentences. I cannot let Buba talk, I cannot stop loving her, I have nobody left to love.

Now, surfacing from underneath the pain is another emotion. It is centred round Eileen and Mona and somebody else in Germany. A little girl my own age who holds my hand on our first day at school and says, 'Don't be afraid, I'll look after you.'

She is my best friend. She lives in the flat opposite and we play together in the hallway downstairs, bumping our dolls' prams down the two flights. She is braver than I am, laughing at the bullies who jostle us in the grey shadows of the school yard. She laughs all the time, Ana, and I learn to laugh with her, to become less solemn.

Then one day she is gone.

'Where is Ana?' I ask.

Buba smooths my hair. 'They've gone, they've moved.'

'But she didn't even say goodbye.'

'And I have good news, Liebchen – tomorrow we move into their nice big flat. You'll have your own room, won't you like that?'

The thread of desolation which runs like an underground river through my life begins here with Ana. It surfaces periodically when Eileen leaves, when Mona is killed. Now again I am faced with it in flood as I see that I must begin again.

Can I go to Max after all? Can I throw myself at his feet in Manchester and begging his forgiveness offer him my heart, a poor thing but his? I must risk rejection, anger, contempt, I must go to him, it is the only option left.

Buba is sitting smoking; Mutti is in the back kitchen washing up.

Buba smiles at me, pats the seat beside her.

I shake my head, stand in front of her. 'I'm leaving, Buba.'

She takes the cigar from her mouth, taps the lighted end gently, carefully, into the surface of the ashtray until it is extinguished. 'You have spoken with Father Jack?'

I nod.

'Then how – it is nonsense you speak.'

'I am going to Max. I'm going to tell him everything and I'm going to beg his forgiveness and – '

'You tell him what? And he tells who else? You are a foolish young girl, you have not thought of anything. It is over between you and this young man. It cannot be. It could never be.'

'I'm going to pack.'

As I take things out of drawers and pile them on my bed I hear Mutti and Buba begin to scream at one another. The ugly German sounds fill the house, reinforcing my commitment. I take a minimum, a survival suitcase. I leave my room without looking round.

At the bottom of the stairs Buba is waiting. 'You are overstrained with all that has happened.' She smiles at me, an old Buba smile.

'You are so delicate, always I have worried about your health, the delicacy of your emotions. Now all this is too much for you.'

She reaches out to embrace me and I walk into her arms. I bend my head smelling her familiar scent, cigars and lily of the valley face powder. I close my eyes and as I do I feel a prick where my neck and shoulder meet.

'For the best,' Buba says. 'A nice rest, expert treatment and you are restored to us.'

Is that Mutti I hear crying in the background?

I have suppressed and I have had suppression imposed on me. When I woke up I remembered nothing of what had happened immediately before. I think now that it must have been the injection which blotted things out.

I found myself in a bed, unable to move a muscle because of the pain that engulfed my body. I moved my neck a centimetre and it was as if my neck were on fire. I willed myself to stay absolutely still and began to examine my pain which for some reason I wanted to hold on to. It gave me satisfaction because by concentrating on it and naming it I was able to push back the unnerving feeling I had of floating, unanchored.

This was much worse than the pain for it induced a state of terror, suggesting unimaginable horrors yet to come. I concentrated on the pain, examining its degree and nature.

Like pleasure pain helps you to get reacquainted with your body. Mine, I said, feeling the soreness in the soles of my feet, in my eyelids, in the roof of my mouth. Mine.

My body and I knew who I was. I lay in a darkened room and named names: darkness, room, bed. Not my bed, narrower, harder.

I re-entered my pain, letting it flow over me, wanting it to absorb again that frightening, conscious intelligence which had begun to burn like a naked light bulb.

I drifted into sleep then, or at least out of consciousness. I seemed to do that for some time, coming and going, coming and going. Maybe the pain was so bad that it literally knocked me out.

Then I found that the pain was not so bad as it had been. I lay in my by now familiar bed and moved my head slowly around. I was in a room that had no direct light but was filled with a blue glow which came through a glass panel over the door. There was a chair against one wall and a long cupboard. The window was curtainless with bars outside.

I tried to sit up but the pain threw me back. Perhaps I had been in some sort of accident. I began, tentatively, to run my fingers over my body to see if I was bandaged or splinted in any area. My skin felt sore, rough too but unbandaged. A fire? Was I suffering from burns?

Slowly I moved my body up in the bed until my arms were able to be around the rails of the bedhead. I grasped and pulled myself upwards. It felt better to be in a sitting position but the air around me was cold. I pulled the blankets closer and wondered where the coarse nightdress that I was wearing had come from. Every time I moved it scratched my skin.

Light was now beginning to come in through the window. Beyond the bars I saw the bare branches of trees and beyond the branches the lightening skies. It was still winter then, no leaves on the trees.

After a time I became aware of sounds. It seemed incredible that I had noticed nothing before because as I listened the noise became deafening. From beyond one wall came the sound of shrieking and chanting; on the other wall someone pounded with rhythmic and insistent ferocity.

'It's like a madhouse,' I said to myself. And as soon as the words were spoken I realized with chilling clarity that that's what it was.

I slid down into the bed and pulled the blankets over my head. They could not keep out the noises, though, nor the terror that had taken hold of my heart. Had I been committed?

It seemed likely.

Was I mad?

If I was I'd be the last to find out.

Eventually the poor things must have tired themselves out because the noise grew less and finally stopped altogether.

There was an interval of silence, a calming, restorative silence which I imagined spreading and spreading until it had embraced the whole building. Too soon however it was replaced by different noises – a discordant striking of metals, tin on tin,

tin on enamel, and above this, heavy and deliberate footsteps and loud cheerful voices.

My door was flung inwards and two nurses walked into the room. I knew they were nurses because of the uniforms.

'Well, Bella,' one of them said, 'and how are we today?'

'Where am I?' I asked, sitting up.

I saw them looking at one another. They both turned to smile at me.

'Good girl,' said one and the other patted me on the head. 'This is some improvement, Bella's talking to us today,' she said.

They never answered my question as to where I was but they gave me other information. I had been in for a fortnight and they had all been worried about me because I had had a bad reaction to some drugs they had put me on. I'd come out in blisters all over my body, a most severe allergy and hard to treat.

That would account for the pain.

'Do I have to stay here?' I asked. 'It's so noisy at night it's impossible to sleep.'

I saw the signal pass between them again. The older one answered. 'I don't think by the look of you this morning that you'll be up here much longer. I'd say when Doctor sees you he'll move you down.'

True to the spirit of the place, being moved down meant being moved up in the madhouse.

The other nurse took a handful of my hair and pulled it back. 'I'm going to do something with this. Plait it, maybe. It's lovely hair but Sister will be wanting it cut off if we don't make it a bit tidier.'

Those two were good, kind women, if unimaginative. There may have been sadists among the staff in that hospital but I never came across them.

'We'll get everything ready in here so's it'll be ship-shape for your visitors.'

'I'm having visitors?'

'As soon as you've eaten your breakfast,' the older nurse replied.

The shock of the breakfast when it arrived put the thought of the visitors out of my mind. It was served on a tin tray and in plastic dishes. The plastic was old and scratched, the cup stained with ancient tannin. There was a bowlful of lumpy grey porridge, a slice of white pan smeared with margarine and a plastic cup half filled with grey, lukewarm tea.

Years afterwards, when Shields and I were discussing the shock that first meal gave me, she laughed at my fastidiousness. At that time, she informed me, in eating houses throughout Ireland people were paying good money for identical food. It was either that or Jammet's and nothing in between.

I had never been either to an eating house or to Jammet's, Dublin's fabled haute cuisine restaurant, and Mutti's cooking was a bad preparation for Irish institutional food. I tried to eat it and I did manage to drink the tea. I already sensed that obedience and docility were taken as outward signs of returning sanity and that if I didn't clear my plastic plates I was lessening my chances of being moved downstairs.

I was looking around for somewhere to stash the food when the door opened and Mutti walked into the room. One of the nurses stood on the threshold but didn't come in.

In slow motion Mutti crossed the room. She was wearing a grey costume with her fox furs round her neck. She looked so beautiful, indeed incongruously beautiful in such surroundings.

She stretched out a hand. It was real, warm. 'Mutti.' I put it to my cheek. 'Mutti.'

'My little Belle.'

I stretched my arms to kiss her but I was distracted by a movement at the door. I looked over and I saw them standing there, together. Twin devils. I wouldn't look up at their faces. I had sworn that I would never look in those faces again but I could see their horrid hands. Plump and skinny, pink and yellow, busy, destructive, annihilating hands.

The bodies of the twin devils began to move away from the door and into the room. They were coming towards me, arms out to get me.

No.

I punched the tray away and stood up in the bed. I picked up a cup and flung it at the devils, then a plate. I laughed as a missile struck and a blob of margarine stuck to the shiny black suit.

'Get out, devils, get out. Go away or I'll kill you both.'

When the nurses rushed at me I could still spit until one of them shoved a gag in my mouth.

The other one shook me. 'Your poor grandmother and a priest. You'd better learn to behave, Bella my girl.'

But I knew that they were the ones, those devils, who would learn, every time they came near me, I would scream and spit and shout and kick until in the end I would tire them out and they'd leave me alone for ever.

When Mutti came to visit me on her own about a week later I explained that I thought my behaviour had been brought about by seeing the two of them like that, together. If my grandmother had come by herself I might have behaved differently.

'She can't.' Mutti shook her head. 'She's afraid to see you on her own so she brings him along for protection.'

After that I made every effort to impress the staff with my docility. I knew that if I spent much longer on the top landing I would really go mad. Every night at about twelve the moaning and sobbing and shouting started and continued until dawn the following morning. Sometimes through exhaustion I fell asleep but most of the time I lay awake, moved by pity and terror, a hapless witness to the throbbing pain of the world.

No matter how little sleep I got I was up and dressed with my bed made by the time the nurses came in with my breakfast tray and I learned to swallow every morsel of food put in front of me. I smiled and handed back an empty tray with thanks and I could see them trying to figure out – is she really getting better or is this just the cunning of madness?

When I was eventually moved down I found that it was like being back at school with rules and a timetable. I even had a best friend, a frail old woman who picked me out on my first day in the dining room. After that she kept a place for me at meals and she held my hand as we walked to occupational therapy or to church. She was gentle but slyly funny about the staff and I often wondered what she was doing in here until one day she told me her secret: she was really Princess Margaret Rose but I wasn't to tell anybody because they might come and steal her tiara.

I took the tablets they gave me, two white in the morning and a red-and-white at night. The medical director decided that I was to have no visitors until he reviewed the situation, which suited me. Sometimes as I walked the long, brown corridors with my friend I wondered at my contentment. Nothing seemed to touch me; I had even begun to eat the food without noticing how awful it was.

Then the medical director reduced my medication and I was no longer content. I suddenly became aware of everything, the ugliness of my surroundings, the oddness of my companions, the numbing boredom of my days, the total lack of privacy. More worrying than any of this was the fear that I might never get out of this place, that I was here for ever.

It was about this time, I think, that Shields came to work in the hospital. Because we were about the same age we were drawn to one another and it was she who used to let me skive off from occupational therapy. When she was on day-room duty I used to slip out after the first half-hour and steal upstairs to the dormitory. The relief of being on my own, even for twenty minutes, was like plunging a burnt finger into icy water. I used to sit at the window and look out at the dark branches of the trees. The heating was always turned off upstairs except at night but I welcomed the cold as I welcomed the view through the window to the wild world outside.

There was space out there, square miles of space. I imagined myself floating up towards the cold blue sky, the same blue, despite her warm heart, as poor Mutti's eyes. I had come to know Mutti, but it was too late. She came to visit me and we sat in silence, nothing to say. She never wore lipstick and her hair had grown out a dank brown. She was nearly as thin as I.

They didn't clean the windows in the madhouse, maybe they couldn't get at them because of the bars. I pressed a finger against the glass and smeared a line from glazing bar to glazing bar. My eye followed my finger's progress downwards and then was caught and held by something, some tiny white thing that fluttered on the other side of the dirty glass. It was the movement rather than the colour which caught my attention, for nothing moved up here in mid-winter. No leaves fluttered on branches, no birds flew past, we were too high even for a swirl of litter caught on the breeze.

I squinted down, cupping my hand around my eyes to block out shadows. It was a tiny snowdrop that had come into bloom, the tiny white head swaying on the spindly green stem.

And there were other shoots breaking through the unprom-ising soil in the window box. I reckoned that by the end of the week there would be a whole garden blooming out there.

'If I could grow things,' I said to Shields when I came down for my dinner. 'Instead of the occupational therapy, I mean.'

'I don't see why not. Jesus, I don't blame you for wanting to get away from that lot. They're driving me bananas and I'm in the whole of my health.'

Mutti brought me a gardening book and two packets of seeds, nasturtium and lettuce. The man in the seed shop had told her that these were the easiest for beginners. The next time I saw the medical director I asked him if I might do a bit of gardening.

He looked alarmed. 'What sort of gardening?'

'Just some seeds, flowers and lettuce. If I could have a few boxes and some soil and turf mould.'

'But you wouldn't want to go straying into the grounds – we couldn't allow that.'

'Nothing like that.'

They allowed me to set up my greenhouse in a disused porch of what had been the front entrance to the house before it had been turned into a hospital. The nurses could keep an eye on me from the upstairs windows.

They were all very pleased with me – I could tell by the way they nodded and smiled approvingly. Shields said to me, 'Things are looking good for you. Keep this up and you'll be out and home before you know it.'

Then they made their big mistake, they thought I was ready for visitors other than Mutti.

I was out in the porch, humming to myself, thinking what a difference the bit of gardening had made to my life. A robin had come in through the open door and stood near me, peering at me hopefully. It was quiet, the only quiet place in the hospital.

I was sitting back on my heels, watching the little bird, when a shadow moved up behind me. The robin, frightened, flew off, and the shadow hunkered down beside me.

'Well, Belle.' A long yellow hand came to rest on the ground inches from my own. I knew that hand.

I took my gardening fork and stuck it with as much strength as I could into the back of that hand. I hoped that I might hit a vein so that I might watch as yellow bile flowed out. All I remember was being yanked backwards as screams filled my ears.

Poor old Shields got into trouble for letting me have the fork and my case was reviewed in the face of this clear evidence of my insane cunning.

It was decided that I would benefit from some ECT. I wasn't consulted, naturally; perhaps my grandmother as my doctor gave her consent.

It was Anto who rescued me, who took one look at me and pushing my hair back out of my eyes, said, 'You shouldn't be going through this nonsense. What you need is a bit more fresh air to put the roses back in those cheeks.'

'Gardening?' I asked timidly.

'What's that you say?'

'If I could go back to my gardening?'

'Only if you promise to grow me some scallions for my tea. I've a weakness for scallions straight out of the ground.'

I thought I was all done with the past but I've just remembered something else. The last visit I had from Mutti. I had moved to the lodge by this time and I was settled into my new life. She had kept in touch after I left the madhouse, calling sporadically, never staying very long, just long enough to scent my little house with that well-remembered amalgam of smells. On this occasion she seemed less hesitant, more defined, as if she had made up her mind about something. I was glad to see also that she had started wearing lipstick again and that her hair was that lovely golden blonde that comes out of a bottle.

She sat at the table and lit a cigarette, not talking, waiting while I made coffee. She took a little sip, dabbed at her raspberry-red mouth. 'I've come to say goodbye. I'm going to leave Ireland, I'm going to London. Never have I liked it here, too small, too claustrophobia. London is big, it will suit me better.'

I nodded, it seemed a good idea to me.

'Before I go – ' She was playing with the cup and saucer, not looking at me. 'Before I go – ' She looked up at me. 'Can you forgive me, Belle? I shouldn't have allowed her.'

There was no need for this. 'Don't, Mutti, it doesn't matter.'

'No, I must speak. I could never stand up to her, even you, the child, had more courage than I. I wanted you to run away to Max so that you might never find out but you wouldn't do that. And then to commit you. She said, "You want us to be thrown out of this country if they start listening to her mad talk? There is a place for such madness."

'And I went down to the kitchen and turned on the wireless so that I would not hear them coming for you and I drank from your grandmother's brandy bottle so that I would not hear my own heart.'

I reached across the table and covered her hand with mine.

She raised her chin, offered me a wobbly smile. 'I'm not all bad, though. When that new doctor came to us and said you were not mad, that he wanted you released, I fought her to let things go ahead, to let you begin with your new little life.'

She looked round my house. 'Your little life.'

Happy with my little life in those days, I felt a stirring of curiosity about that other life that I had left behind.

'Where is she now? Still working away?'

Mutti shook her head. 'She has retired and the house is sold two years ago. We live separate lives. It is as she wanted. With Father Jack all the time. They go out in her car for Sunday-afternoon drives. They go to the pictures. He has learned to cook and he cooks meals for them both.'

She laughed but without amusement. 'It is very strange, very odd to see them. And your grandmother has become more German, almost as if she never left. I think she has cut out of her life some twenty years and she lives now before the war. As if nothing had happened and even her son was still alive.'

Abruptly she stood up. 'I must go.'

'I'm sure you'll be happy in London.'

'I too, I'm sure.' She began to smooth her gloves over the backs of her hands, then turned to peer over her shoulder, checking on her seams.

'She was always a strange woman, always extreme. Poor Papi . . . and he was a doctor too and he did not like some of the things she was doing, he did not approve. He told me once it was because of worries over the blood. The blood was not so good, as they used to say in those days. Maybe not so pure as his own blood, for example. All that black hair. Oh Belle, your black hair.'

I took her in my arms, to calm her and because maybe I didn't want to hear any more.

'I should have been strong enough to protect my child and I wasn't. If only you can forgive me.'

I held her until she stopped crying, then kissed her goodbye as if I were the mother sending her off into the big, wide world.

'And we'll write,' I said at the door. 'As soon as you get settled send me your address.'

But we both knew she wouldn't. It would have been pointless, for neither of us could go back, jump the chasm which separated us from the past.

I watched at the doorway as she walked up the path and disappeared among the trees.

*   *   *

That's it, I've closed the book. I'm ready now for tonight's party.

SAINTHOOD   We were both nervous and both pretending we weren't. Shields arrived at my house in full battle dress. She wore a short tight dress made of some shiny orange material, black opaque tights and very high heels. Her newly hennaed hair clashed with her dress but I had to admit she had something – nerve, verve. I wouldn't go so far as to call it style.

'Is that the new dress?' I asked.

'You don't think it's too short?'

'Well – '

'My legs are about the best part of me, so I don't see why I should hide them. Oh God.' She caught sight of herself in a mirror. 'Oh God, Belle, my make-up looks awful in this light, I'll have to start again.'

I poured her a vodka and left her to get on with it.

I had decided to dress down, in case anybody might think that I was making an effort. I had no party clothes so I just wore a black jumper and skirt. I had black opaque tights too.

Shields called me from the bedroom. 'You'd better hurry up and change, we were supposed to be there half an hour ago.'

'I'm ready.'

She came out to stand over me. 'Jesus, I know we're all in mourning because he's going – '

'I'm not.'

'– but I wouldn't give her the satisfaction of making it so obvious.'

So I put on three strings of pearls and changed my tights and shoes.

*   *   *

The house was big, halfway up a suburban road with a view of the sea. It looked as if it had been built in the thirties, a smart, well-designed house though shabby now and in need of paint. The front garden contained nothing but scrub grass and a wildly burgeoning pyracantha.

'Hurry up,' Shields said as I was paying off the taxi. 'I knew we'd be late.' She trundled off down the path and banged the knocker, sending paint flakes flying.

Anto answered, full of fake bonhomie, not quite meeting my eye but giving my arm a squeeze.

'Welcome, come on in. Linda's around here somewhere.'

Linda. It would have been quite daring to have your daughter christened Linda in those days when other mothers were settling for some version of Mary: Maureen, Marie, Maria.

Most of the hospital staff was gathered under a pall of tobacco smoke in a large room at the end of the hall. Whoops greeted Shields' appearance and she shimmied like a young colt, shy and delighted.

Over the noise Anto said, 'She must be in the kitchen, let's go and find her.'

She was standing with her back to the fridge, talking to two male nurses. She was pretty, or would have been once. Pretty pink-and-white skin, pretty neat features, a good-little-girl demeanour.

She slipped her arm through Anto's and welcomed us in a baby voice. I could imagine how appealing she had been at nineteen or twenty. Dear, she called Anto, admonishing him for not taking our coats. Behind the soft blue eyes something glinted cold and sharp.

After we had put our coats away and Shields was whisked off by some youngsters I wandered into an almost empty living room. It looked as if it had been decorated with care some time ago and then forgotten about. Three walls were papered in green-and-white stripes and the fourth was painted a matching green. The chairs and sofa were covered in gold Dralon and the carpet was the sort of shaggy pile variety that used to be fashionable in the seventies.

Had she been discouraged by marriage to Anto? Given up on him as he had gone about his saintly way, indifferent to fashion and success?

Other people's lives. I was amazed at my own reaction. My speculations were cool, pleasant, passionless. I had had to come here tonight to realize that I was well and truly over Anto.

And all the hours I had spent hating that poor woman, envying her, wondering about her, guessing what she looked like and how good she was in bed.

I jumped as she came up behind me. 'Food,' she said in her baby voice. 'There's some food in the other room.'

'I was just admiring your room.' I smiled falsely, not wanting to be a bitch, just making conversation.

She looked doubtful for a second, then seemed to take my comment at face value. 'I'll get you a plate,' she said.

As I was following her out of the room she turned and smiled at me. 'I always loved the gardens,' she said. 'They used to be so depressing when Anto moved into the hospital, especially those big old dark trees along the avenue.

'The way you made flowers grow up through them. I really liked that.'

I was ready to go home after about an hour but I couldn't prise Shields away. She was going to have a hell of a hangover in the morning and she was going to need a lot of reassurance as to how she had behaved but tonight she was determined to have a last fling. I watched her as she tried to organize a conga. Each time she got a number of people lined up one young doctor towards the front would keel over and bring down half a dozen bodies with him. Finally she yanked him out and pushed him into a chair. A certain ruthlessness with which I was familiar was creeping into her behaviour.

I turned my back on her and let her get on with it.

Somebody had opened the kitchen door and I wandered outside and into the garden. It was a murky night with light from back windows filling the garden with a yellowish glow. Not cold, dampish. Irish winter weather.

I sat on a wall and looked back at the house. I could see bodies bobbing around inside and others hanging out of upstairs windows. The party could be deemed a success.

As I saw him coming towards me across the grass I moved along the wall to make room for him.

We sat together saying nothing, looking back at the house.

After a while I asked, 'Will you miss this?' waving towards the house.

'I'll miss you.'

I didn't feel the same about him. I wouldn't even think about him much, now that I had so much else to think about, so many puzzles to solve.

'If only – ' He stopped, then continued. 'Do you ever think how things might have been?'

'Isn't that the exercise you set me, delving into the past?'

But that no longer seemed to interest him. 'Do you ever think – us? When I met you first, we were both so young. I had been married three years and I knew then – we both knew really.' He took my hand and I let him. This was our goodbye after all.

Shields must have got her conga going. The music flowed into the garden, drunken voices accompanying a piano.

'Linda's a good woman but I've never been able to give her what she wanted. I knew that very soon, we both did. We were too young, I suppose. Then I met you.'

He stroked my hand, pushed back a curl from my forehead.

'I used to hope in the early days. I went on hoping for years. Partly conceit, I suppose – how could you turn down such an offer.'

The conga appeared at the back door and began to snake its way across the patio. The leader did a sudden right turn as he came up against a wall and there were howls from behind him as people lost their balance.

Anto turned my hand over and began to draw lines along my palm. 'What might have been,' he said. 'Have you any idea why?'

'Why what?'

'Why you wouldn't come away with me.'

The conga had turned again and was now heading around the side of the house into the front garden. I watched until the last person had swayed out of sight. Then I turned to smile at the man beside me.

'What are you trying to do, re-write history? You know perfectly well that you would not leave Linda.'

'Belle – I begged you for years. I never told Linda because you wouldn't let me but she knew there was someone else, I don't think it bothered her. Linda is very self-sufficient.'

I took his hand in both of mine, gave it a squeeze then returned it to his lap. 'Let's not say any more about it. It's too long ago, it's over and done with, Anto.'

He sighed, then stood up, touched my head with his hand.

'Perhaps you're right. All too long ago.'

He moved away from me through the yellow, diffused light and as I watched his still-young body crossing the grass I remembered all over again why I had fallen in love with him.

And I wondered if how he remembered it was true or simply

a parallel version of our story. If, in fact, truth, far from being universal, was something locked within each individual heart.

I gathered up my wrap and my bag and made my way round the side of the house and down the path on to the road.

Shields, I decided, could make her own way home.

A NOTE ON THE AUTHOR

Ita Daly is the author of *The Lady with the Red Shoes*, *Ellen*, *A Singular Attraction*, *Dangerous Fictions* and *All Fall Down*. She lives in Dublin.